LOCH ISLAND
(I Shall Dance At Your Wedding)

Ginny Vere Nicoll

✳

Feel Good Books

Published by Feel Good Books

www.feelgoodbooksonline.com

ginny@verenicoll.co.uk

©2014 Ginny Vere Nicoll

First edition

All rights reserved

ISBN: 978-0-9563366-2-0

Cover design by Tamara Hickie
(www.hickieandhickie.com)
from an original watercolour painting
by Ginny Vere Nicoll

Printed by

LIQUORICE

www.theliquoricepress.co.uk

ACKNOWLEDGMENTS

With huge thanks once more to my talented daughter, Tamara Hickie for another lovely cover design, taken from my own imaginary watercolour painting of 'Loch Island'.

Enormous thanks to my two amazingly patient proofreading editors. What a thankless task! Also to Tim and his team at One Tree Books in Petersfield. Thanks must go to my family for putting up with my endless hours of seclusion and I have to mention, yet again, my faithful little four-legged companion, Miss Marmite, constantly and uncomplainingly by my side on her blanket!

Finally I'd like to thank all the kind people who helped in my research both in the Highlands and on the mystical Island of Skye. They all gave so much towards the atmosphere of the book. My visit up there was especially memorable.

Also by Ginny Vere Nicoll

The Smile
ISBN: 978-1-4251-7153-7

Under The Olives
ISBN: 978-0-9563366-0-6

The Coldest Night Of The Year
ISBN: 978-0-9563366-1-3

'LOCH ISLAND'

'I Shall Dance At Your Wedding'

CHAPTER 1

"Let's not fly, let's go North; we could go to Skye. I've never been." said Adriana. Silence reigned. The others all stared at her.

"What – not go abroad?" asked Julian, in somewhat shocked tones, taking out the inevitable cigarette.

"You'll have to go outside to smoke," Guy quickly interrupted. "Don't even think about it in here. It's my club and you know what happened last time, I was the one who got into trouble."

Alicia ignored this last rebuke directed at her husband's best friend and jumped up, her bright blue eyes alight with excitement.

"Good idea Arri. Why not? No airports or passports, no crowds and no hassle. Lovely sea air: few people and no euros, Swiss francs or any other confusing currency to worry about. I could even take my sketch pad."

"Yes, not a bad idea at all," agreed Guy with a touch of his unmistakable Irish accent. "October is a funny time of year, weather-wise, anywhere in Europe. We could take the car and scoop up Rose and Olly on the way. They're well back from their extended honeymoon and will be thinking about another break by now. It must be almost a year since their wedding."

"I suppose we could do some fishing, especially if it rains," Julian suggested, letting out a resigned sigh and longing for a cigarette. With little enthusiasm, he ran his free hand through his unruly fair hair and looked across at his fiancée to judge her reaction. She wouldn't be too keen on sitting beside him in a peat

1

bog in the pouring rain, while he fished. She'd think it thoroughly boring. It didn't suit either of the girls to sit around doing nothing. They were both definitely 'doers' as he well knew, amused by his own private thoughts.

"Hang on a minute!" cried Alicia, now excited and determinedly striking while the iron was hot. "Emma and Marc, with Poppy, are going to be somewhere up in the Highlands in October. I only spoke to her yesterday. They are staying with a relation; some uncle I think. I wasn't really listening as to where exactly, but wouldn't it be great to get to see them all? We could stay in a pub nearby. It would just be so lovely to be together again. Just imagine, peace and quiet and in our own country for once! What do you think?" Alicia glanced around, they were all now looking interested and Julian had even put his intended cigarette away.

"Yes, you're right, it would be great, but I think we'd need to rent somewhere; a shooting lodge perhaps, with some help, so you girls don't have to cook all the time," Guy said sensibly, knowing how much Alicia hated to spend too much time in the kitchen when she was on holiday.

The four young friends sat together, in the one and only allotted 'female sitting room', in the bar of a men's club in the West End of London. The men had been catching up on work matters earlier and the girls had been shopping. They were all looking forward to lunch together and to discussing the prospects of their proposed October holiday.

"Where is the ladies room in this unfeminine establishment?" Adriana asked, "or perhaps they don't have one!" Alicia leapt up with a laugh. "Don't be ridiculous. Of course they do and I'll show you. I think that I need to inspect the facilities too."

The two men watched heads turn, albeit discreetly, to observe the attractive pair as they walked past the members sitting area and out into the corridor. The club was of course peopled mostly by men. Female family and friends were only invited to lunch or to dine with members on specific days of the week and were only allowed to sit in one place. Out of the ark! All these rules and regulations in this day and age, thought Julian chuckling.

"I think we should bring the girls in here a bit more often as they cause quite a stir in this rather worn and old fashioned men's watering hole. I have to say, it is a bit like a rather run down boarding school. I keep expecting my headmaster to appear and confiscate my cigarettes."

"I know what you mean but it actually suits me when I want to be quiet or need a secluded meeting," Guy answered. "Nobody bothers me here and very few friends are members which is also beneficial to my needs. Incidentally, just while the girls are out of earshot, I quite like the idea of our going to Scotland in the autumn. What do you think Julian?"

Julian straightened his tie. He hated wearing the wretched thing because it made him feel trucked up and uncomfortable. He was too hot in his jacket as well and would have liked to have been able to take it off, but he knew that the club protocol wouldn't allow him to do so. 'Stuffy old men', he muttered under his breath, taking the over-plumped cushion out from behind him and chucking it onto a nearby, vacant sofa. He turned towards Guy.

"Yes, well, on reflection I also think it's a good idea, but as long as our other halves are happy. I've always been fascinated by the North Western part of the country." He paused to take a sip of his drink.

"Actually, there's an island up there I've long wanted to visit: Loch Island. Ever heard of it?"

"No I haven't. Where is it exactly?"

"Somewhere up there off that coast but I can't remember who told me about it. It's quite small, about five or six miles across and three times that in length; it apparently emerged from the sea a long time after the other islands. It's inhabited mostly by seals and some interesting bird life, perhaps the odd shepherd and a few sheep in summer. But most importantly, it sports a huge fresh water lake at its centre."

"And full of nice brown trout, I have no doubt!" retorted Guy with a snort.

"Yes, but it sounds an interesting area altogether and there won't be many tourists around in October. We'd be left to our own devices and could enjoy some serious relaxation in spectacular surroundings. Perhaps we should get hold of Emma and Marc, find out exactly where they are going to be and see if the relation, with whom they're staying, knows of a nice cosy shooting and fishing lodge which we could all rent."

"Sounds great," answered Guy. "I'm definitely up for it and perhaps the elusive uncle could point us in the right direction for a bit of help in the house as well. We could go deep sea fishing if the weather allows. We could take the dogs, do some wonderful walking and explore castles and various other ancient monuments. The girls would love all those crofters' shops selling tweed and Shetland wool. Alicia could take her paints and Adriana loves her photography. Personally I shall enjoy sampling the whisky. No! Actually I can't think of anything I'd like better at the moment, especially if we can join up with the others – a thoroughly laid back type of holiday this time and with no drama for a change."

The girls were returning so they all moved in to the restaurant. The room was large and unadorned: spartan, with no nonsense tables and chairs and some very sombre looking portraits glowering down on the diners. Alicia raised her blue eyes to the picture on the wall above their table.

"Well, I'm not going to sit with that one staring down at me, I can tell you. I'm going to sit with my back to the horrid old man." She grabbed a chair nearest the window while the head waiter rushed to assist, stifling a grin as he did so. He'd heard what she'd said.

Adriana sat opposite her friend.

"Thanks very much, now I've got him." Adriana got up again and moved to one side, while the waiter hovered. "It's weird! Look: his eyes are watching me wherever I am. Why on earth do artists want to paint people like that?"

"Because they get a bloody great commission, that's why! Now sit down for goodness sake," Julian insisted. "People are staring."

"Perhaps we could turn him around on the wall. That would, no doubt, go down really well," suggested Alicia, laughing with glee at the very thought of such an unpardonable sin.

"Stop it you two! Behave and, by the way, that is an extremely famous picture, mainly because the man's eyes do follow you wherever you are in this room."

"Well he gives me the creeps," replied Adriana allowing the linen table napkin to be placed across her knees.

"Thank you," she said politely looking up with a smiling apology to the maître d. She was rewarded with a surreptitious wink.

Guy, stifling a smile, shook his dark curly head. He loved being in this ancient relic of a building, in the heart of London. He'd had many intriguing private meetings here. Nobody would ever suspect a clandestine rendezvous in such an un-cool, slightly inferior, men's club. No one could possibly feel intimidated in such a place so, as far as he was concerned, it served its purpose well. On this occasion he was with his wife and his best friends. They were about to have a surprisingly good lunch with excellent wine and would be beautifully looked after. The menus were duly handed around, then with the important decisions of what to eat and drink dealt with, the four friends sat back happily to plan their forthcoming trip North.

"Well," Adriana piped up, "I for one am really glad not to be going to some chic international destination this year because I will have been fighting with squirrels and not fit for polite company for a bit after that."

"Fighting with squirrels! What on earth are you talking about Arri," asked Alicia taken aback. Adriana leant forward grinning.

"I shall be trying to stop the wretched little Squirrel Nutkins from pinching all our walnuts from our one and only precious tree." Julian chuckled continuing to tease his fiancée.

"Believe it or not, she literally gets up each morning at the crack of dawn trying to beat them to the pitch. Only thing is I keep telling her that it's a pointless operation to get up so early, as squirrels can see in the dark and they don't kip all that much in the winter anyway. They won't even stop for breakfast when they are busy hoarding."

"Sounds rather like those dreadful pushy people who get up especially early to bag all the poolside loungers on package holidays," Alicia giggled. "How funny you are Arri. I'd love to be a fly on the wall or rather in the tree!"

"Yes, well you can come and help if you want, but the thing is that when I've won the battle and harvested all the nuts my hands remain black for at least another month. Gloves don't help, they're too cumbersome." Alicia glanced down at her perfect pink fingernails and laughed again.

"No thanks then to the job offered!"

Guy, smiling, sat quietly listening to all the carefree chatter about the hilarious squirrels versus Adriana saga. He took the time to study the two beautiful long legged creatures at his table: his wife Alicia, the cooler, chic blond with her perfectly cut shiny hair, the slimmest of figures and eyes the colour of the Grecian sea; he adored her. Then Adriana, just as attractive, but completely different with a very sexy voluptuous shape, hazel coloured eyes and long tumbling, tawny coloured mane. He glanced across at Julian with his fair unruly mop falling over one eye - how lucky they both were. But Arri and Julian still weren't married and it seemed to be the longest engagement that he'd ever heard of. Julian appeared to have unrevealed reservations about actually tying the knot. It was, Guy imagined, something to do with his parents being unhappy for most of their married life. Perhaps he should suggest a trip to Gretna Green, so they could get it over and done with, if they wanted to in Scotland.

He and Julian were complete opposites. His closest friend and work mate was tall, lean and athletic, inclined to moroseness on occasion, but not lacking in humour: and fearless, perhaps verging on the reckless when the chips were down. While he himself was dark, stocky, steady and strong in character with, he hoped, more than his fair share of courage. In their 'other work' Julian and he complimented each other; they were, without doubt, reliably good when working together on a mission.

The two young women presently at his table were also not quite what they seemed. They and their two absent close girlfriends who, with any luck, would be joining them up North, were probably the most gutsy women he knew. Had they been born into a different age, they would both have been in their element working with the resistance in France during the last war. He was proud of them all.

"Guy! You're miles away," Alicia broke into his thoughts, "what are you looking so serious about?"

"I was just thinking," answered Guy without hesitation, "how wonderful it will be to all be together again, this time in the back of beyond, without a care in the world, for at least a whole fortnight and I hope that the others can come too."

"Yes," replied Alicia with a smile, "I do so very much hope that Rose, Oliver, Emma and Marc will all be with us, then we shall be complete."

"Don't forget the little one," Adriana said, smiling.

They all laughed and nodded in agreement. Julian topped up their drinks and raised his glass to the others.

"Yes, you're right, how could we ever forget that little miracle?

To Guy's god-daughter Poppy Rose!"

"And," said Alicia, taking a sip and with shining eyes looking at her husband, "to shared past adventures, which made all our relationships so very special, our holiday and to the future." Everybody was quiet for a minute remembering, then the Irishman purposely cleared his throat.

"To our absent friends, to the present and hopefully... to a peaceful, happy holiday for us all," Guy added with feeling then drained his glass in one.

CHAPTER 2

It was autumn in early October; a crisp clear sunny day in the highlands and the telephone was ringing insistently.

"Marc, can you answer it?" called Emma from the kitchen of his uncle's shooting lodge. "Goodness knows who it is. I haven't given the number to anybody except our parents and Alicia and we only spoke to them a couple of days ago."

Emma could hear Marc obviously pleased to speak to whoever it was, so she turned the cooker plate to low and wandered in to the sitting room to listen. It was Guy and, judging from Marc's enthusiasm, there was a new plan afoot. Her husband was positively beaming. She sat beside him; he turned and with his free hand stroked her cheek. His tanned face was alight with enthusiasm. He took back his hand and ran his fingers through his own dark auburn hair; his unusual flecked eyes twinkling.

"But this place is huge," he was saying, "it's got eight bedrooms, all with bathrooms. We only use three and we have it for as long as we wish. You can come here; it's stupid to try and find another place now. Anyway, I know about the one that you had booked. It's lucky it's fallen through as you wouldn't have liked it anyway." Emma was nodding assent, grinning from ear to ear. "Of course she'll be pleased; she'll be thrilled. It will be wonderful for us all to be together again and under the same roof."

Emma grabbed the telephone.

"I've been listening. What a brilliant idea you all coming here, it's a much better plan. I'm so excited and Guy your god-daughter, who is nearly running now, I might add, will be ecstatic. Just imagine Uncle Guy and Aunt Rose both at the same time. What a treat for Poppy and for us. When are you coming?"

Guy, at the other end of the telephone was hesitating slightly, worried in case Emma and Marc would rather have had the place to themselves for a bit longer. Emma, aware of this, put her hand over the mouthpiece and whispered to Marc.

"They're fussed about interrupting our romantic holiday, for goodness sake!" Then she quickly removed her hand and resumed the conversation.

"OK, come whenever you like, but as soon as possible; we'll be waiting. I'll hand you back to Marc for the directions and things. Love to you both. Bye."

Emma tip-toed upstairs to check on Poppy while Marc was giving Guy what sounded like extremely complicated directions. Surely such a high tech person as Guy would have a sat nav. She peeped around the door of her child's bedroom relishing the reassuring smell of a recently bathed, warm, milky baby. The cherubic little girl was lying on her side, one arm raised above her red golden curls, while the other hand clutched the soft pink pig that Rose had brought back from a trip to Barcelona. Emma covered her sleeping daughter where she'd kicked off her blanket, kissed a rosy cheek and went to her own room before going back downstairs.

A content happy face looked back at Emma from the looking glass. Should she wear her long dark hair loose tonight or tie it back as Marc best liked it? He always said that he preferred to be able to see as much of her face as possible. She adored her husband so she brushed it till it shone then tied it back. Standing up, she then turned sideways to glance at the long mirror on the wall. Emma held her tummy in, not that she really needed to. She knew that she was now a little more voluptuous, but she had regained her figure pretty quickly after producing Poppy. All the rushing around after a young baby, she imagined, was enough to get anybody back into shape. Not that she'd remain this way for long, all being well. How lucky she was to have carried her first child full term given the horrific dramas endured in early pregnancy. At that time she'd been in the mountains of Switzerland with the very same friends who would soon be here, filling the house with their laughter. What would she have done without these friends? Emma knew that she was truly blessed, both with her husband, her daughter and with this most special group of people. Quietly, she said an appropriate prayer every night of her life.

❄

Jessica, the daughter of a family friend, staying with them to help look after Poppy, was already mashing the potatoes for supper when Emma came back downstairs. Marc was fiddling around with a bottle of wine he'd taken out of the fridge.

"Thanks Jessie, that's great. You really are the best masher of potatoes. Do you want to eat with us or are you too involved in a TV program in your room?" Jessica looked up at her employer gratefully. She really liked this couple and she adored Poppy. They were the loveliest people to be with and never took anything or anybody for granted.

"Actually, I'd like to take mine upstairs if you don't mind, Emma? I can also hear Poppy more easily if she wakes. You two can have some peace and make your plans. Marc tells me that you have several friends coming. That should be fun. You know, I could ask my sister to come up to help with the cooking if you like. She's really good."

"What a brilliant idea that would be, then I wouldn't worry about leaving you on your own if we all go out a bit. Do you think she'd come and at such short notice?"

"I don't see why not, she was really jealous of me coming up here with you and she's not doing anything at the moment. I'll go and ring her and see if she's still free," Jessica answered helpfully. Marc smiled as he listened to this conversation.

"Well, what a turn up for the books, but are you sure you're happy about this?" he asked Emma just a little concerned. "It's quite an invasion. Let's hope that Jess' sister can come as I don't want to load all the work on you. After all it is your holiday as well as everybody else's."

"Good heavens! Of course I'm happy," replied Emma immediately, "and if Jessie gets her sister up to help with the cooking as well, we'll be all set. It will be wonderful fun to have all my most favourite people here. You'd better just check it's alright with your uncle though and find out about the fishing rights."

"Alec won't mind a bit. He loves to have people around. He's been lonely since my aunt died," said Marc. "In fact he'll be delighted, as he says that the fishing on this beat has never reached its full potential, so maybe Julian will catch something huge and we can make history."

The travel plans were made. With two dogs, they couldn't all fit in one car, so Alicia, Guy, Julian and Adriana were going to drive up in Guy's four-by-four, while Olly and Rose were going to catch the night sleeper train to Scotland. Rose hadn't been on it for years and so the journey would bring back memories of her childhood.

They'd all taken a full fortnight off work. Alicia had promised to make some notes on the Western Isles and coast of Scotland for a future travel article. Rose had arranged to keep in touch with her interior decorating business just in case of a problem and would pick up her emails on her iPad. Guy and Julian always remained in touch with the unnamed and unexplained contacts in their army life, but both Alicia and Adriana were used to this and it no longer worried them too much. Arri had somebody covering for her in her literary agency and she had brought a couple of new manuscripts to read, in case they were housebound on rainy days. Olly was owed extra time off as he'd worked two weekends in a row before coming away.

Rose was excited. The very idea of being with Emma, Alicia and Adriana again was just good beyond all expectation. They were her three closest friends and she and Olly also got on very well with their other halves. The added bonus would be to spend time with her small god-daughter Poppy? Rose truly loved the child; they all did. So she could thoroughly spoil her.

Rose had a slight boyish figure and with her short curly hair and freckled face she was a walking advert for some health product. She leapt athletically up into the train after her luggage and set out to find her sleeping berth. She looked at the ticket, it wasn't far and she was in the right carriage. With the friendly attendant's help she stowed her baggage in the neat little compartment and then sat down to wait for Olly.

There was plenty of time; he was coming straight from his office. Rose knew he wouldn't be late. He was meticulous about starting journeys without a panic so she began to enjoy the adventure of being on the night sleeper to Scotland for the first time in so many years. It hadn't lost its appeal. Anything could happen on a night train, she felt. As a child she had always imagined weird goings on, but tonight she had Olly to protect her and she was determined to make the most of the romantic ambience as well. After all she was still a 'bride' as they had only been married for just over eleven months. Smiling happily, in preparation for Olly's arrival, Rose took out the ice cold bottle of champagne, two glasses and the smoked salmon sandwiches which she'd made earlier. The holiday was about to begin.

Their other four friends were already on their way, stopping for a night with people they knew in North Yorkshire.

❄

Guy's car was about the biggest four-by-four on the road but even so there wasn't much room left for people after the luggage, fishing rods, gumboots, warm coats and two dogs were all packed in. Adriana's small wire haired dachshund snuggled up on her knee but Guy's golden retriever had to sit in the back, half on top of the mound of luggage. Barley didn't seem to mind and, looking rather superior, chose to ignore little Fudge sitting blissfully on Adriana's lap. As long as Barley managed to get into the car the big dog was quite content to stay where he was, to sleep and to look periodically out of the window. Julian sat beside Guy. They shared the driving and the girls tried not to back seat drive, although when the men on occasion argued with the sat nav they couldn't contain their mirth. Especially, as just after they'd set off, they'd disregarded the instructions and had ended up in the Holloway Prison car park. There was just nothing like being with your dearest friends on the very first day of a long holiday. It was almost like being a child all over again.

CHAPTER 3

Jessica's very capable sister arrived the day before the guests. Beth obviously was a cook. She looked the part and was the complete opposite to her thin, shapely and very trendy fair haired sister. She had a cheerful, attractive face, with dark twinkly eyes and wild curly brown hair tied back with a bright scarf. These other attributes, together with an awesome energy, more than made up for her rather over indulged body. She had a great sense of humour and fitted in with everybody, including Poppy, who immediately fell for her charm and the home made chocolate brownies which she'd brought up for them all.

Beth had also arrived by train but had hired a car so that she could be independent and do all the shopping whenever she needed. Emma also thought that it would be good for the two girls to be able to go out when they had a day or night off. How far you actually had to go to get somewhere where there was even a bright light, she wasn't quite sure. So she decided to go over to see Marc's uncle, to glean a bit more information about the area, as they hadn't been there long and had hardly even ventured out to explore. Marc was going to meet the overnight train in the morning and the others, who were driving up, would arrive around tea time.

Emma rang Alec who immediately invited her over for coffee. She'd left Marc and Jess in charge while Beth had set off to find the shops!

Alec Neilson lived a mile and a half away, in a typically dismal grey Scottish pile of a place called Glencurrie. Emma's first thought as she walked in was how cold it was and thank God they were in the cosy lodge instead of this mausoleum of a building. She had quite expected a lugubrious butler or a formidable housekeeper in black to answer the door when she rang the bell. The jangling

...med to peel away in some dark cavernous corner of the ...ng; quite a hike, Emma thought, from the actual front door. ...when it finally opened she was met by a woman of a certain ...ge with a bright smiling face. Mrs Haddington introduced herself at once, ushering Emma quickly inside and firmly shutting the big door behind her with a resounding clunk. Mrs H, as Emma was told to call her, had been with the family for a long time as had her husband Stuart who, together with a young boy who occasionally came in his holidays, looked after the garden. She was the shape of a dumpling and dressed a little like a modern-day Mrs Tiggy Winkle. Emma liked her efficient but friendly openness. A reliable, comfortable and comforting person, she felt, especially in times of trouble. What an odd thing to think on first meeting a person, Emma thought to herself, as she was shown in to the sitting room where her husband's uncle was waiting.

Alec was as tall as her father-in-law John and quite similar, although more serious looking perhaps. Emma knew him to be both kind and hospitable. She also understood that he had adored his wife and still felt lost without her. Consequently Marc had said that he was delighted to have them all close by in the lodge. He rose smiling to meet her.

"Hello Emma! How lovely to see you. I trust you are well and I hope that you are all comfortable and that my great-niece approves of her holiday home!"

"Good morning Alec. Yes thank you we all adore the lodge; in fact we are so settled that you might never get rid of us!"

"And how wonderful that would be," he answered good-naturedly.

"Come and sit down and Mrs H will bring us some coffee."

Emma glanced at the family photographs on the table beside the sofa as she sat down. There was a lovely one of Alec and Caroline with their grown up children.

"I wish I'd known your wife," she said sadly. "I know how very fond of her Marc was."

"And she of him," he replied, thoughtful for a moment. "Ah yes, Caroline loved your husband almost as much as our own children. He was by far her favourite nephew. Also never forget that she knew all about you and had even seen a charming photograph, taken when your families all met up in London, just when Caroline had first gone into hospital? I even told her of how you two met and fell in love in Greece. She thought that your romance was extra special and that you sounded perfect for Marc. So you see you were already part of our family so far as Caroline was concerned."

"Thank you Alec, that's such a lovely thought and makes me feel almost as if I knew Caroline, although we never actually met."

The door opened and Mrs H came in with a tray laden with coffee and biscuits. She was nodding her head, as she put the tray down, obviously disapproving of something. Alec didn't miss a thing, Emma quickly realised.

"What's up Mrs H? Somebody's put your nose out of joint unless I'm very much mistaken. Let's have it then." He glanced across at Emma and winked as Mrs H stood up straight then fixed her employer with a beady eye.

"It's those immigrant people," she stated immediately. "Stuart caught a couple of them snooping around the outhouses again. They said, from what he understood, that they were trying to get to the village of Dromvaar by the sea. Well, they were way off route out here, so he sent them packing and was going to go up and see Mac in the pub tonight, as he said he thought they looked suspicious. But where are these folk coming from I ask myself? They look like gypsies and in need of a good bath." Alec chuckled and Mrs Haddington, having said her piece, bent to pour the coffee.

"I expect they came in from Europe off the boats," Alec remarked, "most probably looking for work and, I expect, intending to take advantage of our hospitality in the way of benefits. We're a soft option for these middle Europeans who suffer a very poor way of life and I'm afraid, Mrs H, it's not a problem getting into this country either with or without a passport these days. But perhaps you'd ask Stuart to pop in for a word before he finishes tonight." Mrs Haddington gave a loud harrumph and answered firmly.

"I shall certainly do that, Colonel Neilson. Thank you." She handed both of them their coffee and went to leave the room, muttering about how she failed to understand why these people couldn't stay in their own country, as she did so. The door closed quietly behind her. Emma looked across at Alec and giggled.

"You see, I am well protected up here," laughed Alec handing Emma the plate of shortbread.

"Yes, well I wouldn't be worried either with Mrs Haddington around. What's her husband Stuart like?" she asked, genuinely interested.

"All brawn but with a full load of common sense. He's the salt of this earth, as honest as the day is long and - loyal like no other. The pair of them have been here with me forever and I can't imagine what I'd do without either of them."

"That's really special," murmured Emma and meaning it.

On the way back to the lodge Emma thought how reassuring her visit had been. I'll know where to come if ever I'm in trouble she thought and then pulled herself up short. 'What trouble? Why on earth should she think like that again? Stupid!'

Beth was just drawing up in her little rented Fiat when Emma arrived back at the lodge. She got out and went to help her in with the shopping.

"How did you get on?" Emma enquired of the young woman, who was smiling broadly.

"Brilliant," answered Beth looking pleased with herself, "and I found a really good-news fisherman, named Fergus, who had a great catch he'd just landed. He said to tell you that if anybody wants to go trolling for mackerel he's your man. Here's his mobile number."

"Well, you have been busy," Emma replied taking the rather scruffy looking piece of crumpled paper. It smelt distinctly fishy. "Anything else interesting to report?"

"Yes, Dromvaar is a lovely little village with everything that we might need and apparently it's also got a great pub."

"Ah ha! No doubt your tame fisherman told you that. Did he ask you out then?" Emma couldn't resist teasing the cheerful Beth who had the grace to blush.

"Not exactly, but he did say that he's there most evenings." She laughed.

"Excellent. So we can take it in turns looking after Poppy and go and indulge in wild nights in Dromvaar then. Just what the good doctor ordered, I'd say."

"Just what exactly did the doctor order?" Marc asked appearing with Poppy in his arms.

"There's a great pub in the village. Hello darling." Emma said softly, taking the little girl from him, then to Marc, "can you help us get all this inside? It looks like Fortnum and Mason has nothing on Dromvaar and it's going to rain. I just felt a spot."

They had just managed to get the last bag into the house when the heavens opened.

Their four friends driving up to Scotland were well on their way but also suffering from the elements.

"What awful weather. I hope it's not going to go on doing this the further North we go." Adriana peered out of the car window across the bleak Yorkshire moors.

"Well, I don't know about anybody else but I'm looking forward to stopping for the night, having a bath and a hot meal,"

Alicia said sleepily.

"Let's walk the dogs before we get there, if it stops raining," suggested Julian. "At least the fish will be on the rise with all this wet stuff," he added somewhat morosely, as an after-thought.

"You and your bloody fishing Julian," remarked Guy, "you're in the wrong trade. But we've only got another ten miles, so yes we'll let the dogs out if it eases up enough. I just hope your relative has opened a decent bottle of whisky."

"Don't worry Guy, he will have. He and Jayne are without doubt the most hospitable people I know and she's a great cook too," Adriana chipped in enthusiastically.

"Good," replied Guy with feeling. I'm extremely glad it's not my cousins we are staying with, as you'd be lucky if you got a sandwich let alone a glass of any sort. They wouldn't appreciate our dogs either."

"Yes, they were dreadful," agreed Alicia, "and they argued all the time. We're never going there again." She laughed remembering the hideous evening spent in the over-the-top interior decorated manor house in Gloucestershire. "I just can't wait to be in Scotland with all our friends and the wee darling Poppy who we can spoil mercilessly."

It had been an exhausting journey and, because of the torrential rain, had taken much longer than expected. They were all tired and hungry.

❇

Rose sat in their sleeping compartment waiting for Oliver to appear. She'd seen the ticket inspector and the cheerful attendant, who had been so helpful when she first boarded the train. He had told her to make herself comfortable and that he'd be along to see her again as soon as her husband arrived.

Rose had just decided to start on the smoked salmon sandwiches she'd made when the connecting door burst open and there was Olly.

"Heavens Olly! What on earth are you doing? There might be someone else in there!"

"There is," laughed Oliver making way for the same member of staff who had just unlocked the door and now stood behind him beaming. He nodded to them both and backed out leaving them alone.

"And guess what?" Olly continued making sure that their door was well and truly locked, "because we're not long from our honeymoon we have been upgraded so we have been given connecting rooms – how about that?"

"Goodness how extravagant," replied Rose, overexcited.

"No," responded Olly, "it's only a little extra because the train's not full and we are newly married; well fairly newly married!" Rose was rummaging around in the little Scotrail bag on the bed.

"Look, look... a toothbrush, paste, a flannel and ear plugs, would you believe? There's even a basin in here." She stood to lift up the little fitted dressing table underneath the window, so as to show him. Just then there was a knock on the door. Olly opened it to another smiling attendant.

"Good evening, Sir. Now would you be liking a call in the morning and a cup of tea for your lady wife, perhaps as we go through Glen Garry?"

"Yes, thank you, but what time exactly would that be do you think?" Olly realised that it could be at an ungodly early hour.

"Usually about half-six, Sir; depending on our journey." Rose was jumping around in the compartment behind her husband.

"Yes please! Oh yes please! And would there be any chance of a biscuit do you think? With the tea I mean?"

"But of course, and you shall have the best shortbread that Scotland has to offer," the man added with a grin.

After he'd gone Rose couldn't sit still.

"What shall we do now, Olly? The train's not due to leave for another half hour."

"Well, I suggest that we go along to the lounge car and have some supper, as I'm starving, but I need a wash first."

Rose uncovered the hidden treat whilst Oliver washed his hands.

"OK, but first let's have this. Look what I brought with me?" With a flourish, she brandished the bottle of champagne, cooling in its ice bag and undid the hastily wrapped pack of smoked salmon sandwiches, which she'd just been about to start.

"These can be our first course," Rose announced with sparkling eyes holding them up for him to see. Olly took one, bit into it, then picked up the bottle to pour her a glass of champagne.

"Alright," he laughed. "Let's make a night of it then; we're on holiday!"

When they had eaten all their sandwiches and were well over half way through the bottle of champagne, Oliver stood up and looked around the tiny compartment.

"What are you doing?" asked Rose innocently.

"I am just considering where and how in this wonderful five star suite I shall ravage you first." Rose giggled.

"Shall we wait till the train moves off then? I don't like the thought of all these people just outside... look..." she said, letting the blind up with a ping.

"Christ Rose! Put it down for God's sake!" He leaned across to grab the blind to tug it down again, as he did so making eye contact with two KGB look-a-likes walking close by outside. "You have quite put me off my stride you silly girl." Olly laughed good-naturedly adding, "not that it will take much to get me in the mood again." He reached out and Rose, giggling, ducked away.

"OK, OK but let's have dinner first. I'm still hungry."

"Alright, let's go along to find our table."

The last doors were slammed shut and locked then the train gave the most almighty lurch, creaked, sighed and set off slowly out of the station.

Oliver took his wife firmly by the hand and led her along the narrow passageway to the dining car where there were a few passengers already quietly eating. It was Friday night; people were tired after a busy week. A smiling lady in uniform greeted them and led them to their table where a bottle of white wine was waiting, already chilling in a cooler. The menus were brought and the two young people, enjoying every minute of this new experience, happily chose what they would eat. They sipped their wine and watched the lights of London flash past, soon giving way to empty darkness made even more exciting by the hurry and the rhythm of the wheels on the line. Rose's cheeks had a warm glow of happiness. Oliver studied his wife, with her shining eyes, as she stared out of the window. He considered himself the luckiest man on earth. An hour and a half later they returned to their sleeping compartment.

"At last," Olly said standing up, peeling off his clothes and putting out his arms. "Come here my darling I cannot resist you for another single moment. This is a new venue and I wonder what might be the best way to start with?" Rose had already wriggled out of her jeans and jacket. She looked across at her husband and met his twinkling grey eyes.

"Come and get me," she cried above the noise of the rattling train, bracing herself against the edge of the bunk. He crossed the small divide, pressed hard against her and taking her face between his hands began to kiss her waiting mouth.

A night of uninhibited passion began. In spite of the

seemingly small space allowed them, there proved to be endless alluring possibilities for two fit athletic bodies. Rose considered this over-night sleeper train to Scotland to be one of the most romantic and exciting journeys to be had and she was determined to make the most of it. Whenever Oliver had Rose to himself he became completely lost in desire to luxuriate in her body as if for the very first time. She was extraordinary in her different, ever-changing needs which she always adapted to the occasion offered. For him it was like having a hungry little lioness who liked to be devoured and also to do the devouring. She showed an enormous capacity for love and loving and he could never have enough of her.

CHAPTER 4

"What a night!" Adriana never ceased to be amazed by the sheer stamina of both Julian and Guy when they decided to make the most of the evening! Alicia let out a sigh.

"And it seems that neither of them have a hangover either which is really annoying. I don't know how they do it, do you?" she asked of her friend beside her in the car. There were a couple of grunts from the front. Guy was concentrating hard, as the rain was once more sheeting down making driving difficult. Julian was navigating as they'd decided to give the motorway a miss in view of the conditions. Adriana was, once more, vigorously rubbing cream into her walnut stained hands.

"But I don't think our hosts were feeling too good this morning, poor things: having to get up early to look after that needy little boy of theirs must have been tough."

"Yes," Alicia muttered looking away and out of the window, "and I have to say that breakfast with their whingeing child rather puts me off wanting to have children just yet." Adriana said nothing and looked down at her hands.

"Thank God for that," muttered Guy under his breath in the front. Julian, ignoring the conversation was busy scrutinizing the map.

"OK Guy, forget the sat nav for the moment as it's going to keep trying to take us back to the motorway. Take the next right then straight through the next village and on for about fifteen miles, then I'll look again." He put the map down and peeled the wrapper off a peppermint. This was turning out to be some long journey and he could have done with a cigarette, but Guy wouldn't let him smoke in his car.

"I vote we ring Marc when we stop for lunch. Perhaps we should suggest meeting at the pub tonight and then he could lead us in, as he says the wretched machine gets lost in the hills and they have no proper post code up there anyway."

"Good idea. They have some help to look after Poppy, so why not suggest supper out, as we'll be late, then it will save any cooking as well? What do you think girls?"

"Excellent plan," agreed Alicia, "but I'll ring them now, on my mobile then Emma won't have started organizing dinner."

Emma picked up the telephone at the first ring.

"Hello Emma it's us, how are you?"

"Hello 'us' we're fine, thanks. Rose and Olly have only just arrived. The train was late because of a tree across the line. We've lit the fire and now we're playing scrabble, can you believe? Where have you got to? Are you having a foul drive 'cos I'm afraid it's not so good up here either?"

"Dreadful. Torrential rain and we are definitely going to be late, so we thought a good plan might be to meet at the pub, perhaps in Dromvaar, for supper and then you could lead us in. That's if you can leave Poppy, of course. What do you think?"

"Yes, that would be great as you'll never find us otherwise, particularly in this weather. Also it will give my lovely cook Beth a bit longer to settle in with her sister. She says the pub there is great. I'll find the number and book a table. Roughly at what time, do you think?"

❄

Mac, the local bobby, in charge of several villages including Dromvaar, stopped by at the Royal Stag just before midday. He reckoned that the barman would be relatively free to talk to him. He wanted to see if he knew anything about Colonel Alec's immigrants. Where were these people coming into the country and where were they living? What did they do and most importantly who helped them get here? He'd like to check whether they even had a passport. The Colonel had told him what to look for if it was false. Mac was an old fashioned sort of policeman. Modern day patrol cars which charged around the place, oblivious as to what was really going on and based in the cities, were no good in his part of the highlands. He knew just about everybody in the area, had a good many friends and missed nothing. Mac determined to keep it this way. He was off duty and in civilian clothes but none the less, out of habit, he parked his old Land-Rover around the corner from the main entrance to the pub. He didn't want to frighten any of the young people off as they were the ones who got around and were most likely to notice things. He left his Labrador, Donald, in the car. He didn't want the old dog in trouble again for creating chaos by chasing the pub's obnoxious marmalade cat. At his last visit, the wretched creature had shinned up the curtains and pulled the rail down, narrowly missing nutty old Meg's head. Seeing as the old girl 'did' for the pub, this didn't go down too well.

Mac was past middle age, tall with greying hair at the temples and, in spite of his wife Maggie's excellent cooking, had so far managed to keep his figure trim. He had a great sense of humour and was well liked. But he had a gut feeling that perhaps things weren't quite as they should be.

"Hello Mac," called Dougie as the policeman approached the bar. "I see you're in civvies, so I imagine you'd like a pint of the usual?"

"Yes, please Dougie, I do have a wee spot that needs topping up. Actually, I wanted to ask you something." He watched as the barman concentrated, taking extra trouble to fill the glass to the brim. Mac felt his mouth watering in anticipation. Dougie carefully handed the frothing beer across the bar. Mac took a thirsty great slug and reverted to his native tongue.

"Och!... that's guid. Bless ye." He looked at the drink lovingly, smacking his lips, then cleared his throat: back to business.

"I was wondering, Dougie - if you had any thoughts regarding these immigrant people who seem to be appearing out of nowhere. The old Colonel's had a few problems with them sniffing around, up at Glencurrie."

"Ay, they seem harmless enough. One of them's a gardener I hear, a nice enough lad. He's been in the pub. I dinnae ken about the others. Haven't had much contact, although I see them around once in a while. They keep themselves to themselves, I believe."

"Yes," agreed Mac, "which makes it very difficult to assess exactly what they're doing here in these parts."

"Looking for work I s'pose," replied Dougie, losing interest as another perspective customer walked in, stopping to hang his coat up on the row of hooks by the door.

"See if you can find out a bit from the lad then Dougie, if he comes in again. Find out where they've come from and where they live if you can."

"According to Ailsa they don't speak much," answered Dougie turning to look at Mac again. "She says the laird has one or two helping around the castle. He sends them down sometimes to pick up an order. They'll not be living in the village here or Ailsa would know about it. But I'll let you know and keep an eye open as I always do, Mac. Now how about another?" Mac nodded and Dougie went on to tell him that the young people in the Colonel's lodge were all booked in for dinner and so Fergus had brought in some nice fresh fish. The chef was pulling out all the stops as it was a good booking for the time of year.

CHAPTER 5

"We're nearly there," announced Julian turning to awaken the sleeping girls. "Take a left here Guy, then it should be the next village."

"Well done, you haven't lost your touch. You're still a bloody good navigator," Guy declared, relieved to have almost finished the journey. Although they had shared the driving it was still a long way from London to their destination, which was almost on a level with Skye.

The party from the lodge were all seated at a long trestle by the fire waiting expectantly for their friends to arrive. The pub was buzzing and there wasn't an empty table to be seen. It was lucky that they had booked. Since a renowned sous-chef had bailed out of London and taken over the restaurant, The Royal Stag had become a popular eating place. The talented Ginger (for obvious reasons) O'Cleary, said he'd had enough of the rich and famous and everybody on the take in the West End. He had come up for a break and met Fergus who had introduced him to Dougie. The pub was under private ownership and the absentee landlord and landowner was badly in need of a chef at the time. He was a rich man and spent much of his time swanning around the continent followed by a string of unsuitable women. Dougie had been told to stop bothering him and to get on and find a decent cook. Ginger, as far as Dougie was concerned, had dropped out of heaven and now their takings had more than doubled, just to prove it. It also meant that his wife Ailsa didn't have to worry about the pub. She loved being at the tweed mill and much preferred to keep her work life separate from that of her husband.

Fergus, who'd been propping up the bar when the English party arrived, had just come across to introduce himself and to remind Marc that he was 'ready, willing and able', as he had put it, to take anybody out fishing whenever they wished. 'Just for a wee sum mind', he had added, with a charming wink, much to the amusement of the girls. The fisherman, Emma could see, had a certain outdoor humorous allure. No wonder that Beth was slightly taken with him.

❄

Finally, just after half past eight, the weary travellers walked in to complete the group. There was a hush as all heads swung round to see who the driving rain and cold autumn wind had blown in on such a night. Even after travelling all day the two blonde women caused a distraction. No self- respecting Scot was going to neglect his God given duty to stare at something beautiful. Emma and Rose had already endured this ill conceived attention and were delighted when both Alicia and Adriana underwent the same treatment, as they walked to the table. Seldom had eight people been so pleased to be together. The excitement was infectious and the noise level in the pub was immediately raised even higher. Now their holiday had really begun.

The Royal Stag consisted of three rooms with various nooks and crannies off each one. Although grey and somewhat dour on the outside the inside was surprisingly atmospheric, warm and welcoming, with open fires kept well stocked up. Dougie came across immediately to greet his new customers.

"Och you must have had a terrible journey," he declared, taking it upon himself to help the newcomers off with their coats. His confidence had grown since he no longer had to worry about his chef. Dougie now had a good team waiting on the tables and behind the bar, so he had begun to consider himself as more of a maitre d' and Ailsa was proud of him.

The dining area was in a separate section to the overcrowded bar, where the few chairs were taken, so that people were mostly standing around the counter and leaning against the banisters. It took Alicia and Adriana a full five minutes to thread their way between people and the tables to find the downstairs wash room.

"I'm afraid there's a bit of a queue," giggled a young girl coming up towards them.

"Right, thanks, you go Ally. I'll wait up here and have a people watching moment."

"OK, shan't be a minute." Alicia ran on down the stairs. Adriana stood at the top looking around her. Friday evening: a familiar sight in most western countries of the world; a cross section of predominately the younger generation all enjoying themselves after a hard week's work. But the very broad Scots accent was different here, quite musical really, Adriana thought. Mostly locals she noticed, discreetly studying those nearest to her. She wished Ally would hurry up as she'd soon be crossing her legs. She should have taken the opportunity offered at the last awful grubby garage, but hadn't been able to face either the likely even grubbier facilities, or the rain, when she left the comforting warmth of the car.

She glanced around. Three darker skinned foreigners, standing in a huddle, to one side of the open staircase caught her attention. Unlike others, they looked ill at ease which was why she had noticed them. They were talking in low voices and rather furtively looking around as if waiting for someone. 'Up to no good', was the thought which sprang immediately to mind. The door opened at the bottom of the stairs and Alicia re-appeared. As Adriana started down, it brought her nearer the creepy looking group and she hesitated. Another older man and a small, oddly attractive looking, pale faced girl were now joining them, with a child of about ten in tow. The appearance of the youngster in the pub was being heatedly discussed, with much gesticulation and then he was sent out with the proverbial flea in his ear. Adriana felt sorry for the boy. He looked sullen and sad. The girl appeared excited. The others were all shuffling around to make room, looking relieved. As the man leant towards his friends, Adriana looked away aware that she was staring, but she distinctly heard him say in a heavily accented, guttural voice, "the red ones are here." He'd had to speak up to make himself heard. Then in a marked Irish brogue, the girl also piped up. "Yes, to be sure the squirrels have been extra busy this time; plenty of young ones they have." She was unbuttoning a thick anorak and was grinning as if she'd imparted what sounded like extremely welcome news. The men smirked back, at which point they went out of sight. A man leaning against the banister was looking down at Adriana with interest so she quickly averted her eyes and continued on down. Alicia was coming up towards her.

"What were you doing Arri?" Alicia swept up beside her, "that man up there obviously wants to pick you up," she teased. "Don't look back, he's staring after you. See you back at the table." Adriana nodded smiling, her mind elsewhere as she pushed the door of the washroom open again. How odd though. Why on earth would people like that be interested in squirrels of all things? Whatever could it have meant 'the red ones are here'? Some sort of message perhaps? And... what on earth was that young, if tough-looking woman and child doing with such people? Curious she thought, rubbing her still stained hands together, remembering her own recent bad experience with the wretched little animals.

Unless she was very much mistaken, except for the Irish girl, these unsavoury looking individuals were misfits up here. Middle European perhaps? They certainly didn't look or sound Polish. At home they had a young plumber who was from that country. The Poles were decent folk and worked hard for their money. She hadn't recognized the language. No, these people were from even further afield. It was curious because they seemed decidedly uncomfortable about being here. However on this coast surely anybody could sneak in off the ships which docked in the larger ports.

Perhaps these people weren't strangers at all. No one else seemed to be taking much notice of them, but then maybe the locals minded their own business. Her imagination was out of control again - supposedly it was because of past adventures and the secret other life that both Julian and Guy shared. She should be used to it by now, when on occasion the two men moved out and simply vanished. But they were on holiday and she must stop looking for trouble where none existed. Even so the shifty looking individuals gave her the shivers. There was something not exactly aggressive about them, but they exuded vibes of unease and an allure of unpleasant intrigue. Anyway, it really wasn't her concern. She must concentrate on other more important matters; like tying Julian down to a date for their long awaited nuptials to take place. This holiday would be a good occasion as they would be with their closest friends, who would all support her.

The small incident soon forgotten, Adriana returned to the table, where a glass of wine awaited her and where her friends were already scanning the menus. The menu looked delicious with a good selection of fresh fish. Today's catch sounded perfect.

After dinner the pub had emptied out and, while the group of friends drank their coffee, Fergus and Dougie came across to discuss the possibilities of a deep sea fishing trip for their party. Alicia's cool blue eyes discreetly appraised the publican and the fisherman, while they were busy talking to their men. Fergus for a start was fit as a fiddle, his face and unruly dark hair weathered by the sea, his cheeks now enhanced by the heat in the room. Certainly he was a man who enjoyed a joke, judging by the gist of the present conversation. He wore a high-necked jersey over faded blue jeans and had obviously been home and scrubbed up before coming here. Dougie on the other hand was running to plump with an equally cheerful open looking face, though coloured, she suspected, by his fair share of the alcohol he served rather than from the healthy air outside. His pale hair was receding slightly at the temples; he was in an open-necked, striped shirt and an old pair of cords. Two good, wholesome looking people, 'what you see is what you get' Alicia thought, now listening to the fishing discussion.

"What about this bit of inland water on Loch Island?" asked Julian, impatient to get his plan into action. "I've heard there are mega-sized brown trout for the catching." Adriana groaned and put her head in her hands. Guy laughed. Julian was always at his most charismatic when talking about fishing, his favourite subject. His eyes all lit up.

Fergus looked surprised.

"I canno' believe it, did you hear that, the man wants to go to Loch Island? What about that, d'you ken?" Dougie looked equally astonished.

"Well then, young man. D'you know then that the island was out of bounds for many years, along with another, because of that anthrax scare now long past?"

"Yes, I did know that," answered Julian, "but surely the anthrax ban was lifted many years ago?"

Adriana interrupted.

"Julian, I cannot understand why, what with all the other places you can fish up here, including Marc's uncle's much sort-after beat, you still want to go to this barren island; whatever for?"

"It's obviously got giant sized trout," Olly chipped in. 'Boring' Alicia mouthed at Rose who nodded, yawned and cuddled up closer to Olly.

"Well, well I'll be blowed," continued Fergus fixing Julian with a respectful smile. "A man after me own heart."

"The thing is," said Dougie, "that island only has a few sheep in the summer and it's deserted now. There's nothing on it at all and it is a fairly unforgiving place to be. No one goes out at this time of the year as it's a fair rough crossing and you have to go in from the West." Julian wasn't giving up. He turned to Fergus.

"Fergus, you have a decent sea going craft, I'm sure; couldn't you be persuaded?" Emma looked up at Marc, with her dark eyes, willing him to crush the plan. She, for one, didn't fancy the idea of being thrown around the sea in a smelly and dilapidated old fishing boat. She'd be as sick as a dog.

"I suggest we think on this plan, perhaps sleep on it and see what the weather does over the next couple of days," he said diplomatically, running his fingers through his thick, auburn coloured hair.

"Agreed," Guy replied, "there speaks the doctor and I don't know about anybody else but I'm ready for my bed. Dougie, perhaps we could have the bill?" Julian looking slightly crest fallen, but having given in reasonably gracefully, handed over his and Adriana's share of the money and went out for a quick smoke while the other men paid. Emma and Rose jumped up to retrieve all their coats. Alicia and Adriana bent down to look out of the window while they waited.

"Good heavens!" said Alicia, "it's actually stopped raining!"

Adriana peered out.

"Well at least for the moment it has and I can assure you that I certainly shan't be going out on Fergus's old tub, not unless the sun is shining and, judging from what people say, that doesn't seem to happen too often up here, at least not at this time of the year."

CHAPTER 6

It was late. Alec lay in his old four-poster bed pondering this strange gut feeling he had that something was wrong. Caroline used to say that he had second sense. True - these perceptions, which had often alerted him before an incident in the past, had seldom proved him wrong. They'd often come to the rescue of both he and his men during his long stint in Iraq. He thought about the conversation he'd had with Stuart the day before, regarding the two strangers who his gardener had caught snooping around the outhouses, supposedly wanting work. They were undoubtedly looking for something to pinch, Alec thought. Most likely it would be machinery to flog, from out of the barns.

He must ask Stuart what he had found out from the local bobby, Mac. If nothing was forthcoming he'd get in touch with one of his contacts near Aberdeen, over the other side of the country to see if they were having the same sort of problems over there. He'd like to find out what sort of checks were in place for people coming in off the ships. Alec was tired after a day spent in Edinburgh on family business and his shoulder, where he'd taken a bullet towards the end of his time in Iraq several years before, was giving him gip, so he hadn't ventured out again to see Stuart before he'd gone home. However, if there had been anything important to report he was quite sure that his housekeeper, Mrs H, would have already informed him.

Alec missed the army and all his friends in the regiment. They all talked the same language. But more than anything he missed Caroline. In all the years they'd had together she had been his soul mate. He just wished they'd had longer together as she would have loved having Marc and Emma up here, with his little great-niece Poppy. Alec sat up and took a deep drink of cooling water. Mrs H would put too many blankets on the bed: he was always too hot. He must remember to get her to make up the spare-room for his brother, Marc's father John, for he was due to arrive the next week. Alec was much looking forward to the visit but it was such a pity that his sister-in-law Ana couldn't be with his brother this time, tied down as she was in Greece, with all their children. But he felt very lucky to have so many of his family around and he was looking forward to organizing a dinner here in the house, to which he'd ask all Marc's friends from the lodge. With these positive thoughts in his head Alec kicked off the top blanket, turned the light out and, as he'd been trained to do, dropped quickly into a relatively dreamless and restful sleep.

❄

Jean Haddington wasn't satisfied with the conversation that her husband had just had up at the pub with Mac. She wasn't about to let it lie either. She set about vigorously drying up the mugs they'd used for their hot night time drinks.

"What is it with Mac, Stuart? He should be finding out more about what goes on around here. He's too laid back for a bobby; sees good in everyone or looks the other way and, mark my words, those people you saw sniffing around here aren't up to any good. The Colonel agrees with me."

"I know," he answered, "I hear what you say, but these people have done no wrong yet, so Mac can't do anything except keep an eye on them, when they're around that is. You know that."

"Tch! You're as bad as he is! You don't see what's under your nose. Something will happen and then it will be too late. We don't want all these foreigners taking jobs and money off the local people around here anyway. Why can't they stay in the cities?"

Leaving his formidable wife still muttering in the kitchen, Stuart went on up to bed. He was tired and stiff with pains in his knees these days. It was the damp. He wasn't getting any younger and didn't have the energy of his wife, who was ten years his junior. He wasn't in the mood for any more of this conversation which was going nowhere, but he had to agree he hadn't liked the look of the shifty strangers either. Why would they come here? The fishing port of Dromvaar was a tight-knit, jealously guarded community. Strangers of their sort would never be easily accepted in the village and certainly not at the commercially run shooting and fishing lodges either. Most likely they'd be looking for work in the hotels and pubs further afield, thought Stuart. The small towns were thriving with more than their fair share of fish and chip shops, pizza establishments and the inevitable supermarkets. Still, he'd keep his eyes and ears open and ask the Colonel to get some more substantial locks for the barns.

The lone girl sat quietly at the bar, finishing a glass of neat whisky with ice. Dougie had already rung the bell for last orders. This customer was a hard-looking type who could certainly hold her drink, thought Dougie, studying her surreptitiously while he put away the last of the glasses. Completely at ease and exuding confidence; apart from which she'd been drinking steadily all through the evening, just like a man, coming up to the bar herself each time to reorder. Dougie assumed that she must have come in with somebody at the beginning of the evening, when they were full and he'd been too busy to notice. But for the most part she'd been sitting on her own, talking to no-one. Not unattractive, a bit what he'd call scrawny and undoubtedly sexy if slightly butch, with her short boyish hair and huge spooky eyes. Maybe she was of the alternative persuasion; she certainly looked like she was on something other than alcohol and he didn't like all those earrings. Dressed in a leather jacket and torn, skinny jeans, she had a distinct Irish lilt to her voice. Interesting, but he certainly wouldn't be wanting one of his family bringing this one home for supper, he thought unkindly. Not that he was lucky enough to have any sons or daughters. He must remember to tell Mac, for he'd never seen this lass before and he had to admit that he was somewhat intrigued. Perhaps she was just passing through but somehow he reckoned not. He started turning the lights out and the girl got down from the bar stool, nodded at him and went. He watched her through the window as she walked away. She stopped for a moment in the lee of the pub wall to light a cigarette. Then she was gone. The sheepdog stirred from his place by the fire and came across wagging his tail, knowing it was nearly time for his last walk of the day. Dougie sighed and bent to pat the dogs head tutting, "Och, that one gives me the creeps she does, for goodness sake my old friend they don't make them like they used to anymore. Come on then. The sooner we get you out the sooner we can get to our beds. Ailsa will be upstairs and wondering where we are."

CHAPTER 7

Fergus was sorting out his tangled nets. They would soon dry off in the sun then he'd go to eat breakfast, at Molly's cafe. He could see everything from there if he sat at the table in the bay window. He'd hang around in the hope that the southerners might come down from the lodge to arrange a trip out to Loch Island. It would be a good day, the wind was light and, looking up at the sky, he reckoned the rain might just hold off till evening. He was annoyed with himself for not having asked about the cook. He'd been quite taken with Beth when she'd come in for some shopping. She'd seemed a sensible sort with a good sense of humour. It was time that he had another girlfriend, hopefully with no difficult strings attached as in his last relationship. If nobody had appeared in the port by the time he'd eaten breakfast, he could always run a selection of fresh fish up to the house. They would most likely be eating in tonight and he was sure that Beth would be pleased to see him.

Breakfast at the lodge in the huge open plan kitchen was a moveable feast. Marc and Emma had already eaten with Poppy and the others all appeared in dribs and drabs. The girls were enjoying being lazy and the men couldn't wait to make a plan.

Julian went across to stare out of the window and study the cloud formations, whilst considering his options. He mustn't sound too keen but he was desperate to get out there and find the lake on the island. He turned to the others.

"The weather looks settled enough. How about an excursion on Fergus' boat just to get our sea legs and see how the land lies out there?"

Adriana smiled at her fiancé's feigned nonchalance. He was never still, always had to have a plan of action and would take a long time to wind down into holiday mode. Whereas his other male half, Guy, appeared to be able to forget work matters and relax almost instantly as soon as he had the chance.

Adriana looked across at Alicia who winked back knowingly.

"No thanks, we'll stay here with Emma." Olly looked up at Rose pouring coffee into a large mug from the Aga top.

"What about you Rose? What would you like to do today?" Rose put the coffee pot down, grinning.

"Need you ask? Stay here with the girls and Poppy of course, thanks." Guy was smiling.

"Alright. Well it looks like it's to be a men only outing. Are you on Olly?"

Before Olly could answer there was a roar like thunder outside and a battered old truck appeared up the drive at speed.

"Who on earth is this?" Guy got up to stand beside Julian at the window.

Beth was already out of the backdoor and waiting to greet the new arrival.

"I think," said Emma leaning over Guy's shoulder to look, "that it is our friendly fisherman who is also much taken with our lovely cook."

They could see Jessica with Poppy on the swing at the bottom of the lawn, discreetly staying well out of the way. Fergus jumped out of the truck and to their amazement gave Beth a peck on the cheek. Before Beth could catch them staring they all dived away from the window.

"Well!" remarked Oliver, "I think that this unexpected visit makes our plans for the day much easier to organize."

Fergus was delighted to partake of a cup of coffee and in doing so keep Beth company, whilst she made up sandwiches for the men to take out on the boat with them. It had been a good idea to bring up some fresh fish for the evening meal at the lodge. Fergus was delighted with the way things were turning out to his advantage - in every way.

❄

There was a cool but gentle breeze blowing as Fergus set his boat for Loch Island. Everyone wore warm clothes and the fisherman had donned his favourite old wool hat, knitted for him by Molly up at the cafe in the port. Molly spoilt Fergus. She liked to mother him; she felt it her duty as he didn't seem to have a wife, a girlfriend or even any other relations in the area. Fergus was grateful and revelled in the attention.

Guy looked around the old but extremely efficient and well maintained fishing smack. He liked Fergus who had already enlightened them with his story. He'd come to Domvaar by mistake. He'd arrived having boarded the wrong bus in too much of a hurry, escaping his past life. He had no roots to worry about, no belongings to speak of, had fallen in love with the place and had literally just stayed. Molly had taken him in whilst he'd found his feet. He had paid his way by doing odd jobs for her in the cafe, crewing the lifeboat and helping the other fisherman until he could afford to buy his own vessel. Now he felt he was at home and was completely accepted as one of the community.

It was good to be on the water again, although not of the Med's glorious blue or the Aegean's aqua, the sea here was of a cold steely grey. Guy loved it even more for its ever changing alluring and life threatening persistence. He liked to pit his wits against its force and had a rare understanding of the moods of any large expanse of water. This perception had saved him from trouble on various occasions.

They were soon nearing Julian's Loch Island, half circling it's coastline and coming in to a hidden little beach on the West.

43

Fergus expertly anchored the boat and took them across to the beach by dinghy. He insisted that he'd prefer to stay on the boat, in case the weather turned and, with the currents, the anchor dragged. All they had to do was keep an eye on the weather and wave from the beach when they were ready to return.

The island had a well worn sheep track leading to the inland lake which was only a mile and a half due East. From the nearest hillock you could see it. They shouldn't get lost. There was nothing: nobody living on the island at present, although there was talk, at government level, about it becoming habitable once more at some point in the future.

Julian, with his fishing rod and tackle couldn't wait to start off along the track.

"You go on ahead with Julian," Guy called to Olly. "I'm going to climb up that hill to have a look at the rest of the island. I'll join you two later. When you have had enough start back the same way, then we can't miss meeting each other."

❄

The girls were busy making their plans for the day.

"Let's go into the port, get some air and find Poppy an ice cream or something," Rose suggested, after they'd been through a considerable supply of Beth's excellent coffee, whilst catching up with news from four different households.

"Good idea," answered Emma. "It will give Jessica a break and Beth some peace to organize dinner for the men who, no doubt coming in off the sea, will be famished. What's the betting they stop at the pub on the way back though? I heard them making a plan to meet there after Marc has finished his stint at the surgery. He's promised to help out, just for two days a week while one of the other doctors is away."

"Even better," said Adriana. "Longer for us to relax and wallow before they have a chance to hog the bath and mess up the bathrooms. They'll have sand coming out of their socks and nasty salty wet clothes."

＊

The port consisted of a colourful row of fishermens' cottages above and looking down on the little harbour with all its brightly coloured boats and mooring buoys. The lifeboat station, on the water, was directly below the pink house at the end. A cafe, a shop and the small fish and vegetable market were all further along, on the same level but well back from the road and the protective sea wall. Because he was part of the lifeboat crew, Fergus said that he was lucky enough to have been allowed one of these little homes when the last inhabitant had 'moved upstairs', as he had put it. The rest of the village including the Post Office, pub, surgery and the old school house was tucked away in the lee of the hill behind. Fergus also informed them that their policeman, PC MacDonald, was based in the next larger town of Portmoor along the coast.

Inland, on the far side of the village, there was a working tweed mill, with a large tourist shop and restaurant. Also half a mile away along the river, there was a whisky distillery. On top of the hill behind the sheltered port was a half derelict castle of which the locals were very proud, as it was said that Bonny Prince Charlie had spent a night there. Whether this was fact or fiction, together with the tweed and whisky business, it was still a great tourist attraction in the summer season.

The so called 'laird', a certain Lord Strathkellan, lived in a large, rather ugly monstrosity up on the hill near the castle, aptly called Castle House. In spite of the rather dour grey building, the house had a beautiful garden open to the public during the summer months. Tickets for this favour were sold in the tourist shop at the tweed mill, in order that the laird should not be disturbed. The house was always locked and well protected, on the garden side, from curious visitors. Emma already knew him not to be a friend of Marc's uncle. For some reason in the past they'd had a major fall out. Marc thought that it had been because the laird had designs on his aunt some years before she had become ill.

The ice cream was to be found in Molly's snug cafe where it could be eaten comfortably in the warm. Molly was a lovely cheerful Scottish lady, with grey hair, dressed in a heather coloured jersey which was adorned with a scarf fixed with a broach of the Scottish thistle. Her long apron enveloped her sturdy figure and a sensible pair of brogues peeped out from beneath. Sixties music was playing in the background. Emma left Rose and Alicia there to enjoy this treat with Poppy, while she went on to the Post Office with Adriana. The Post Office was a hive of activity. Adriana held open the door for an elderly couple just leaving. The telephone was ringing and the post mistress, ignoring the ringing bell, was trying to deal with four large parcels which had been brought in and, she said, had to travel South to London. She was trying to stick labels onto the unsuitable packaging, with some difficulty it seemed.

"Tch'. Who'd ever want to send such large things to London, of all places and in a bin bag?" she asked, thankfully leaving the offending goods to one side so as to serve her new and much more interesting customers.

"You're from the lodge then too!" Mary Macquire announced, surveying Adriana with a beady eye without expecting an answer, whilst she began to count out the stamps. News travels fast up here, Adriana realized. They both nodded assent, smiled politely and Emma introduced Adriana who couldn't resist commenting on the messily done up parcels awaiting collection.

"I do agree, they are so badly packed. Perhaps it's wool and tweed from the factory?"

"Och naw," answered Mary Macquire, "they do their own packaging and send by proper delivery. These were brought in by a wee wisp of a girl who insisted that they were very important and that a friend would be collecting. But she put something in the children's charity shop box here, so I said that she could leave them, providing that is, that they are taken away within opening hours. She had a poor young boy with her who, in my opinion, could have done with a bit of charity himself.

Adriana experienced a sudden jolt of disquiet.

"Was this girl Irish, Mary? Petite and with short dark hair?" Emma looked at her friend somewhat bewildered.

"Good heavens! What's all this about Adriana? You've hardly been here two minutes. How can you know this girl?"

Mary was nodding knowingly. "You are very observant my dear – this girl was indeed Irish and a tough nut into the bargain I'd say. She wasn't about to take no for an answer and I felt sorry for the child. He looked in need of food and water and a bit of affection as much as anything. I'm thinking of giving the little chap some odd jobs around here when he's not at school. Payment will be a square meal or two," she added as an afterthought.

"Thought so," replied Adriana, "she was in the pub last night; bound to be the same girl and I heard the Irish accent. She was with some dark skinned strangers who certainly weren't from these parts either."

"Well well! I expect she was with those foreigners then, the gypsies? Och, there's something about those people I don't like..." Somebody else came into the small waiting area, so conversation came to a halt while Mary Macquire quickly produced the stamps they needed. She was a bright little person. She had a kind, open face with neat hair and remarkable brown eyes, added to a reliably strong personality thought Adriana, drawn by the lady's outspokenness. She obviously had the lowdown on everybody in the area.

❄

The two young women walked slowly back to the cafe together.

"You're not sensing some mystery here Arri, are you? Surely not up here of all places? It must be the quietest place on earth. Nothing happens here, especially in winter time; except for the sad demise of some game birds and of course, those lovely majestic beasts' wives - when the hind stalking season starts towards the end of this month."

"No, I'm probably just being ridiculous. After all we have had quite a lot of adventure in our lives already, haven't we? But, I don't know, it was just something about that girl. She doesn't fit in and I got an odd, uneasy feeling that she's here taking advantage of all this unspoilt quietness; even perhaps collaborating with unwelcome strangers and that maybe she's here for no good reason at all ... stupid thinking really, but there it is, you know me. I always say what I think. Forget it ... Oh my God! Poppy's got another ice cream Emma! She'll be sick!"

CHAPTER 8

Guy soon reached the highest point of the hill. He was glad to find himself fit and only a little out of breath as he achieved the summit. The sea air was wonderfully refreshing, after being stuck in a car for the last couple of days. This was just what they needed to recharge their batteries; they all lived busy lives. You really couldn't be much further away from the great metropolis. The lodge was perfect; comfortable, with lovely views out across the moors from all aspects.

Now he sat on a smooth flat rock looking down on the rest of the island, and took out his binoculars. The landscape periodically caught and splashed in dazzling sunshine where the bright rays had escaped from scudding clouds, glowed gold and orange touched with red. A couple of sea eagles swooped far above calling to one another in their muted lonely cry, a sound only heard in vast empty airspace.

The two small figures below, heading East, were now half way on their trek to the loch which was in the shape of a figure of eight, with a shepherd's bothy or a shack of some sort in the loop on either side. Guy observed his friends making steady progress towards the water. The two men stopped suddenly as they disturbed a covey of grouse. They also watched as the birds flew low, protesting noisily, breaking the silence. Looking left, to the North, were layered mountains; a soft purple in the far distance surrounded with an autumn mist. Beyond them, on the far horizon he could just distinguish the North Minch sea. Nearer, as he held the field glasses steady and focused, he could see the remains of a derelict village in a glen. Part of the church still stood proudly amongst mature trees. An old farm looked sad with its barn rooves half caved in, alongside forgotten fields and tumbling stone walls. To the right he could see the way they had come, across from the mainland. Turning to scan the final view behind him, he could even make out Fergus eating his sandwiches on the boat. Guy watched as the fisherman stood to lean out over the side then quickly haul something in. Guy smiled; the man had a line out to catch his supper.

Then a movement caught his attention at the far end of the bay. There was something or somebody else on the beach.

❊

Alec had been on the telephone to the Chief Constable over in Aberdeenshire. Yes, he was well aware that certain rather suspect looking people from far off countries appeared to be infiltrating the whole area. There had been a few problems their way also; petty theft and the odd scuffle in the pubs, but nothing more and the people so far had been found to be carrying bona fide passports and papers. The senior policeman then added that, in his opinion, there were far too many of them allowed in but they had the government and the EU rules and regulations to thank for that. Overseas we were well known to have become a soft touch. There was nothing to be done so long as these people behaved themselves. The local people just had to put up with them and make the newcomers welcome, because he reckoned they were here to stay.

Alec thought it highly unlikely that these strangers would be made welcome and he also considered that there was bound to be disorder. He decided that there was something to be done. He'd get Mac, their local man, to come up and see him in the morning to discuss the situation – just in case. Nobody seemed to have much control of anything in this country anymore and nobody seemed to care much either. He wasn't a man of this modern thinking. He'd been to war and had seen enough unrest and violence to last him a lifetime. He wasn't about to see this small part of his beloved country left to simmer on the brink of any trouble. The local people had become far too complacent and resigned to whatever might come their way.

Alec was looking forward to having the young party from the lodge up to dinner the following night and to telling his nephew that soon his father would also be joining them. Marc had told his uncle that two of his friends they had staying with them were in fact 'very interesting' army people, whose company he would certainly enjoy. Alec knew exactly what Marc had meant by that: the same people who had helped bring an extremely frightening episode in Switzerland to a satisfactory conclusion a couple of years previously, when Emma had been abducted in the Swiss Alps. He was looking forward to some intelligent and informed conversation.

Alec had a great respect for men who put their lives on the line for others. The Colonel was modest enough not to consider himself worthy of such respect, in spite of having featured himself in the Iraq war in intelligence operations. He had been one of a specialized group who were frequently sent forward on hazardous recognisance missions, collecting crucial information which would then be sent back to base. He had merely thought himself suitable for the job and done it to the best of his ability. In spite of this he had lost his brother-in-law and several good men from his regiment. To this day he still wished that he could have done more.

"There was somebody else on the beach!" Guy announced as they met Fergus with the dinghy at the allotted place on the sand. The others got in and stashed the fishing gear underneath the seat in the prow of the boat, while Guy waited, intending to give the vessel a push before jumping in himself.

"Was there indeed?" answered the fisherman, taking up the oars in preparation. "Where did you see this person then? There's no other boat here," he said stopping to look around, "and this is the only safe landing place on the island for it is circled by treacherous rocks, you see."

"I saw distinct movement over there, through these," Guy replied indicating the binoculars and pointing to the far corner of beach.

"I expect it was an animal then," interrupted Olly. "There must at least be some wild animal life here on all this otherwise completely wasted land."

"Also I read that they were talking about re-introducing the red deer here to set up new breeding stock," said Julian. "Perhaps they've already done that?" he looked at his friend curiously. "So, no demons here old friend," he finished, quietly chuckling, whilst settling himself as comfortably as possible in the back of the boat where his cigarette smoke would be taken away out across the water with the breeze.

"So there it is then. Shall we get on back now?" Fergus asked, grinning good-naturedly and waiting for Guy to give them a shove and jump in.

"Right," Guy grunted as he waded out into the water making sure not to fill his boots, "but I'm telling you all, I saw someone and it wasn't an animal."

Back in the harbour they thanked and paid Fergus, leaving him to wash down his boat and prepare his nets ready to go out again early the next morning. It had been both an interesting and rewarding trip as Julian had managed to hook three nice sized fish which they intended to take back to the lodge for supper. The three men then stowed the tackle, the fish and their waders in the boot of the car and headed for the pub to meet Marc.

Oliver went ahead to order; Julian and Guy locked the car and followed more slowly.

"There's no mystery here you know," said Julian as if continuing a conversation already started. "If there was someone else on the beach, why shouldn't there have been? After all we were there." Guy stopped to turn and judge his friends reaction before replying, his eyes steely and grey as he held his friend and colleague's gaze.

"Yes I agree, but why would they bother to conceal their transport? This person was actually dragging a small boat up the beach to hide in the bushes." Guy's eyebrow was now raised in question. Julian stood without speaking for a moment, considering his answer then putting a hand to Guy's shoulder and returning his scrutiny, replied simply:

"Not our business," and he walked on up the steps to find Olly.

"I'm not so sure," Guy called after him, shaking his head in mild irritation and with a wry smile on his face.

The girls reported a good day. They had explored the village thoroughly. They'd been to the whisky distillery, where they'd met the laird; a pompous, unhealthy looking person, with a rather attractive wife called Finola, for whom they had all felt sorry. The man had been collecting supplies for a forth-coming house party and whilst waiting for the order, which had been imperiously given, he had appraised the girls blatantly and embarrassingly in front of his wife before introducing himself. She had merely smiled at them graciously without uttering a word. Alicia, catching her eye, sensed that she was a nice person and had the immediate feeling that she was most probably trapped within an uncompromising world and married to a man she despised. 'No wonder Marc's uncle doesn't like the lord of the glen', Adriana had whispered as they had walked away clutching their house presents to their breasts.

They had then gone to the tweed mill and had lunch at the restaurant. Emma told them that if they chose some tweed, there was a woman in the village who would apparently copy trousers or a jacket in a matter of days, 'like they do in Hong Kong and just as good', she had added. In the shop Alicia tried on a blazer in a heather blue pinstripe material of wool and cashmere. It went beautifully with her jeans and fitted perfectly so they all persuaded her to buy it. Rose bought a V-necked cashmere jumper and Emma bought a large, multi-coloured, woollen shawl for her mother. Adriana decided to come back with a pair of her trousers to be copied. She had found a dark navy herringbone cloth she particularly liked.

At lunch they had met Ailsa Macquire, married to the publican Dougie, who was Mary the post mistress' son. Ailsa's parents, the Haddingtons, worked for Marc's uncle Alec up at Glencurrie. Ailsa was more than happy to add a bit of free gossip to their lunch order. It soon became obvious that everybody loathed the laird and loved his wife, Finola. None of them could understand why she stayed except that she'd been brought up in the area. Her children, now grown up, were away at university and her parents weren't that far away in Edinburgh.

Ailsa was a smart bonnie woman who appeared to run things at the mill most efficiently. She was cheery and pink cheeked, friendly and thoughtful with the staff and obviously welcomed all visitors in the same way. Nobody, she announced, ever left empty-handed and the business was thriving. During the autumn and winter months she explained, when later she joined them for a cup of tea, they were busy supplying the locals and the shooting brigade. Everybody came to order something during their stay and the tourists, of course, were a huge part of their income in the summer season. With a twinkle in her eyes she also told them that working at the mill was much more fun than being in the pub with Dougie, because you met far more interesting people.

✳

The girls arrived back at the lodge to find that Marc had telephoned to say that they were in the pub, as they had expected and would be back in time for dinner plus three large fish. Beth had given them the message, adding that she had already organized trout for dinner. So, when the men came back with their catch, would they please not mention when everybody sat down to eat that the fish couldn't possibly be the ones they had just caught.

"Don't worry," assured Adriana chuckling, "they won't have a clue. You're a star Beth, well done."

"Mine won't even attempt a scrambled egg!" Alicia sighed. "Although I'm sure that he's perfectly capable, just won't admit to it!"

"Marc is a good cook," said Emma. "He'll know, but I'll make certain he doesn't say a thing."

Jessica took a very tired Poppy up into her arms and turned to go, adding over her shoulder. "Luckily a certain small person here isn't quite old enough to let the cat out of the bag. She hugged the little child to her and kissed the top of her head. "I think we'll go for a warm bath and soon have you all tucked up in bed where you can dream about ice cream!" Poppy perked up immediately and pointed at Rose.

"More... ice keem?"

"Oh dear, the secret's out," said Rose looking guilty. "I'm really sorry Emma; she's had much too much I know, but I'm afraid I just can't resist my adorable god-daughter!"

"No problem," replied Emma, "as long as she's not sick, in which case we can let your Godmother clear it all up, can't we darling?" They all laughed. Emma went across to her daughter and taking her little face in her hands kissed her button nose, then tried to be serious. "Now bath and bed with Jess, then mummy or daddy will come and read a story. OK?"

"Kay," the little girl waved, then sticking her thumb in her mouth, snuggled into Jessica's shoulder as they turned to go upstairs.

"She really is the sweetest thing on two legs. If I ever have children I'll be a dreadfully spoiling mother," sighed Rose watching them go.

"No you won't," smiled Alicia then unexpectedly caught a look of raw anguish fleetingly touch Adriana's features, before she followed them up the stairs.

CHAPTER 9

"Would anybody mind, do you think, if Julian and I took our women for a quick flit to Paris for Alicia's birthday next week? It would only be for a night or two and as I booked tickets for La Boheme ages ago I think it would be a pity to waste them."

The four men were in the pub at the bar and all turned their attention to Guy. Olly scrutinized the blatantly innocent expression on Guy's face.

"You have something else to do in Paris, don't you my friend, other than the opera and... buying your wife some sexy underwear for her birthday, of course?"

Julian chuckled and winked across at Guy before answering.

"A family matter boyo, just a family matter."

Marc listened and watched this repartee with interest.

"Yes, just a meeting with my father's old lawyer," replied Guy, taking a swig of his beer, "and these tickets for the opera actually cost me a fortune. I also think that it would give Emma a bit of a break, having less of us in the house for a couple of days. By the way, I wonder if our good friend the doctor has anything of interest to tell us?" Having subtly changed the subject, with a raised eyebrow he looked to his left where Marc sat quietly. Moving to a more comfortable position on the stool, Marc regarded his three friends for a moment before clearing his throat, grinning, then answered.

"Alright! Yes, well detected Guy. I noticed your reaction to Emma turning down the wine last night. We have another one on the way and due in the early summer. But don't say anything until Emma's let the girls into our secret. She was so excited to have you all up here and be able to tell her three best friends at the same time."

"Congratulations," they all chorused.

"To you both and to the adorable Poppy also who will undoubtedly be thrilled with a baby brother or sister," Olly pronounced, raising his glass with the others and drinking deeply. "This calls for another wee dram I think. Now where's Dougie got to?"

Guy knew something was wrong on the drive up to Scotland. His oldest, closest friend and team mate, Julian, was quieter and more morose than usual but he'd had enough beer now to be a little more communicative. Something was definitely up between him and Adriana. They should have tied the knot by now. The problem, whatever it was, had to be dealt with as Guy couldn't afford to have Julian in any way out of sorts, just in case an unexpected job came up and they had to rush off. A lack of attention could cost lives in their undercover work. They already had an important meeting set in Paris with their French counterparts with some serious issues to be discussed. He wanted Julian at his best.

Guy instigated a quiet word with Olly, whilst their other two friends talked fishing, and a good opportunity for a tactful chat with Julian soon presented itself.

Marc drove back to the lodge with Julian and Guy in the back and Olly beside him. As they left the tarmac and set off down the last mile and a half of track, Guy persuaded Julian to get out and walk with him, supposedly to work off the surplus alcohol before joining the girls. As it was almost dark Marc handed them a torch but both men had cats' eyes; they were used to finding their way unaided on even the blackest of nights. As it was, the sky was clear and the moon would soon be up. It was a beautiful night and Guy wished he didn't have to spoil it.

✳

The girls were in the snuggery beside the fire and making plans when the men returned from the pub. There was an air of excitement. Adriana had agreed to be Godmother to the new baby. She felt touched that they should ask her. She longed to have a child of her own, but it didn't seem to be happening and she couldn't understand why Julian wouldn't name the day. Something was up and it was beginning to affect their relationship.

The three trophy fish were supposedly on the menu that night and everybody thought that it was the best meal so far. Beth carried off the white lie to perfection, telling Julian that they were the biggest she'd seen this season. An air of celebration filled the room with the news of the new baby and Guy told of the plan to fly to Paris from Inverness after the weekend. Rose and Emma immediately said they'd give Alicia and Adriana a French shopping order.

Guy was concerned for both Julian and Adriana. But what to advise them to do about their extremely personal problem was another matter. At least his friend seemed relieved to have told him. But Julian also had to tell Adriana what was worrying him as without doubt their relationship was beginning to suffer. Guy felt that another day out on the boat to Loch Island would be a good distraction. He'd suggest it at breakfast the next morning when everybody was less inebriated. A quiet day had been planned followed by dinner up at Glencurrie.

✳

Fergus finished tidying up the boat, then went to his home in the port to shower off and change before going on up to the pub for his usual pie and a pint. He wanted to discuss a plan of action with Dougie regarding Beth up at the lodge. He'd enjoyed his day out with the men but didn't feel he knew any of them well enough to broach the subject yet. He had to admit that the girl had him in a bit of a whirl and he very much hoped to see her again, maybe even take her out if he got the chance. But Fergus felt he needed some advice first and a bit of dutch courage.

Dougie listened closely while drying up some glasses. Then thoughtfully he perched his spectacles on his nose, something he did when he wanted to be serious and always before addressing a sensitive situation. He felt he looked the wiser for this small gesture and so it had become a habit.

"As I see it laddie, you just need to take the bull by the horns. Go on. Just ask her out. She can only say no and you aren't exactly planning to jump her on your first date, are you?"

"No of course not, but what will they all think, up there at the lodge? I don't want to lose business like today which was good money for this time of the year."

"For God's sake man, it's a free world and those men have all got something in their trousers. They're all human beings and decent people. Beth will have an evening off. Ask her, before someone else does."

Another customer appeared at the bar and Fergus was left to mull over Dougie's advice. When the man had been served, Dougie returned to eye Fergus speculatively.

"Well man, what do you say?"

"You're right Dougie, you're right. I'll go up with some fresh catch tomorrow morning and then I can ask the lassie."

"Good," replied Dougie. "Now just as a matter of interest, do you know anything about that young woman over there," he said pointing his finger towards the dining area. "The little one with the sad looking bairn?"

Fergus moved to one side to see more clearly.

"Nope, never seen her before last night. Why?"

"I dunno," answered Dougie, "but I don't like the look of her. There's something about her. My mother up at the post office says she's as tough a nut as she's ever met; not a pleasant word comes out of her mouth. She gives me the creeps and as for that child, the poor boy looks downright scared if you ask me. The girl comes in sometimes with those immigrant people; tied at the hip they are. There's something funny about the lot of them."

"Well," said Fergus, "keep an eye on them and tell Mac; he'll know what to do."

At this point in the conversation Stuart arrived and joined in heartily with his views on the foreign people, some who had been giving cause for concern up at Colonel Alec's. They all knew that the Colonel had played an important part in the Iraq war. At the time it had been very hush hush; so all the locals thought that he must have been involved in espionage of some sort. When Colonel Neilsen came home and received a medal they were all well pleased and as proud as punch. The man had recently lost his beloved wife and everybody in and around the village would have dropped whatever they were doing in order to ensure that his life now remained undisturbed.

❆

It was the following Saturday when the Irish girl came in to Dromvaar next, to see if her parcels had been picked up. There was no school, if indeed the child went to school, thought Mary, but she decided to ask if the young boy would like a little job. She needed her store cupboard tidied up and she would also like her garden weeded. 'Only for a little pocket money, mind, and a sandwich at lunch time after the job was done.' She had said this quickly as the shy child's face had lit up, promising the beginnings of a smile. Anybody would think that she'd given him the chance to escape from prison, thought Mary uncharitably. She looked at the young mother square in the eye, daring her to turn down the offer. No warmth there. The eyes regarded her without feeling; cold as fish and Mary had to stifle a shiver. Then the girl nodded with a grunt, said she'd be back to pick the boy up at five o'clock and left, without a word of thanks, or even a goodbye to her nervous looking son. As soon as she'd gone the child visibly relaxed and Mary was even rewarded with the glimmer of a small lopsided grin. Phew, thought Mary. I feel a bit like a shining white knight on a mission. She smiled encouragingly at the boy and took him off into the kitchen for a mug of cocoa and a cup of tea for herself. Now she'd make it her business to find out a bit about these people and in the meantime try and make this boy's world a better place to be in.

CHAPTER 10

Mrs H loved a party and this one, she was going to make sure, would be perfect. The colonel still looked sad and he deserved some fun. He'd always looked after her family. So she'd do anything for him in return. No one dared say a bad word about the Colonel when Jean Haddington was on the warpath. Marc's nice young wife had sent up some beautiful flowers; Stuart had come up trumps with fresh vegetables from the garden; she'd planned a lovely menu and Ailsa was going to come to help her later.

Beth and Jessica were going to give Poppy her bath and put her to bed, so that Emma could have a peaceful time getting ready. Fergus, much to Beth's delight, had promised to drop some fresh kippers up for breakfast and had asked her to go for a drink with him while the others were out and Jessica babysat. Everything seemed to have slotted nicely into place.

❅

Mary Macquire decided to go up and see Dougie once she'd shut up shop and before opening time at the pub. She was dead worried. After a day spent with the young lad Sean, her initial intuition that something was very wrong became real. He was a gentle young lad who spoke hardly at all, out of shyness she felt at first, but then she decided he had a speech defect which was probably psychological. Mary had watched him carefully to make sure he didn't take anything as he worked, but she soon realized that the only thing he was really interesting in, was helping himself to food. If she left a plate of biscuits within reach they were soon gone. He was a growing lad and always hungry, just as her own children had been at the same age. He was a funny looking boy, somehow all lopsided but if only she could gain his confidence she felt that a smile would be reward enough.

It was hot in the store room and when Sean took off his jacket he was just too slow tucking in his shirt – Mary had seen the bruises.

❄

Dougie was reading the paper. It was his quiet time, an hour before opening the pub for the evening session. Ailsa wasn't back from the mill yet. He heard his mother's footsteps approaching the back door. As always she had a determined stride, accentuated when something was up. He looked up and sighed, waiting for the usual alerting cough before she knocked and opened the door.

Mary knew that this was Dougie's only peaceful time, when he'd rather not be disturbed, but it couldn't be helped. Even Ailsa kept out of his way for a bit after he'd had his tea. Just to give him time to think while he polished his shoes, as her daughter-in-law put it. Not that Dougie ever polished his shoes.

Mary felt so sad that they were unable to have children and she knew just how much they both minded. But the pair of them were well liked by everybody in the village. Her adored son, Dougie, had always been the life and soul of every party ever since he'd grown up. He was so hospitable and that's why he made a perfect publican. Every year they went away on an exotic holiday and so at least there was some compensation for not having a family, thought Mary. You were free as birds to go where you liked, if you had the money and Dougie did well from the pub especially since the restaurant had taken off.

"Hello Ma," called Dougie as she knocked, "come in, come in, you know I'm here."

"I do indeed," replied Mary walking in and kissing him on the cheek.

"Sit down; now what is it this time mother?" Dougie asked benevolently.

Mary settled herself in the big armchair opposite her son and looked at him quizzically over her glasses.

"I think that I have discovered something very serious Dougie and that's what I have come to talk about. The problem is what to do about it."

❄

Everybody queued up outside Poppy's bedroom to kiss her goodnight before they all went to change for dinner.

"It's a bit like visiting the Queen you know," said Rose as she gathered the little girl into her arms when her turn came to say goodnight.

"Pincess," said Poppy clearly then "pince," pointing at Guy as he came into the room.

"Oh good!" replied Guy, "that's made my day Poppy, if I'm a 'pince' then you'll always be my 'pincess'." Jessica drew the curtains and Emma and Marc appeared to say prayers, which had to name everybody in turn and so went on for a long time. A delay, which Poppy already understood, was considered acceptable by both parents.

❄

"Well," said Alec raising his glass, "here is to you all. Thanks so much for coming. It's great to fill the house with happiness once more and," he turned to where Jean stood, just inside the dining room door, ready to serve the food, "to Mrs H, for the wonderful spread which I know she has prepared." The cook beamed her pleasure as they all thanked her.

"Och, away with you all," she said and scurried out to get the first course.

Rose, sitting beside Alec, took a moment to survey the room while he was engaged in conversation with Alicia on his other side. The room was oblong with a huge bay window at one end. Emma's bright arrangement of flowers stood in pride of place on a beautifully polished circular table within the curved bow. Ancestors peered down from oil paintings on the long ochre coloured wall in front of her. Behind Rose was a large open fire with fragrant birch logs smouldering lethargically and over her shoulder she also glimpsed misty scenes of Scotland decorating the walls to either side of the fire place. It was a lovely room with an atmosphere created, Rose felt, from many years of countless evenings when friends and family had joined together for different occasions.

Mrs H had surpassed herself, dinner was delicious; local smoked salmon to start with, followed by roast pheasant with all the trimmings and a special house pudding called the 'Glencurrie winter pudding' - a concoction of steamed sponge with blackberries and thick cream. After dinner the girls went back to the drawing room for coffee by the fire. Alec stayed in the dining room to enjoy a glass or two of port with the men and to indulge in some unusually interesting conversation.

Everybody enjoyed the evening. The food and wine were perfection and the house filled with laughter. When Ailsa came in to help her mother clear up she soon found herself caught up in the infectious merriment. The evening had undoubtedly been a huge success and her mother, responsible for the delicious meal, was at the heart of it all.

When the lodge guests left late in the evening, a day's fishing had been organized on the home beat for the following week, after the return of the group going to France. There would be lunch at the house to which the girls could come or not as they wished. Julian's face had lit up with the prospect of some salmon fishing, Guy noticed.

Alec was happier than he'd been in a long time. The young people were a great boost to his flagging spirits. They were all attractive, polite and good fun, interacting in the most comical way. That night he went to bed content, relaxed and even comforted in the knowledge that for the moment he had plenty of kindred spirits around - strong, brave men who also understood the darker side of life led within the constraints of their secret activities in the armed forces. They were intelligent, fit and savvy servicemen who could be relied upon whatever the circumstances. He'd taken his medal from its box in his dressing table drawer and touched it - remembering. Remembering the reason it had been received and remembering his adored wife's proud face, in the front row below the dais, as it had been given. Oh, to be young again and fearless. Then he picked up Caroline's photograph, placed his finger on the dimple, at the edge of her smile and whispered, "and for you my darling I could have conquered the world, if only we'd had more time."

❄

As the party returned in convoy to the lodge, they met Fergus coming towards them after dropping Beth off at the house. He was grinning and stopped, winding down the window of the ancient truck.

"Evening to you all," he called, "the weather is set fair for the next few days so perhaps you might have a mind to return to Loch Island?"

"Good idea. That would be just great. Thanks Fergus. Can we speak in the morning, if that suits you?" Julian asked hopefully from the driver's seat.

"Maybe we could go again tomorrow if it's to be a good day?" suggested Guy. Fergus had appeared at just the right moment so far as he was concerned.

"Aye, that will be fine, I'll be ready for you at 10 a.m." He gave them a funny salute and still grinning went on his way, quickly, before any of the women could change their minds.

"Well," said Alicia, "he's obviously had a good evening out with Beth."

"Are you sure you'll be up for it again tomorrow?" asked Julian quietly, hardly daring to believe in his luck.

"Yes," said Guy thoughtfully. "Actually, Julian, I'd like to visit your island again."

"Good. Thought you might." Julian answered with a satisfied grunt.

"Well you needn't worry about us, we have our own plans, don't we Alicia?" said Adriana with a slight edge to her voice, which didn't go un-noticed.

"Of course we do," answered Alicia, quickly covering for the awkward moment and wondering what plans they were supposed to have made.

Beth was making a cup of cocoa in the kitchen. She was pink cheeked and grinning to herself. Not wishing to intrude on her romantic thoughts, they all waved and, stifling smiles, went up to bed.

CHAPTER 11

The following morning Oliver thought it best for Guy and Julian to go on their own, with Fergus, to Loch Island. He had a sense that something was not quite right and for the moment he had felt that he wasn't to be included. After all, Guy and Julian had known each other for many years; they were not only close friends but colleagues in that most difficult, yet most alluring other world into which they sometimes disappeared. He decided to stay with the girls. They'd take the dogs for a walk then most likely go to the pub for a snack at lunchtime. Jessica and Beth were going to take the afternoon off. Emma was going to have a quiet afternoon with Marc and Poppy. He'd appreciate some private time with Rose and was looking forward to a short excursion together which they had already planned for their wedding anniversary.

Once out from the harbour the water was choppy and the air cool. Both Julian and Guy felt it was a good thing that the girls weren't with them and were glad of their own warm clothes. Fergus, in his own unique version of a warm, woollen hat, was in fine form. Things were going well with Beth and with this extra money he'd have more than enough to take her out to supper when the next opportunity arose.

As they chugged out to sea and around the island to come in from the West, they could see the silhouette of a large ship anchored further out. As they watched, it took up anchor and began to head slowly away to the North.

"I wonder what that is? A tanker or a trawler?" Guy took out the binoculars.

"Maybe it's the Hibernia supply ship," answered Fergus concentrating once more on their own passage. "I see her out there sheltering sometimes, before going on up to the North Sea oil rigs."

"No, it's not The Hibernia," answered Guy. "It's something bigger, and that's a Russian flag they're flying. I wonder what they are doing out here so far from home? The weather is good so they're certainly not needing shelter."

"Perhaps they're pumping out the bilges, or after making good headway, biding their time before their next port of call?" suggested Julian, losing interest.

"That's the Isle of Lewis they were anchored off, isn't it?" asked Guy, still watching the retreating ship.

"Ay, and I've seen them there a few times now. They'll not be far from the main shipping channel, not in that bloody great vessel. It'll do at least thirty knots," added Fergus shouting to be heard, "but they don't bother us and so long as they're not after our fish we've a mind to leave well alone. We don't want any international incidents up here, you know!" He gave a loud guffaw and turned into the bay as Guy swivelled around and once more raised his glasses to his eyes, this time training them on the beach. He thought he saw movement down there but he couldn't be sure. They were just too far away and perhaps he was imagining things. Julian, standing close beside him was looking at him quizzically.

"What are you looking for; why the sudden interest?" he asked, knowing that Fergus couldn't hear him speak above the engine noise. Guy grunted.

"Something not quite right here my friend, something not quite right; can't put my finger on it at the moment, but just that reliable old gut feeling. You know what I mean?"

"Um, yes I do hear what you say, but I suggest we remember that we are on holiday here please, so for pity's sake don't go looking for intrigue. That Russian ship probably has every right to be there... now I have some serious fishing to do." He gave Guy an enthusiastic grin and turned away to watch the depth sounder for Fergus, while he readied the anchor.

They were now nearing the shallow water and Guy once more raised his binoculars. Not a sign of any movement where he could have sworn he'd seen someone last time. But he'd have a look around while Julian was fishing and get some exercise at the same time.

"No hairy monster on the beach then?" asked Fergus, laughing, noticing his interest.

"No, just some guillemots and some razorbills," answered Guy quickly. "What about seals at this time of the year?"

"You might see some grey ones basking on the rocks if it's sunny and calm." He looked up at the sky. "The weather is improving again now and October is their main breeding season."

Fergus anchored the boat and they all piled into the small dory with Julian's fishing gear, then set in towards the sand, where Fergus let them off as before.

The two friends walked for a few minutes in silence along the track towards the inland lake then, where the route divided left, Julian stopped and turned to his friend.

"Now don't even pretend that you want to come and watch me fishing, so what are you going to do? Or don't I need to ask? That path looks like it cuts right back to the bay, by the way," he said pointing, "and there's probably another branch somewhere that goes towards the abandoned village which you can go and explore!" He said pointing to his left. Guy chuckled.

"No you're right. I've got better things to do than go after your Loch Island monster. I'm going to investigate the far end of the cove first, then take a closer look at that deserted village. Depending on my findings, after that I'll either climb that hill again to our right and wait for you there until you've had enough or I'll come to meet you along the track from the loch. Anyway, we'll be able to see each other and you can always use the mobile."

"Alright, I'll try and catch something a bit bigger this time. See you later, but don't go finding us any problems please, remember..." Guy cut him off.

"Yes I know, I know - we're on holiday, but you, my friend, have some serious thinking to do while you're there hooking our supper, so don't forget that either. This problem of yours needs sorting out - and soon." Julian, bit his lip and shook his head as he turned to walk away down the path.

"You're right of course, but there's no easy way around this one."

Guy watched Julian walk away, his shoulders slightly hunched. Deep down he was an unhappy man and Guy was saddened for his friend.

Guy headed off intent on finding some evidence of a living presence other than wildlife. He hadn't been seeing things and it hadn't been a bloody seal manoeuvring that boat up to hide it in the bushes. He could see Fergus' fishing boat rocking slightly out on the water, the dinghy tied alongside. No sign of the fisherman himself, probably having a sleep after his late night out with Beth, thought Guy.

The path Guy was following soon deteriorated into nothing other than rutted old rabbit runs, interspersed with holes and tufts of coarse grass. But he quickly regained the sand dunes with their larger scrub and windswept, misshapen trees. These provided some camouflage on either side of a narrow, pitted strip of old tarmac winding alongside the beach. Now he could walk quickly without fear of being seen. If, that was, there was anybody there to see him.

There was a cool wind blowing in off the open water, bringing with it the taste of salt and the smell of the sea. On his left bundles of dried cord-grass swirled and danced hectically along beside him. Periodically the clumps caught on driftwood or rock and held fast, until stronger gusts of wind lifted them free to continue an agitated ballet along the sand. A white tailed eagle, hunting, swooped down from the sky until, disturbed by Guy's intrusion it turned and flew away in the opposite direction. Guy raised his glasses and watched its retreat as it shrank and disappeared from view, merging with the distant hills; a lovely sight and quite rare. He scanned the road ahead leading to the end of the bay. Not even a rabbit in sight. Nothing moved beside the water.

The tide was up so Guy knew it unlikely that he'd find footprints around the bushes where he'd seen the person hiding the boat, on the previous visit. On reaching the spot he found there to be a submerged slipway, a disintegrated pontoon with a rusted collection of old paint pots, buckets and a broken broom. A few pieces of ancient mooring rope were still tied to half deflated colourless buoys. Not a thing of interest: nothing of any use at all.

Just then he caught sight of something shining in the water, around some rocks a little way out. Seals. Grey seals playing amongst themselves watched over by what looked like a gaggle of sea birds. Guy studied them for a few minutes through his field glasses. They were playing with something in the water, like a ball. But it wasn't a ball; it was a faded mooring buoy with a length of chain attached. He could now hear a clinking as they nudged it around in the water. Caught in the sun, the chain gleamed silver and new.

A small sandy track led away from the pontoon in the direction of the village. Impossible to tell if anybody had walked this way recently as the wind blew flurries of sand around, disguising his own footmarks as soon as he raised his feet. Guy walked until there was little cover and he could just make out the village ahead in the distance. He'd already been gone for nearly an hour. It was time to retrace his steps. Just as he turned a small white object on the ground caught his eye, snagged against a broken branch in the undergrowth beside him. It was a discarded, empty but pristine, packet of Marlborough cigarettes. Here was the proof. There was, or had been, somebody on the island - and recently. Ever more thoughtful and now most curious, Guy headed back up towards the loch.

❋

Julian hadn't seen him approach. Such concentration and such a mundane, inactive sport, considered Guy as he crept up, not wishing to disturb his friend until his presence was noticed. Even from behind Julian still looked dejected and Guy pitied his personal conundrum. But now there was something else to consider. He sat and waited patiently, watching quietly; there was no hurry.

A tug on the line and Julian began to carefully reel in a little at a time, until the fish was well and truly hooked. He gave a slight yank and the rod bent. The fish was on and Guy watched in admiration as his friend played it for some minutes before he went to help with the landing net. This time it was a big one and Guy could see how Julian's spirits were immediately lifted.

"That was a spectacular bit of fishing my friend. Well done! You've got yourself a whopper this time." Julian was grinning from ear to ear.

"Yes, wasn't that great? And at least ten pounds in weight I should think." He looked a different man. He unhooked the fish and whacked it on the head till it lay still, then looking up, said quietly "and, you're right, I've made my decision; I have to tell her and not just go on hoping."

"Soon?"

"Yes, very soon."

"OK, but don't underestimate Adriana in her reaction. She's a strong woman and devoted to you. She may surprise you. Now look what I've found," he said, holding out the cigarette packet, "and I don't believe that seals have your nasty habit either, do you?"

Guy went on to tell Julian about the brand new chain on the mooring. Then they packed up the gear and started back to meet Fergus in the dinghy.

Fergus also had been busy – he'd trolled for mackerel further out in the bay and landed a few dozen fish. He'd had the kettle on and they all drank tea and ate the excellent sandwiches made up by Beth. The afternoon was sunny and warm. The wind had eased as promised. Later Fergus let out the fishing lines again, as they made their way slowly back to the port.

That night Julian took his courage in both hands and when they'd gone to bed he told Adriana of his dilemma. She was, as Guy had said she would be, understanding and sensitive, strong and staunch and he loved her then more than he'd ever loved her. Yet he still refused to marry her.

CHAPTER 12

Guy decided to stay in Paris for two nights. Rose and Olly wanted to go to the Isle of Skye which seemed to be good timing, as Marc's father would shortly be arriving to stay with his brother at Glencurrie. Alec, John with his son, daughter-in-law and grandchild could have some family time! Guy and Alicia, Julian and Adriana would be leaving very early in the morning to catch a flight for France out of Inverness. When everyone returned the men were all looking forward to the day's planned salmon fishing up at Glencurrie. The girls were as yet undecided about whether or not they would wish to be sitting on the windswept river bank all day giving encouragement to their menfolk.

Rose was excited. She'd always wanted to go to Skye. As a little girl Speed Bonny Boat had been her very favourite song. She had even sung the song at school, at an end of term musical evening. So Oliver had to accede, whether or not he wanted to go. They hired a small car and set out after breakfast on a glorious October morning, just as the hills in the distance were turning from a night shroud of purple to a bright, shimmering gold.

"Isn't this just beautiful, Olly? I could almost live up here you know."

"No you couldn't," answered Oliver quickly. "You'd hate the cold in winter and you'd miss your busy social life in London with all your friends."

"Do you really think so?" continued Rose thoughtfully.

"Yes I do," replied Oliver firmly. "Winter is a long old haul and the days are dark up here. Now can you please concentrate on where we are going." They had come to a small crossroads, with no signs except those directing people to the various shooting estates.

"Which way?"

"Towards the sea Olly – it must be straight on."

"OK, but please read the map. We should be back on the proper road in a minute."

"I can't wait to get to our little hotel can you? I have heard that you can go down to the sea and watch the otters playing. Wouldn't that be wonderful?"

"Yes my darling it would, but first we have to get there, so please read the map and get it right so we don't go hundreds of miles in the wrong direction."

"I wish we had a sat nav!"

"So do I," answered Oliver with some exasperation, "but the Kyle of Lochalsh, through which we have to go, is definitely on the map!"

The other travellers had already left for Inverness.

Marc arranged to pick up his father from the station at teatime, while Emma was busy planning a return dinner at the lodge for Alec and John the following evening. She wished that Anastasia could have managed to come over to the UK with John. But Emma understood that it had been impossible for her to leave the younger children this time. Ana was a serene, beautiful person who adored her whole family; her step-grandchild Poppy included. She always brought the charm and allure of Greece with her. Emma loved her company; they were close friends and had been through much together before becoming related by marriage.

Jessica was having a great time with Poppy who had demanded to be taken to see Stuart's new puppies up at Glencurrie. Beth was going to drive them over before going in to Dromvaar to do the food shopping: and just possibly have a quick cup of coffee with Fergus at the same time, Emma thought delightedly. The two girls were such a cheerful duo to have around. They really added to the sunny atmosphere of the place. She'd miss the others being away, but it was only for a couple of nights. Emma was very much looking forward to seeing her father-in-law and he would be so excited about the new baby.

"There's no hurry to get back Beth, it's only me and Marc for lunch and we can have a salad. Why don't you and Jessica take Poppy to the Mill for something to eat there? Ailsa said last night that she was longing to meet Poppy." Beth flushed scarlet and Emma now knew for certain that things with Fergus were rolling along in the right direction!

"OK, if you are really sure. That would be great Emma, thank you. We'd love that, wouldn't we Jess?" Jessica nodded and looked pleased while Poppy jumped up and down chanting 'ice keem, ice keem', over and over again. Emma put up a hand.

"Alright but one only please Jess." They all laughed and the little girl clapped her small chubby hands in delight.

Marc walked into the kitchen having heard the gist of the conversation.

"Ice cream, ice cream? you'll turn into one you sweet little girl." He gathered Poppy up in his arms while she struggled to be free.

"Daddy, daddy let go me, let go me." He laughed and dumped her wriggling little person into an old arm chair by the window where Fudge was sleeping, but he merely raised his head, licked her face and went back to sleep again. Barley came across wagging his tail, happy to fill in as Poppy's playmate.

"So now everybody else is sorted, how about I take my lovely wife out for a meal at the country house hotel the other side of

Dromvaar – then I shall bring her back for a rest?"

"Brilliant," replied Emma. "I'd love that, but I don't need a rest yet, I'm fine."

"We'll see about that later, my darling," he winked at the girls and went out followed by both dogs, who were hoping for a walk.

❄

Dougie had called Mac and asked him to drop by in the morning, before they opened up at noon. He had something important which he wished to discuss.

Dougie's mother had put the fear of God into her son when she had described the bruises and welts on that poor child's back. She had gone over to Sean and before he could flee she had taken his arm lifting up his shirt to have a better look. The boy had cringed as she went near, almost as if he thought she was going to hit him. Mary Macquire had been horrified and the child had been distraught that she had seen. Rather than upset him further she had decided to remain outwardly calm, say no more and distract him with more food, otherwise she thought that he might have run. Well done mother, thought Dougie; very well done indeed. The bitch of a woman had collected the boy later, as arranged. Mary, with difficulty, had said nothing and the pair hadn't been seen since. For the moment they seemed to have vanished and nobody knew where they lived.

Mac said not a word while he listened to the story, his face becoming more solemn by the minute. Then he took out his mobile preparing to call up the social services. Dougie put a hand on his arm.

"Hang on there a minute Mac, we don't know yet who these people are or where they hang out and for the moment they seem to have disappeared into thin air. Don't you think we should locate them first and perhaps do a bit of investigating ourselves? I'm sure that Stuart and the Colonel will help. I'll also have a wee word with my chef, Ginger. After all, he's Irish and might have heard a thing or two about that girl?"

"Och Dougie, you're probably right, but I'll go along now and see Mary. She'll give me a good description which I can then discreetly put around within the force." He shook his head. "That poor wee lad and about nine, ten years old, d'you say?" Dougie nodded sadly.

"Right, I'll be away then. Keep your ears and eyes open and if you hear anything at all call my mobile. It's a sensitive situation. I have a bad feeling and it's not just about the child either. Be careful, ye ken, we don't want to frighten them off."

"I won't do that, don't you worry," the publican answered. He turned back to his work behind the bar muttering to himself. What his mother had told him had really upset Dougie. There was he and Ailsa desperate for children and not having any luck. He'd like to ring the neck of anybody who abused a child. Ailsa would be as upset as he was.

At the mill Ailsa was having trouble with the laird. He always came down to make a nuisance of himself when she was there, never when she wasn't. It alarmed her, just a little, that he seemed to keep track of her movements and always seemed to know when she was around. He'd tried it on a couple of times when he'd been the worse for wear: it was quite obvious that his whisky drinking was out of control. Luckily, on each occasion she hadn't been on her own when he'd found her in the store room. One of the others, already alerted, had come in to the rescue. Still, he'd managed to get her up against the wall and put his hand down the front of her shirt before help arrived. Now he was trying to get her to bring his order up to the house herself after hours and she knew that his poor wife was away. The trouble was he held the purse strings so to speak. Ailsa also had to be careful. The mill did very well out of the income from the garden tours and the owner of the mill, Eileen Mcloughline was a good friend to the man's wife. They had grown up together. But Eileen was a good sort and sensible. Ailsa knew that if she couldn't handle the situation she'd have to go to Eileen and come clean. Her boss, although a great friend of Finola's, couldn't stand the laird herself. Ailsa deduced that Eileen probably knew a lot more about the thoroughly incompatible marriage than anybody else. If anybody needed a good friend it was Finola Strathkellan. Of that Ailsa was quite sure.

CHAPTER 13

Guy had planned Alicia's birthday down to the very smallest detail. He'd booked them all into a small boutique hotel off the Rue de Seine near St.Germain for two nights. Alicia loved to hear the bells ringing out across Paris. They could see the top of the church and bell tower from their bedroom window, with its tiny little roof terrace. Tickets for the opera at the Bastille were reserved for the second evening. They had caught the early flight from Inverness and were soon settled in their rooms with plenty of time for a quick lunchtime snack at the brasserie around the corner, before the mens' meeting. The girls were going to visit 'la Dame à la licorne' tapestries in the Cluny museum, followed by some shopping. Then they would all meet for drinks back at the hotel in the early evening.

Alicia stood staring at the incredible medieval works of art in their darkened room with protective screening and illumination.

"The colours are still unbelievable; it's hard to believe they're actually so ancient, isn't it?"

"I know," agreed Adriana. "It somehow makes you feel that we haven't really progressed very far doesn't it? Imagine anybody achieving anything like this today." Alicia was leaning as near as she could, screwing up her eyes concentrating on the extraordinary detail.

"You know they made all their own dyes using basic pigment. The colours are so vibrant and so much purer than ours now and I love the intricate work on all the animals."

"Yes they really are so beautiful, such mind blowing craftsmanship." Adriana sighed. "I really don't think I feel like looking at anymore in the museum this afternoon, do you?"

"No," answered Alicia, "we should have really looked at the tapestries last. Now I would be disappointed in anything else. Nothing can match this. Let's go and have tea or coffee while we collect our wits, then go shopping."

They strolled back towards their hotel through the nearby shopping streets around the boulevard St.Germain. They headed for the Rue de Seine with its many restaurants, wandering slowly past, peering in through the shop windows when something caught their eye. It wasn't quite warm enough to sit outside. A café on a corner looked the most inviting as the busy period was now over and it was empting out. The door opened and a group of young girls appeared laughing and talking together in some foreign language that certainly wasn't French. Adriana turned around to watch them go across the street in their short skirts, tight jeans and impossibly high heels. They were an attractive group; a short haired young woman, in the middle of the group answered them, telling them to try to speak French or English. Adriana couldn't quite see her face but she sounded Irish. Perhaps they were students on a cultural tour, she thought, wondering where they came from – what fun that must be. They'd also been shopping judging by the many carrier bags.

Alicia had gone in ahead, to find a table. She had taken off her coat and was already ordering coffee in her very reasonable French as Adriana followed her inside.

"This is just great isn't it? Such a treat to have some time to ourselves for a bit." Alicia was looking forward to a decent cup of coffee.

"Yes it is," answered Adriana sitting down. "Guy is inclined to over-organise us. I wonder what he has planned for tonight?"

"He said they'd take us dancing after dinner, which would be fun, wouldn't it?"

Adriana looked at her hands and said nothing.

"Arri what is it? There's something wrong. I can feel it. Is it Julian...? It is, isn't it? I can tell from your expression."

The coffee arrived and the waiter fussed around making sure they had all they needed then moved off to another table. Adriana slumped forward letting out a sigh. With hunched shoulders and her elbows on the table she looked across at her friend wondering what to say. Alicia was determined to find out what the problem was.

"Come on Arri, you can tell me, you know I won't say squeak!"

"Oh dear! What a nightmare it is, but alright...." Adriana sat up and took a sip of her coffee.... "I'll tell you, but you have to swear to keep it to yourself."

"I swear."

"Alright, well... the reason that this wedding is never going to happen is, I think..., because we don't seem to be able to have a baby and...," she began to sniff alarmingly so that Alicia quickly handed a handkerchief across, "we really have been trying. Julian thinks it's his fault because he had mumps as a child. He told me the night before last. He says that he doesn't want to saddle me, as he puts it, with a childless marriage," she finished in a rush. Alicia looked horrified.

"Oh Arri, I am so so sorry. How awful for you both, but are you quite sure about this? I mean has Julian seen a doctor and had everything checked?"

"Yes, we both have. I'm fine but the specialist said that, although it's unlikely that Julian can father children, it's not impossible and of course there are various things we can do... but now Julian just says we must carry on as we are and see what, if anything, happens. But he won't marry me unless he can give me a child. He's adamant about it." Adriana looked stricken. Alicia reached across for her hand in sympathy.

"Oh Heavens! You poor thing! But how do you feel about it?"

"I'd marry him anyway and I've told him that. I love him Alicia, you know I do. He knows I want children, but so as far as I'm concerned if it doesn't happen we'll just have to adopt one."

"God! What a vile situation for both of you. It must be seriously difficult living together with this hanging over you. Do you think he's talked to Guy? They're so close I can't believe he hasn't." Adriana let go of Alicia's hand and blew her nose loudly. Several people on a nearby table turned around to stare. Alicia glared back at them.

"Yes, I think he probably has. I just hope that Guy can knock some sense into the stupid man."

"Do you want me to tip the wink to Guy anyway?"

"No thank you, at least not for the moment and actually I have a possible plan that might or might not come off. But it's not something I'm going to tell you about so don't even ask me."

"Oh Arri, don't make any rash decisions on your own will you? You know that you can tell me anything."

"Yes I do know that. But this is something I have to do on my own, so just keep faith please. That's all I ask."

"Alright, but you only have to say. Now let's drink up and go to do that shopping, so that we can walk into the hotel later with loads of carrier bags. Then they'll have a fit." They both giggled at this and Alicia called for the bill.

Adriana felt a whole lot better having confided in Alicia. A little thrill ran through her body and she determined somehow to make her very unorthodox and devious plan happen.

Alicia, dropped the sad subject, but still couldn't help wondering what on earth Adriana had in mind that could possibly help save the situation. A vague feeling of unease settled in her stomach and a breath of chill wind crept down the back of her neck.

"Are you cold?" asked Adriana noticing her shiver.

"No," answered Alicia. "Just worried."

"Don't be, it's not your problem. Come on, let's go shopping. We've got two hours until the shops shut," Adriana replied with an unusually steely glint in her eye.

❄

The girls hit the shops with enthusiasm. It was her birthday the following day, so Alicia bought herself a chic little black dress for the opera. It fitted like a glove. Set on cheering up her friend, Alicia then persuaded Adriana to purchase a really cool pair of evening trousers, in a lovely dark red, with a tie suede belt and a cream silk shirt to complete the outfit. They bought shoes for themselves and presents for Emma and Rose, Marc and Poppy. They would also find a small gift for Jessica and Beth, either tomorrow or in the tax free, before flying back to the UK. When they met the men in the bar of their hotel in the evening they did indeed have many carrier bags.

"We've spent all your money!" laughed Alicia flopping down as she reached their table. Guy and Julian looked at each other in alarm.

"And there's nothing you can do about it, 'cos nothing's going back and all the shops are shut now anyway," Adriana added with relish, her good humour completely restored with the excitement and feel-good therapy of it all. "Now what can we have to drink?"

❄

That night, after dinner on the left bank, at a restaurant managed by an old friend of both Guy and Alicia, they went dancing at a chic new nightclub. Adriana was intrigued once more as to how Guy seemed to gain entry into these stylish places wherever they went. There was seemingly no difficulty about being welcomed in alongside the smart Parisians. He always seemed to know somebody with the necessary credentials.

It was as they were leaving that Adriana noticed the party in a far corner. They hadn't been there when they arrived. Two Oriental looking men and several startlingly pretty very young girls who she'd seen before, coming out of the Brasserie earlier in the day. Not an unusual sight in an upmarket nightclub, but it was the girl with short cropped hair, who seemed to be in negotiation with the men, who caught Adriana's eagle eye. She must also have been with the group earlier in the day. But more importantly Adriana had definitely seen her somewhere else as well. A far cry from this chic nightclub; it was in the pub in Scotland on that very first evening, when they'd arrived in Dromvaar in torrential rain.

The door shut behind them. Adriana was – breathless, waving her hands around excitedly. She couldn't get it out fast enough. Julian put his arm around her shoulders.

"What is it, my darling? What on earth's the matter, are you feeling alright?"

"Yes, yes of course I'm alright... it's, it's the woman, the... the woman in the corner," she spluttered, "I've seen her before."

"Which woman? What are you talking about? Who? Someone you've seen in London? Well what of it – who is it for Heaven's sake? Why on earth are you in such a state?" Guy, alerted by the astonished look on Adriana's face, quickly ushered them all around the corner, away from the nightclub door which was opening and closing as people came and went. Then he put his hand gently on her arm and took charge.

"Shush a minute, hush everybody. Arri, what woman? What do you mean, seen who before? Where have you seen her exactly?" Adriana breathed in deeply and exhaled with an impatient sigh.

"The woman – it's the girl in the corner on the left as we came out. She's with two Asian guys and several beautiful young girls – she's the scruffy one, with a child, who I saw in the pub with the immigrants on that first night in Dromvaar. She's creepy: out of place both here and in the pub. I'm telling you she's up to no good. Something really evil's going on. I can feel it. I thought it then and I think it even more now that I've seen her over here, in this chic nightclub with these two Orientals and those innocent young girls." There was an intake of breath and silence prevailed momentarily.

"Adriana, are you absolutely sure about this?"

"One hundred percent certain. I never forget a face, especially one like that," she added for good measure. "I also saw them all earlier, coming out of a brasserie when we went to have a coffee in the Rue de Seine. I didn't get a proper look at her then, as I was looking at the girls, but I'm sure she was with them."

"Right," said Guy, "did she recognize you - do you think?"

"No," Adriana replied quickly. "She was too busy talking, on all three occasions."

"OK, Julian! get us a taxi would you? I'm just going to go back in and have a quick peep. Wait for me here and Ally darling... lend me that scarf around your neck would you? I shall surreptitiously find it under the table where we were seated. I won't be a minute." Stuffing the silk scarf in the pocket of his overcoat Guy knocked three times on the door and went back in.

※

They were all sitting in the taxi around the corner when he returned a few minutes later jumping in, giving the address of their hotel, as he did so.

"Well?" asked Julian as the taxi pulled out into the late night traffic, "what did you find out in..." he glanced at his watch... "precisely six minutes?"

Guy, was silent for a moment as he handed Alicia her scarf. 'He's good... so very good', thought Alicia watching her husband proudly and hardly daring to take a breath. The air was chill and anticipatory. Guy, looking somewhat smug, then turned towards Adriana.

"Arri, well done, you're very observant. The word has it that these young girls have come in from middle European countries: Bulgaria, Romania, Albania mostly, even Slovenia, Hungary and the Ukraine. They have been specifically groomed, for what requirements you don't need to know," he commented seriously, "but you can imagine. Adriana was correct in her assumption that some sort of negotiation seemed to be taking place between the Oriental looking gentlemen and the young Irish woman who seemed to be taking the lead. According to our friend the manager, whenever this particular guest darkens their door, she always appears in control, dead cool, tough and certainly is no lady. I have to say that she certainly looks like she'd concede nothing in a man's deal."

"My friend is unhappy about having these suspect people in his club at all, but unfortunately the Orientals were introduced by one of the founder members a couple of months ago, when the club first opened. Apart from anything else, nobody wishes to get involved, as needless to say these two are not people with whom you'd wish to tangle. The man who introduced them is responsible for much of the funding behind the club."

"Good Lord!" exclaimed Alicia, "what a lot you did find out in such a short time. Did you get a good look at the Irish girl?"

"Yes, a quick glance, from a distance," replied Guy, "but I never forget a voice, particularly an Irish one and, for now, I was more interested in getting a look at the Far Eastern men, as they are part of the bigger picture."

"What are you going to do about all this?" asked Adriana. "Even Mary Macquire, at the Post Office back in Dromvaar, is suspicious. No question they're all bad news. Did you see how young those girls were?"

"Yes, and I know that the vagrants who, you say were with this Irish girl in Dromvaar, are also giving cause for concern. I need to find out where they come from. There isn't, as yet, any evidence of wrong doing. Further very subtle investigation is necessary and I shall definitely have to find out why this all seems to lead back to Scotland. I have no doubt now that there's a link." He turned to Julian.

"There's also that Russian ship that we saw anchored off the Isle Of Lewis, when we went across to Loch Island. We need to check it out as Fergus said he'd seen it anchored there before, so it wasn't just sheltering." Julian, having digested all this, got out a cigarette in preparation for vacating the taxi and merely said resentfully,

"Bloody fucking hell, here we go again. Let's give up for once and for all on so-called holidays. They're not worth the struggle." Adriana snuggled up beside him.

"Come on my love, you know that you and Guy are itching for some action!"

"The only action I want, "he returned glumly, "is fishing on that ruddy loch!"

❄

The next day nobody had to get up early and it was Alicia's birthday. Guy decided to play down the events of the previous evening for the time being, when they were all together, but he would certainly mention his findings later that morning to his colleagues in their high profile group meeting. The girls had breakfast in bed and the men met downstairs, for an unhurried croissant and coffee, before going off to their French counterparts' headquarters.

It was a lovely clear autumn day, cool and crisp but with no unpleasant wind-chill. Alicia and Adriana wandered around the streets near the hotel. There were a couple of interesting art galleries; the gushing Frenchman in one shop was absolutely certain that he had a prospective buyer in Adriana and moved in fast with a slick hard-sell spiel. She had listened politely, pretending to understand, whilst he chatted her up. Alicia realizing her friend was lost, had come to the rescue and with some difficulty they managed to regain the street with Adriana's dignity intact and her credit card still in place. On reaching the pavement, once away from the window, they had dissolved into helpless giggles. There were several delicatessen and gift shops to browse in, where Adriana insisted Alicia choose something for her birthday. She spent ages; there were so many things to look at in the beautifully arranged windows, let alone when they went inside. Eventually she decided on a fragrant candle surrounded in engraved glass, with a silver lid.

The men returned in high spirits to meet them once more at the Brasserie for lunch. That afternoon after dropping the shopping off at the hotel, they all went to the Rodin museum in the Rue de Varenne. The girls were insistent that they wanted to see 'The Kiss' again. It was a work of art that never ceased to work its magic for Alicia, in particular, as she had now turned from her painting to sculpture, when she had the time away from her journalism. She was fascinated as before by the smooth and wonderful detail. How could something in cool marble be so evocative, so warm and so life like, so mesmeric in its beauty? Auguste Rodin was truly a genius. She longed to feel the work of art, to run her hands over the perfect shapes of the two entwined bodies, but of course you couldn't touch; there was a roped off area around the plinth. So she gazed at the magnificent creation and filled her head with the memory of it – until the next time.

❊ ❊ ❊

CHAPTER 14

Rose and Oliver were stopped by the police when they arrived at Balmacara, just before they reached the bridge at the Kyle of Localsh to drive across to Skye. It appeared to be just a random check; but Olly wasn't so sure as they asked a lot of questions and even looked in the boot. When they were waved on again he glanced in his mirror.

"They're looking for somebody," he said.

"How do you know that Olly? They were just checking, that's all."

"No. You see that large police van parked in the layby?"

"Yes." replied Rose turning around to have another look as they passed by. "What about it?"

"That vehicle carries all the equipment to track just about anything anywhere in the world," said Oliver importantly. "Communication facilities like you wouldn't believe."

"Goodness Olly, how on earth do you know that?" But Oliver wasn't about to enlighten his wife further as he had better things on his mind.

"Come on, my darling, pay attention we're nearly there and I can't wait to get to our room." She leant across and kissed him feeling the same.

"I know. Me too. Look, look Olly," she was pointing. "There's the bridge all lit up in the sun and just look at the mountains across on Skye. They're pink and the ones behind are black. The nearest are called the Cuillin hills. I've read up about them; can't think why they're called hills though, can you? They're huge."

They crossed over the water, to Broadford, then turned down towards Sleat where they found their idyllic little hotel. It was as perfect as they could have wished, for their wedding anniversary treat. Their room was in a different building and looking out over the water, just a few feet away across a narrow strip of lawn. They had two floors; their bedroom was up a little flight of stairs. The bed was big and comfortable and the room like a beautifully romantic attic. Underneath there was a sitting area and a bathroom with everything they could possibly need.

"This is beyond all expectation," was all Rose said, looking around and pretending to ignore what was in her husband's mind! Then she caught his eye and raced upstairs to jump on the bed enthusiastically.

"Come on up, quickly Olly," she called. "Hurry up, then we can go and explore." Oliver ran up the stairs two at a time flinging his clothes off as he went and landed in one bound on the bed beside his wife. Hungrily they set about each other, thrilled to let the world go away and with no one to disturb their passionate lovemaking.

Oliver lay regarding his sleeping wife. She was so vivacious, so quick to respond, such fun to be with and she was just so physical. She never turned him down and enjoyed making love as if it was a golden adventure each and every time and it was never the same twice. He looked at his watch. Perhaps he should wake her and they could go out for the walk before he got other ideas once more. As if she'd heard his thoughts Rose opened one eye.

"Hello!"

"Hello you", he answered kissing her smiling mouth. "Shall we go out now or...?"

"No Olly, no come on let's get some other exercise or we won't eat any dinner and I want to find out about the otters!"

"OK," he ruffled her unruly dark hair, heaved himself up off the bed and went across to the window.

The evening was drawing in, the loch shone like glass and the gentle afternoon light was already changing the hills beyond from pink to a soft purple. It was beautiful. Olly was so happy to be at this lovely place with Rose, but there was a small feeling of unease deep down in the pit of his stomach. There was a small prickle of discontent between two of his friends and there was also something unsettled in the air surrounding them all. There was neither rhyme nor reason but, Oliver supposed, this was what premonition was all about and it lay uncomfortably on him.

Rose appeared at his side. "I love you Olly."

"And I love you too my darling, very much indeed." He turned her around and pulled her into his arms, kissing her as if he'd never let her go. The walk would have to wait.

Mac waited for Mary Macquire to attend to her last customer before she shut for the lunchtime break. It was one of the staff from the mill and she was telling Mary that she was worried for Ailsa with the unwanted attentions from the laird. Mary was giving of her best advice.

"Well m'dear, I don't think that I should interfere. Ailsa is a big lassie now and should be able to look after herself, but if what you say becomes too much of a burden then I'll have a word, don't you worry your head, just keep me posted!" At this Mary let out a chuckle of laughter and appeared from behind the counter to see her customer out and began to shut up the shop.

Mac, pretending to ignore the conversation he'd just heard about Mary's daughter-in-law and the Lord Strathkellan's unwanted attentions, waited patiently while she pulled the blind down and locked the door.

"Come on in Mac, we'll go in the back and I'll make you a cuppa." Mary put the kettle on then turned to her old friend.

"No news then?"

"No news, I'm afraid Mary, not a sign of any of them."

"Tch, I'm really concerned for that poor wee one, Mac. Those people are up to no good, do you know and what might they have done to shut that young boy up if he knows more than what's good for him?"

"I know Mary, I know. It doesn't bear thinking about, but there's no use in worrying about something which may never happen. There might just be a feasible answer to everything."

"Nae Mac, no!"

"Well, we're just going to have to wait and see." He drank up his tea, got up and picked his police hat up off the table. "Och we canna dae naught until we find them."

"I know Mac; you'll do all ye can. Now away with you. I must do some of my paperwork and I haven't long."

❄

Ailsa was on her own in the little store room off the kitchen when Alistair Strathkellan stealthily appeared once more, unannounced.

"Hello there Ailsa! I've been looking for you." Never mind the jocular greeting. The man had something menacing about him, Ailsa thought instinctively. He held out his arms and lunged for her but Ailsa was quicker, she managed to knock a broom over right across his path. He tripped and fell sideways in an ungainly heap and was reduced to scrabbling around amongst some pots and pans and large bags of flour, swearing like a trooper. The noise could have woken the dead.

"Oh dear, your lordship, are you alright? What a terrible tumble you went. I'll get one of the lads to help you up as my back might let us both down," she said and strode out stifling her laughter and muttering, "that'll teach the old bastard."

Beth and Jessica were there having lunch with Poppy and heard the commotion coming from behind the kitchen. Beth jumped up to see if she could help, but Ailsa waved her away and called for Jock, the odd job man, who was stacking some boxes out behind the till. Jock, grinning from ear to ear, patted Ailsa on the back as he went past and, obviously accustomed to this state of affairs, went to the Laird's assistance at once, rubbing his hands together with glee. A short time later when they both appeared from the back, Jock looked in control of the situation but the laird, covered in flour, looked shifty and distinctly embarrassed.

"Well," whispered Beth, trying to keep a straight face and concentrate on finishing her lunch, "what do you make of that?" Jessica let out a half smothered laugh and kicked her sister hard under the table. They both burst into giggles, joined by a delighted Poppy, who had absolutely no idea whatsoever what they were laughing about. The laird, considerably redder in the face than before, marched out with very little dignity left intact. Jock held open the door for him and Ailsa collapsed into a chair. Even Poppy was silent as they listened for the noise of the retreating car. Ailsa then regaled them all with what had actually happened and ordered pudding all around and an ice cream for Poppy. The story would get better with the telling and Ailsa very much hoped that it would put paid to the laird's amorous advances for some time to come. Receding hair and freckles, overweight and purple in the face, she could well imagine why Alistair Strathkellan had to look elsewhere to satisfy his needs. Poor Finola. What an awful ordeal his romantic advances must be.

CHAPTER 15

Alec and John were close and delighted to see each other again. Alec had spent some time with his brother and family on their Ionian island in the height of the summer, but they hadn't seen each other since. Marc had met his father at the station and then stayed for a drink up at Glencurrie, before leaving the two older men to their own devices. They were going to have a quiet evening catching up. Jean Haddington had made some soup and a fish pie. There were fresh stewed peaches and cheese and biscuits to follow. Mrs H liked Colonel Alec's brother and she had always kept in mind how much he loved her fish pie.

The following evening dinner would be down at the lodge. The men would go early as John was keen to be there for his grand-daughter Poppy's bath and bedtime story.

Stuart and Mrs H had planned a day off for the following day. He and his formidable wife were heading for Edinburgh to spend some time with their son, Ailsa's twin. Stuart had been in, before dark, just to re-assure Alec that everything was well and truly locked up and also that there had been no more sign of the immigrant people. Perhaps, having had no luck around these parts, they'd moved off elsewhere. Mac, who was of the same mind, would come past just to check the following evening. He said to tell the Colonel to call his mobile immediately if he saw any signs of the foreigners returning.

Alec thanked Stuart and settled in for the evening with his brother. They enjoyed the excellent fish pie and when the meal was done sat either side of the glowing fire, in the sitting room, with a bottle of the local whisky on the table between them.

There was much to talk about - the sorry state of Greece, its government and present policies, which had begun to badly affect John's own life with his family over there.

Alec repeated his heartfelt wish. "You know that there is the lodge if you ever want to come back to Scotland. It's a perfect size for you all and it's in good nick. The schools are excellent up here for the younger ones and Andros can have a whole herd of goats - if he so wishes!" John laughed.

"You're very kind Alec, but you know how I feel: it's Anastasia. I'm really not sure that she could cope with the cold and endless winter up here. She'd be a fish out of warm water as the children might be too. Ana loves the house under the olives and I just can't imagine her anywhere else. She hardly ever leaves the island and then only for visits to her family on the mainland."

"I understand," said Alec disappointed, "but if things become too difficult, it will always be here for you. Perhaps you might consider coming over for the children's Easter holidays? The house doesn't have to be rented all the time."

"That is a wonderful idea and I'll suggest it to Ana on my return. She might well agree. She misses Marc and Emma and longs to spend more time with our darling little grandchild. Now what's this about trouble with travellers from Europe?"

"Ah! Well... I'm not sure exactly. Some rather suspect people appeared a while ago, but now, for the moment at least, they seem to have disappeared again." Alec replied. "I just have a feeling all's not quite right with the world around here, at present. I can't put my finger on it but I sense there's a certain disquiet in the air; something undercover perhaps, if you know what I mean? I've had a chat to Guy and Julian. Do you remember those young men? They were the two who brought the Swiss drama to a satisfactory conclusion, helped by Oliver and Rose as it turned out. They're all staying at the lodge with Emma and Marc but are away now for a couple of days, but they're based there and will soon be back."

"Yes, of course I remember them all. Julian, Guy, Alicia and Adriana were all at Emma and Marc's wedding in Greece... and at Poppy's christening in London. I think that Rose and Guy are both godparents, so that's where we first met Rose with Oliver. A very lively interesting group of people and so much fun to be with. I'm looking forward to seeing them all again. I'm only sorry that Ana can't be here with us this time as she would enjoy them too." He took another sip of whisky and chuckled, "and don't, whatever you do, let me forget Poppy's present at the bottom of my suitcase or I shall be in frightful trouble."

Alec leant across to refill his brother's glass.

"Yes, I wish Ana was here and the children, then we would be complete. However, I do realise that it is difficult for her to get away with your second family being so much younger and of school age."

"Never mind, I hope that you'll all come out to the Ionian again next summer. We'll have a great time. There's nothing that Ana likes more than to fill our house under the olives with cheerful family laughter and Andros has named a new baby goat especially for Poppy."

"What a lovely idea," Alec responded. "No doubt she'll be thrilled."

"Now what about these 'negative influences lurking in the wings', then? Or should I say unwanted visitors? What are the authorities doing about it, Alec? You are extremely isolated up here."

"Well, it's difficult you see, with no evidence of actual wrong-doing so to speak. But Guy and Julian are two very able young men who more than understand the special operative side of army life, if you get my meaning. That is their unofficial line of work. They have better connections now than I have and I'm very pleased to have them around at the moment; it's reassuring. I'm out of all that sort of thing now. I have tried to check out these new rules and regulations about middle European people coming into the country up here, but I seem to encounter a brick wall as far as unauthorized information is concerned. All responsibility seems to be passed back to London. I might need a couple of your old contacts to help out, if that's possible? Bearing in mind, of course, how much younger you are than me." John laughed.

"All of twelve years younger! Yes, I am still in touch with a few people. You only have to ask and I'll get on to it."

"Good, now how about another whisky before bed? Help yourself while I just go and check that Mrs H has locked up, as I can hear the dogs barking. Do ring Ana, as I'm sure she'd like to know that you are safe arrived. Tell her we miss her and send her my love."

The back door was firmly locked but the dogs were frantic to go out. So Alec let them go, making one hell of a noise. He stepped out onto the path leading to the courtyard of barns, peering into the dark. Just then the moon put in a coy appearance creating a sudden haze of light and Alec could have sworn he'd seen a dark figure scale the gate. The dogs were leaping up and down in a frenzy. Having heard the commotion, John suddenly appeared at his side.

"What was it? A cat or a fox?"

"Neither," Alec answered, "too big; much too big." He said worriedly, hauling the dogs back into the house.

"I'll call Mac in the morning. Whoever it is won't be back tonight, not with these two noisy buggers around."

Nonetheless, as they went back in Alec unlocked the gun cabinet, took out his shotgun and some blank cartridges, just in case the dogs needed some backup in the small hours.

❊

It had rained in the night and any footprints around the gate would have been obscured. After breakfast Alec and John, together with Mac, checked the barns thoroughly. Nothing was missing and the locks hadn't been touched. Mac thought it most likely to have been an amateur, a lone individual, on the lookout for an open door or window and something easy to pinch. A quick grab and run job, but he hadn't bargained for the dogs and so had scarpered.

"What about the foreign people?" John asked.

"They seem to have vanished into thin air," answered Mac, "and they wouldn't have gone near the house in any case: they'd have known about the dogs. They would have made for the barns. There would have been two of them and they're pretty darn quick at picking locks." Although he wasn't convinced, Alec had to go along with this, at least for the moment.

"You can put your gun back in the cabinet now Colonel. I'll have a car pass by a couple of times during the night, just to be on the safe side," Mac said, obviously thinking that this would be considered acceptable. His phone rang, a hurried conversation ensued, then excusing himself he rushed off importantly saying that he was needed down in the port.

John and Alec watched him speed off in his little panda car.

"Well," Alec declared, "that's that then. Mac hates that car. He much prefers his own jalopy. It's not quite Scotland Yard up here, is it?"

"No," replied John, "but definitely better than the Greek equivalent, I can assure you."

❄

In Paris, the four friends spent the rest of the day up in Montmartre; just wandering around the little shops and stopping frequently to rest, for coffee, crepes or pastries, in the many quaint little cafes.

The opera, 'La Boheme', later that evening, was nothing short of spectacular. One of the best productions ever; it was perfection in every respect and greeted with a standing ovation after the finale. They had dinner in a restaurant around the corner from the Opera House. The first course was organized before the performance. The table remained reserved and during the interval they enjoyed their main course. At the end, after the final roars of the crowd had subsided they returned once more for coffee and dessert. Awash with emotion and the glorious music, everybody was quiet for a while. Alicia felt that she'd had the very best birthday and for this one special day her husband had been clever enough to insist on nobody discussing or dwelling on the previous evening's rather dramatic ending. The repercussions of which, she had no doubt, would come before long anyway. But this day and this night had been extra special and nothing could spoil the memory of it. Alicia raising her glass was the first to speak.

"Thank you, thank you my darling husband. This has been the best birthday present and the best day spent with my most favourite people." Guy leaned across and kissed her, handing over a small carrier bag hiding beside his chair.

"This, sweetheart, is for you, but not to be opened here in front of our friends!"

"Happy birthday!" they all chorused for the last time, perfectly aware of the contents of the package.

"I hope that Julian didn't help you choose whatever is in that parcel?" asked Adriana laughing, noticing the well known name on the bag. Julian looked just a little uncomfortable.

"Certainly not," he replied indignantly, "I stood outside and had a smoke!"

On arriving back at the hotel, the girls went up first while the men sat and had a cognac at the bar. Guy began to speak as if continuing a conversation.

"I have decided that there has to be some way onto that island from the East, from the mainland itself." Julian shook his head and smiled.

"You can't let it drop for long can you! But why on earth do you say that?" he asked perplexed. "There's a perfectly good landing on the West where Fergus left us."

"I don't believe that village is deserted but I do think that whatever is going on there has to have covert contact with the mainland, as well as from the sea. There has to be another way in."

"If you say so. We can investigate that. But what do you make of Adriana recognizing that Irish woman? That really is a strange coincidence."

"I think she and unfortunately those young girls are all muddled up in the same racket. But whether or not it all ties up with the immigrant people in Dromvaar and the island village, as yet I'm unsure."

"What about that Russian ship lurking off Lewis?"

"That also needs to be looked into. I think we should talk to Alec again. He understands our work and probably still has some useful contacts up here. I'd also like to get hold of a marine chart and an ordnance survey map of that area."

"OK, but what about the girls? We don't want them to start sounding off around the village when we get back, especially now that Arri recognized that girl."

"No. We need to handle it carefully. You know what they're like when there's an air of intrigue. I'll talk to Alicia. She won't let Adriana go off investigating anything on her own. We'll play the whole thing down for the moment."

"Alright but don't forget Rose and Olly – they won't wish to be left out of anything untoward that's going on!"

"Fuck! I forgot about the intrepid Rose and the over enthusiastic Oliver. No, don't worry I will also have a quiet word with Olly and I suppose Marc needs to be warned in as well."

"Well, we have our fishing at Glencurrie planned for the day after tomorrow. I'm not sure that the girls will wish to be involved all day long, so it might be a good opportunity for a serious discussion in comparative privacy."

"Yes you're right. Now talking about privacy, I think it's time I rejoined my wife upstairs and finish off her birthday with a flourish!"

Laughing together, the two friends said goodnight and went to their rooms, still for the moment on holiday and determined, as yet, not to be taken over by untoward future events. They were in Paris and in another country for a little while longer. Scotland seemed another world away. Guy opened his door happily anticipating his wife in her birthday present, which would without doubt very soon be removed.

CHAPTER 16

Mac was trying to calm Molly. She, poor woman, had come across the body; or rather her dog had found it first. When he'd received the call, Mac had left the Colonel and rushed down to the cafe. There he'd found Mary Macquire and Dougie taking care of the distraught lady. She'd had sweet tea and a biscuit and had soon recovered herself enough to be able to tell him what she'd seen.

Molly had been walking her dog along the strip of sand before the old smokery on the far side of Dromvaar. The cliffs there dipped down to sea level. She liked to walk along the beach and throw sticks into the water for the old Labrador to retrieve and bathe. On reaching the end of the bay the dog started barking wildly at a piece of rough cloth flapping in the wind, wedged amongst the rocks. Molly had thought it to be an old sack snagged, brought in with the tide. But, to her horror, the dog had started pulling at something inside the ripped sodden bag and uncovered a pale bloated arm. She had hauled the dog off, left the gruesome find and run as fast as she could back to the car, returning at speed to the cafe and to the telephone. Everybody kept telling her that she should move with the times and get a mobile, but she had held out saying that she didn't want the disturbance. But, on this occasion, Molly had wished that she'd listened to the advice.

It wasn't long before the whole of Dromvaar and the surrounding area had heard the news. The television channels and local newspapers were soon assembling and Mac, much to his disgust, had been delegated to organize the traffic and help set up an incident room, while more senior officers took charge of circumstances surrounding the discovery of the body. Mac rang the Colonel on his mobile as Alec had particularly asked to be kept abreast of the investigation. After the call Mac felt a little of his lost dignity return. The Colonel was much admired and well liked in these parts and Mac knew Alec Neilsen's contacts to be far superior to this lot, who were pumped up with their own importance and too busy throwing their weight around.

Dougie was preparing for extra mouths to feed and Ailsa, for once, said that she'd help out in the evening if he needed her. Dougie knew perfectly well that it was more a question of his wife not wishing to miss out on any of the excitement.

The body tied up in the sack was that of a very young woman. The police soon accounted for everyone of a similar age in the area. Even though she'd been in the water several days Mac had said that in life the girl would have been considered very beautiful. It was thought that the body could have been swept down from the North with the tide and current and maybe even thrown from off a ship - who knows? Mac was horrified that such a young person, little more than a child, could have been murdered and dumped in the sea. What on earth for? What could the poor mite possibly have done to merit such a cruel death? Time would tell and no doubt, with help from forensics, the truth behind this dreadful deed would soon be discovered.

Mary Macquire was convinced that the murder had something to do with the Irish woman, now disappeared with her child. When she had first heard about the body she had been terrified that it might have been that of the boy Sean. Then when she had heard that the dead person was female, she had wondered if the murdered woman was the Irish girl. Nothing would have surprised her. If that slut had been capable of abusing that poor child, God alone only knew in what she might have been mixed up. That night the whole village was buzzing with the police, the press and all the local people wanting to discuss the latest gruesome happening.

Beth and Jessica had been walking along the harbour wall with Poppy that afternoon when the drama unfolded. They soon heard what had happened and Fergus took the opportunity to come and tell them all the gory details.

Everybody was in a state of shock. Such a thing had never happened before in Dromvaar. The last person to die in unusual circumstances had been the old man who'd lived in Fergus' cottage before him. He'd always said that when it was time for him to pass over he would carry his favourite chair down to the sea and settle himself in it for good. This was exactly what he'd done. The only trouble about this had been that he'd asked to be buried boxed in his chair and the grave diggers had baulked at the shape and size of the hole they'd had to dig!

Mary Macquire said that she'd have Molly to stay, as she didn't want the poor woman having nightmares on her own. Ailsa said that she could spare one of the girls from the mill to help run the cafe the next day, while Molly was recovering and giving statements to the police.

When Jessica and Beth got back to the lodge Marc and Emma were still out. They'd gone to the Glenaigle Country House hotel for lunch and most likely had decided to go for a walk afterwards. Dinner was organized for Alec and John that evening. There was nothing for Emma to do and Beth had Jessica to help her serve it and wash up. The others were all due back the following day.

"What a good thing that Poppy doesn't understand what's happened," commented Beth as she locked the car and followed Jessica and Poppy to the front door. "What an awful thing to happen in this lovely peaceful place."

"Not so peaceful anymore I'm afraid. I think that we should keep out of Dromvaar at the moment, at least until everything has calmed down a bit."

"Well, I shall have to go in to do the shopping," Beth answered, ever practical and just a little too quickly.

"And to see somebody else I imagine?" Jess dug her sister in the ribs. Beth coloured, immediately becoming defensive.

"Fergus works, Jess, out on his boat. He doesn't just hang around waiting to see me, you know."

"Maybe not, but he's really keen; that's obvious and it's mutual, I can tell. I like him too," she said quickly. "He's fun."

Poppy joined in immediately bouncing up and down, clapping her little hands chanting, "Poppy like too, fun." They both laughed and the atmosphere lightened.

"You, little Madam," Beth picked her up and made to throw her away, "may not be able to talk much yet, but you certainly understand, don't you?" She said, tickling the little girl, who giggled helplessly.

"Okay, bath time," Jess took over, "then I'll come to help you with the vegetables." They went upstairs and Beth headed for the kitchen.

Soon after, Marc and Emma arrived back looking both happy and relaxed, until Beth had to fill them in with the latest developments. They were horrified.

Dinner that night was mostly spent discussing the recent shocking event. Alec decided that he was very pleased that the others were all due back from Paris the next day. He thought that he'd ask both Julian and Guy up for a drink the following evening, if they weren't too tired.

❄

Rose was in her element. The weather had improved and they had been told where they should go to see the otters in the early dawn, or in the evening just before sundown. Oliver decided that he wished to be in bed with his wife at dawn, so they would go down later in the day, before it got dark.

They took a flask of tea, some biscuits and a rug and sat on some rocks, at the back of the bay, to watch and wait. There was not a soul in sight. The sun began to sink leaving a vivid orange sky softening to apricot, gulls called to one another as small waves caressed the sand while the sea steadily retreated with the ebbing tide. They nearly missed what they'd come to see, as Olly started getting carried away with the romance of the place. Rose saw the movement out of the corner of her eye, in the place where they'd been told to watch; at the mouth of a small river where it ran into the sea. Suddenly there they were, the otters, slithering over the rocks and diving in, appearing again with their sleek heads bobbing about like children as they played in the water. It was a magical sight. How lucky they were to see a family of four, in their natural habitat and for the lovely creatures to be either completely unaware or unworried by their still, enraptured, audience.

That night at dinner they sat in the little restaurant relishing another delicious meal on their last night in this tranquil hotel with its spectacular scenery, on the mystical Isle of Skye.

CHAPTER 17

Guy received the call from Alec on his mobile, on the way back from the airport. The four occupants were stunned to hear of the dead body washed up on the rocks near Dromvaar. But Guy somehow seemed to be the least surprised.

It was not fully dark when they turned off the main road and headed up towards the estate. The girls, wanting some air, got out to walk the last few minutes up the drive to the lodge while the men drove past and on up to Glencurrie.

Alec and John were delighted to see them both and Alec apologised profusely for having waylaid them on their return from Paris.

"No problem at all," said Guy. "I was coming to see you anyway."

They were ushered to the sofa in the sitting room, by the blazing fire. Mrs Haddington was removing the remnants of tea and tidying up the newspapers. Both the village and the port, Alec told them, were thoroughly hyped up with speculation and gossip.

First he related all that he knew of the dead girl. Guy then described Adriana's surprising sighting of the Irish girl in the Parisian nightclub. Alec, in turn was also taken aback.

"Good God. It sounds like this death could well be a small part of a much bigger story then?"

"Yes, possibly and linked, in some way I am afraid, to Dromvaar. It's too much of a coincidence the Irish woman being in both places."

Alec stood deep in thought for a minute.

"It's odd, but I've had a gut feeling about things around

here for a while now. These vagrants, who seem to have some connection to this girl, are involved in something. I'm sure of it and it's not just petty theft either, as some would have me believe. There's something about them. They seem to be more sinister; not the usual type of travellers we get looking for work from time to time. They're usually old fashioned, friendly people who work hard for a living. Apart from which this lot are too elusive, keeping themselves to themselves as if they're hiding something. You're sure about the Irish woman in Paris being one and the same as the scruffy girl in the pub?"

"Yes, absolutely certain," Julian answered. "Adriana never forgets a face, in spite of the difference in location and circumstance; she doesn't make that sort of mistake."

"No, of course not." Alec took a handkerchief from his pocket to polish his glasses, while absorbing the facts.

"Well, I don't like the sound of it at all, particularly as such young women seem to be implicated. Now, John and I have been in constant touch with Mac, our local bobby. He says that the poor dead youngster had no identification whatsoever and had, without doubt, been exceptionally pretty. This perhaps ties up, don't you think, with the group that Adriana saw being escorted by the Irish girl in Paris." Guy and Julian nodded their agreement. It had to be some sort of an illegal ring procuring girls. Alec continued.

"Needless to say, Mac has already been taken off the case and given more mundane duties, much to his disgust. He has always been my best local contact. He knows everyone, but that's about as much information as I have been able to glean to date. I have no doubt that the incident room will be concentrating, at present, on trying first to identify the body of the girl with the help of Interpol I expect, then discovering where she has come from and by what means. Mac did also say that all the fishermen were being interviewed and asked if they'd seen anything untoward whilst about their work out on the water."

"My instinct tells me that this whole saga has to be handled with extreme caution or we'll get nothing more out of anybody. Perhaps you two would have more luck with the Detective Chief Superintendent in charge of the investigation? They've battened down all the hatches it seems and I've been out of Intelligence for some time now. Although I do still have some senior contacts, yours will certainly be more up to date than mine." Julian had been sitting quietly listening.

"Alec, can you fill us in with a bit more about Loch Island? Both Guy and I have the feeling that the village there might just possibly not be quite as deserted as it looks. Apparently, there's also some interesting shipping which shelters off the far Western side of the island on a regular basis; a Russian vessel in particular."

"Is there really? You two must have eyes in the back of your heads! I know that there is plenty of shipping in the area apart from the oil and fishing industries, especially in summertime. There are frequent ferries to and from all the islands. I've seen cruise liners, of all sizes, in these waters and on many occasions the smaller, luxury Hebridean Princess. She's a beautiful little ship, well not so small actually; she can take fifty guests all in very comfortable cabins. She has thirty-eight crew and the food is reputed to be outstanding. I was going to take Caroline on a surprise voyage for our wedding anniversary. She would have loved it, but sadly that wasn't to happen." There was silence for a moment, no one knew quite what to say, then Alec cleared his throat.

"Yes, well perhaps we could all go on her together one day. That would be fun. But as I was saying - with all the busy sea going traffic out there - I've never seen or heard of anything Russian: at least not close in: and you think there just might be hostile life on the island which links to all this?" Alec stared at Julian, his eyebrow raised in question. He was alert and focused and was thoroughly enjoying being part of all the intrigue.

"Yes, possibly I do." They all sat mulling this over, while Mrs Haddington brought in the drink's tray. John got up to serve everybody and Mrs H sensing the seriousness of the meeting, left quietly closing the door behind her. Julian, deep in thought, went across to help John pour the drinks. He dropped a couple of lumps of ice in a tumbler of whisky and soda and took it across to Alec who, nodding his thanks, took a sip.

"Alec, do you by any chance have an ordnance survey map of the area, which includes Loch Island?" asked Julian, "also, would you have some knowledge of the Northern shipping lanes up and around Stornoway and on across to Scapa Flow?"

"Yes, on both counts," the Colonel said, placing his drink on the small table beside his chair and getting to his feet. "The charts are in my study. I'll get them. Meanwhile," he walked across the room, turning at the door to look back at his brother, "John here is your Navy man and will either know or can find out all that you need as far as shipping is concerned."

John laughed. "Well, I can certainly do my best. What do you need to know?"

John told them all that he knew of the rules and regulations regarding shipping vessels in the whole Northern region, including within the oil rig vicinities. He was also knowledgeable about telecommunications, weather patterns and even the differing allowances for extreme conditions, which might affect ships wishing to seek shelter. He had a pretty good idea of normal routing passages between the further countries too. As for keeping track of any individual vessel - he also knew exactly how to obtain that information - even if it wasn't meant for a wider audience.

Guy had already decided that although the two brothers were of a different generation and retired, they were obviously well experienced and still in touch with younger colleagues in their old departments. They would offer excellent back up and could, he felt sure, be relied upon to help in a crisis.

Alec appeared back from his study with relatively up to date nautical charts of the region. They all pored over the ordnance survey map without speaking. Guy traced the coast North of Dromvaar with his finger, stopping suddenly and crossing over the small strip of water between the mainland and Loch Island, then back again, tapping firmly to mark the place.

"This area here. What are these buildings?"

"That's an old, defunct, smokery."

"What else is there and where exactly was the body found? Show me please." The elder man was in his element. Alec put on his glasses and leant closer pointing then, clearing his throat, bent to concentrate.

"Right. First, to the South, here's Dromvaar. That's where the small ferry crosses the bay. It's actually goes from a tiny landing place, which as the crow flies is only about three and a half miles from the lodge. It comes in here, on the Northern side of the port, under these fishermen's cottages. Tourists and walkers use it and there are parking areas, to each side of the embarkation points, at both ends. Here and again – here," he said picking up a blunt pencil and tracing the passage, back and forth, across the water.

"Beyond the harbour, further North, is a small rise in the land which then dips down again to a long beach. This is the so-called safe swimming bay. This is where Mary Macquire was walking with her dog and here...," he said, now stabbing his finger on the map, "... this is where the body was found, on these rocks at the end of this stretch of sand."

"OK," replied Guy. "Next is the derelict smokehouse. Could there once have been a boathouse on the water? Is there anchorage, a pontoon or a slipway of some sort which could still be used for a small vessel to visit the island? I presume there used to be moorings there?"

"Yes," replied Alec, "there were. I don't know about a boathouse, but it would be easy enough to camouflage a small dinghy amongst the disintegrating buildings. You wouldn't notice it even from the air. But this strip of water down between the island and mainland is closed to all shipping now and cordoned off with marker buoys, as there's a shifting wreck located about here." He indicated the place. "That's why the little harbour was abandoned and died. It was considered too expensive to raise the wreck. There's a deep pool of water so it's fairly safely dug in and trapped, confined within this area." He drew a circle with his finger.

"But the wreck can drag a bit and every few years divers go down to check its position, just in case it has moved further down. The shifting sands and the currents, coming in from the North, are extremely strong there, especially in rough weather. But, as I said, the whole zone is forbidden; no one can go there now, not even to fish. Anybody seen to venture into the prohibited domain would incur a heavy fine." John then chipped in.

"The Cape Wrath coastguard station would be alerted should any vessel stray off course. The North Minch is an unforgiving sea and no place to seek shelter. The ship would be warned of the hazard and the restricted passage which would be clearly marked on their charts. They'd be told to navigate back into the shipping lane. If they didn't comply immediately the helicopter would be sent out to escort them."

"Yes," said Alec, "that whole expanse of water, up off the North Western tip of Scotland, is extremely well policed. It has to be - for obvious reasons. A Russian ship off the Isle of Lewis would need a fair reason for being there and it would have had to ask for permission to clean out its bilges or whatever. We can check that out." He lent down to the chart once more.

"Beyond and above the derelict port is the old lighthouse, see there... and that's about it, really. The next cove merely has a couple of deserted crofter's cottages, sometimes used in the summer and a lot of sheep." Julian moved between them scrutinizing the faded map.

"What's this opposite the old smokery buildings... on the island? It's a small canal or river, isn't it? Is it navigable do you imagine?" Alec looked up surprised.

"Good God no! Well at least I would think that's very unlikely, unless perhaps with a small rubber dinghy... but as I said this narrow strait is out of bounds and has been for years." Julian, screwing up his eyes and frowning, had now moved in closer to follow the thin blue line with his finger. Suddenly he stopped; a glimmer of excitement brightening his normally unreadable face.

"And this here, on the island, looks like another small inland lake, fed by that waterway coming in from the sea and... it's quite near to the deserted village, isn't it?" He tapped his forefinger on the map to show them, then quietly stepped back, smoothing his hair back from off his face, and looking across to Guy. Guy stood watching, a small smile touching the corners of his mouth. He merely nodded in unspoken agreement.

Alec straightened up and was silent. John leant across to look for himself as the others all stood back. The silence was charged.

"Right!" Alec let out a long sigh and walked across to the drink's tray. The adrenalin was flowing and it felt mighty good. Breaking the loaded silence he looked around and smiled at all the expectant faces. "We need to decide what to do about all this. Let's have another drink and then further examine all the possibilities."

CHAPTER 18

"I'm sorry but I don't want to go fishing." The others all looked across at Adriana. Alicia sensed determination in her friend.

"It's just that I hate fishing, I'd rather take a sandwich and go for a walk."

"OK, that's fine, but how about the rest of us going to the mill this morning? I'd like to get a couple of bigger jerseys and Rose, you might like to get something from your trendy wardrobe copied. We could then join the men for lunch at Glencurrie. Jess is going to bring Poppy to join us as her grandfather just can't get enough of her."

Emma could see that this went down well with the others, but she was worried about Adriana who seemed to be in an odd mood. Things were definitely off kilter between Arri and Julian. She'd like to help but didn't know where to start, but it really wasn't any of her business. Maybe she'd have a chat with Rose to see what she thought. Yet it was most likely to be Alicia in whom Adriana would confide, if she felt the need.

Guy was reading his newspaper at the end of the table and looked across at Marc with a raised eyebrow. It was a heaven sent opportunity, a done deal even before they'd suggested it and Adriana was definitely not herself. It would be good for her to get out and to be made to feel useful. He too sensed that things were deteriorating between Julian and his fiancée. He put the paper down.

"Marc, you said that you wanted to go up to look at that old lighthouse. Perhaps Arri could go with you? I'm sure Beth would make you both a picnic. Would that be alright do you think Emma?"

"Of course it would. Would you like to do that Arri?"

"Yes I would actually," Adriana answered brightening, "very much... if Marc would like the company, that is?" She hardly dared look at him.

"Absolutely I would," he winked cheerfully across at Guy. The girls were quite unaware that Guy had taken Marc into his confidence and had actually asked him to go up to the lighthouse, to see from there if he noticed anything unusual about the deserted old port down below.

"We can drive down to the ferry, take it across the bay and then walk. It's a fair way, but good exercise. If we start early we'll be back well before dark." Adriana could hardly contain her excitement. Her plan was working out perfectly, so far.

"Brilliant, I'll go and ask Beth to make you a picnic which my darling husband will have to carry in a backpack." Emma got up and bent down to kiss his head and ruffle his curly auburn coloured hair as she went past.

"Incidentally," putting her finger to her lips, "Beth is having lunch with Fergus today, but don't say I told you." This made them all smile: a new romance in the house.

Guy caught Adriana as she was going upstairs and beckoned her into the study. Arri was momentarily thrown off balance, what on earth did he want? He couldn't possibly be reading her thoughts. But he merely handed over his binoculars saying:

"Arri, I want you to take these. You are my ears and eyes today and make sure you have your mobile and that it is charged. Marc will explain everything. Take your time, it's a lovely day."

"This has something to do with that Irish girl and the body, doesn't it?"

"Yes, possibly, but I don't want to make a big deal of it yet, so please be circumspect in front of the others. I've already spoken to Alicia." Marc then appeared, also looking pleased to be taking some useful action.

"I suspect we may not be allowed onto the long beach as the police will still be there."

"Probably not, but Alec has already checked with Mac. You can walk along the track alongside the sand but not on the beach itself. Coming from the path across the cliff from the South you automatically run onto that route. It divides."

"OK, well I'm ready when you are Arri. I'll go and see how Beth's getting on with our picnic."

"Wear warm clothes, it will get cold up there at the lighthouse later on. You have the map?" Marc nodded. "Good. Keep out of sight when you are above the lighthouse and ring me if you see anything untoward, anything at all. My mobile will be on all the time. I just hope, if it rings, that it doesn't frighten off the fish, or I'll be in trouble," he added with a snort.

It was Ailsa's afternoon off and so she said she'd pop along to Glencurrie to help her mother with lunch for the fishermen and their wives. As usual Mrs H had everything under control; two large cottage pies, followed by apple and blackberry crumble with cream, or perhaps with ice cream, for the little one. There were cheese and biscuits on the side if required.

"How are you managing with the laird now?" Her mother didn't beat around the bush. "I heard about his contretemps with the bag of flour. It went round the whole village. He must have felt a fool. Serves him right, if you ask me."

"Yes, he certainly got his comeuppance, Mum. I keep hoping he'll set his sights elsewhere, but no such luck so far. I just feel so sorry for Finola being saddled with such a poor excuse for a man."

"Yes, you're right and Lady Strathkellan is a lovely woman. But the laird's like a randy old stag and you're a bonny wee lass - to be sure. So I'm not surprised, seeing as how he is, that he's also been eying you up," Jean Haddington finished, raising her eybrow.

"Well it's not funny," replied Ailsa, "there's something weird about the man. He gives me the shivers. Incidentally," Ailsa said changing the subject, "last time I was up there at Castle House with supplies, Jock came up with me for moral support and on the way back he mentioned that he'd seen a couple of those foreigners skulking in the garden. He said that although they behaved as if they didn't wish to be seen, it actually looked like they were working there."

"That's interesting, the Lord Strathkellan employing illegal immigrants. Most interesting. Have you told Mac about this?"

"Yes, I did. I told him yesterday morning, but he was so wrapped up in this murder that I expect he forgot all about it."

"Well then," said her mother, "I think perhaps that he should be reminded that he needs to discover where these people are hanging out, because I've heard that some of them are in cahoots with that Irish girl with the bairn; the one that's disappeared. But maybe I'll just tell the Colonel myself."

Just then they heard signs of the party returning from the river and judging by the general commotion and squeals of delight, it also sounded as if Poppy had arrived.

"All hands on deck then," announced Mrs H. "Put the peas on lassie."

Emma and Poppy appeared at the door to the kitchen.

"Hello again Ailsa, hello Mrs H. We've brought you a present." Poppy ran forward with three late roses from the lodge garden and Emma produced a box of chocolates.

The men were delighted with themselves. Guy had unexpectedly caught a fish, Julian had landed two and even Rose, with Oliver's help, had managed to hook a decent sized salmon just after she'd arrived back from Dromvaar. Two of the fish would be sent off to be smoked in the new smokehouse further North. They were to fish the home beat on the other side of the house after lunch, when both Alicia and Emma said that, in view of Rose's success, they also wanted to have a go. This caused much amusement. Both Alicia and Guy wondered how Adriana and Marc were getting on – but each with different concerns.

CHAPTER 19

The day was perfect; there had been a sharp frost and now the sky was a clear unspoilt blue, with the sparkling sun making the most of the autumnal colouring. The ferry was small but efficient. There were only a dozen people and a few small children, mostly wanting an unusual and fun trip into Dromvaar. None of them appeared to be attired in serious walking clothes. Marc had most of the picnic in his back-pack. Adriana carried the wine, mugs and plastic glasses in a bag over her shoulder. She had been responsible for the alcohol which she considered to be all important on this occasion. Marc looked a little pensive, she thought, but at the same time he also appeared pleased to be out and away.

Adriana knew the attraction to be mutual, but she must play her cards carefully. She experienced a shudder of excitement. Her body felt finely tuned and anticipatory. The vibration of the ferry engine seemed to enhance her longing. She wondered if Marc sensed what she was feeling. Could he read her thoughts? It was a couple of years since they'd been alone together, but in a different place and in an extremely dramatic situation. Something had so nearly happened between them then. Adriana had never forgotten and she wondered if he had.

It was too noisy to speak above the engine noise but she risked a glance in his direction. Marc seemed to be concentrating on the view ahead. The water today was like glass. Looking across to the port it seemed impossible to accept that there had been a death, and a violent one at that, in such a tranquil place. Adriana hoped that on this particular quest they'd see or find some useful evidence which might help with the murder investigation and perhaps in some way provide a link to the soulless Irish girl. Exciting stuff but not half as intoxicating as the plan she had in mind. Adriana took the cloth bag off her shoulder and stowed it carefully beside her. Beth had made sure that she'd given them one of the better bottles of wine.

Once on the far side they set off out of the harbour, climbing the steep cliff path until at the highest point they could stand and see both ways. Behind them the little ferry was already making its way back again and in front, down on the beach, the police presence was still in evidence. Large areas were cordoned off and men in protective suits appeared to be scouring the seashore above the high tide mark. Cars with flashing lights and several ominous looking vans, of varying sizes, were parked at the edge of the sand along a narrow track. A hive of activity.

"Why do police in the forensic department always seem to wear white suits? It's weird." Adriana commented. "They look like aliens from up here."

"Goodness only knows why they have to be stark white," Marc replied. "It does seem pretty impractical. Some idiot in the government I suppose. The protective suit is to ensure that any evidence found remains in an undamaged state as possible. Everything has to be sterile so that anything touched can't be tampered with further, destroying information sometimes crucial to the investigation." Adriana looked impressed.

"Heavens Marc, you are a fount of knowledge."

"I am, after all, a doctor Arri. I have to know all this - and a lot else, I can tell you." He laughed and then turned away from her to point downhill.

"Anyway, look, there is where the path divides, just below us. I suggest we take avoiding action and go the long way around. What do you think?"

"Yes definitely, let's steer clear of all that lot. They look extremely busy and might not be too pleased to be disturbed."

Their route skirted the beach and then climbed again until once more they could also see beyond; this time into the deserted port, above which on the far cliffs stood their goal, the old lighthouse. This time, instead of dropping down to the derelict buildings below, they stayed above and walked along the top of the cliffs. The path was both unused and overgrown, giving plenty of cover. Marc stopped in places to hold the brambles back for Adriana, at the same time carefully scanning the view beneath them. Adriana took the occasional photograph of the layout of the extinct complex, as Guy had asked. Eventually they came to the lighthouse. The door at the back was boarded up, with half exposed rusty nails, yet easy to remove. Inside the building was in surprisingly good repair and Adriana wondered immediately why somebody hadn't already picked up the lighthouse for conversion.

"I should think it's still owned by the Northern Lighthouse Board or whatever. So, as yet, nobody can touch it and a frightful waste of a spectacular location, I agree," Marc said in answer to her question. "I'm starving let's eat." He looked a little like a schoolboy out on a treat, thought Adriana affectionately. But she could feel the tension as they looked around the spartan room. There was an old sofa upon which they spread their coats, then Marc left Adriana to organize the picnic while he explored the views from the lighthouse. The windows were filthy and he doubted very much that any movement from within could be seen from the outside. It was a perfect spot for surveillance. Particularly from the highest level, up the winding steps, he soon discovered.

"We'll eat, then climb the stairs to get a better view," he said. As he spoke Marc regarded his companion. Adriana looked vulnerable. She was nervous and so very sexy. He could feel the vibes. They all knew that something was very wrong between herself and Julian but he wasn't about to take advantage of that situation. Marc suspected that both Alicia and Guy knew what the trouble was; after all they were the oldest of friends, but none of the others had any inkling as to what was the matter. Arri and Julian had been an item for years.

Adriana caught him looking at her and felt slightly encouraged. She had to make this plan work. She couldn't think of another way. Marc opened the bottle of wine. He wasn't sure that it was such a good idea but it was too late to decline. How could he not join Arri in a glass, or perhaps two? That would have seemed ridiculous. After all they were both responsible grown people and there was Emma, his adored wife and Julian to consider - of course.

The wine was excellent as Adriana had hoped it would be and, out of the cold air, it warmed her whole being and gave her courage. They ate companionably and drank more wine, the tension eased and they were soon comfortable together again and laughing; remembering old times when they'd all had other adventures. All was well until Marc, turning too quickly, accidently knocked Arri with his elbow and caught her a smack in the eye. He quickly took her face in his hands and looked into the hidden depths of the hazel green eye to see what damage he'd done. She opened her mouth to speak, a small dimple showed at the edge of her alluring smile. She didn't dare move a muscle, just uttered a gentle sigh and he couldn't resist. The kiss as once before, in the past, began and continued, filled with so much that had lain dormant between them. But then Marc abruptly pulled away.

"We can't be doing this. You're too beautiful and perhaps vulnerable. I'm sorry, so sorry Arri." She leaned up close and took his hand firmly in hers.

"Don't be," she whispered. "I have something to ask that is probably the most difficult thing that I shall ever ask anyone and I wouldn't have had the courage without the wine." Marc stared at her.

"Go on."

"OK, but first please let's finish the bottle." He poured for them both, then waited, hardly daring to breathe, until she spoke again. The atmosphere was electric.

"You are the closest of friends and what I am going to ask is a huge favour, both for me and at the end of the day, for Julian as well. I could be really devious and not tell you the reason behind my action but I hope that you will consider me too honest for that."

Adriana took a deep breath.

"Julian has been told that it's highly unlikely that he can ever give me a child as he had a bad go of mumps when he was young. Because of this he won't marry me and... it's tearing us apart. You must be aware of the tension between us?" He nodded mesmerized by the deep sad eyes as she laid her soul bare. Then he knew what was coming.

"This situation could rip us all apart actually unless... unless you..." she couldn't finish it and the tears begun to fall. He gathered her in his arms and, whether out of sympathy or his own need, was instantly lost.

They made love like two drowning people: immersed in each other. It had nothing really to do with lust or even disloyalty. A smouldering attraction set alight when combined with human frailty and sympathetic sensitivity, creating undeniable desire. More importantly it was the powerful knowledge that, within their grasp, they might have a way of solving this seemingly insurmountable problem. They knew each other well. It was easy to love and be loved. They had always both been more than physically aware and knew instinctively how to please each other. When the moment came Adriana cried out in desperation and he matched her, as they tumbled together, up and over the pinnacle of ecstasy into peaceful relief and hope beyond compare.

Afterwards, they lay awhile without speaking and when they'd rested and recovered began to make love again; this time with a gentle thoroughness and finality. As far as Adriana was concerned, it was perfection. She never would have dreamed it possible to have been given this chance and in such a way and for the second time she gave of herself completely.

When it was finally over, there was no regret just a longing and hope that they might together have created a miracle. Only time would tell. Their secret would be safe between them whatever the outcome.

No one must ever know what had occurred. Whatever the future held there must be no further meeting of this kind. This was the way it had to be in order to live with what they had done. It was time to return to real life and to think of the task they'd undertaken.

They dressed, a little reluctantly and then took the coffee and some chocolate up to the top of the lighthouse. There they sat on two old plastic chairs, pressed close together for warmth and quietly discussed the murder and its ongoing investigation.

It was about one hour later. Marc had just suggested that they pack up and start back, when Adriana picking up the binoculars one last time saw something move out from somewhere underneath the old smokery. It was a small rubber dinghy, with three people aboard. It was too far to see if they were male or female. Adriana and Marc watched in excitement as the boat set out towards the island and headed for what could only be a tiny entrance, in from the sea, hidden from the naked eye by windswept vegetation and scrub. Then it disappeared.

They turned to look at each other incredulously.

"That's it, that's exactly what Guy hoped for, isn't it?"

"It most certainly is. Well done Arri, we nearly missed it. Now we should get back." He leant across and kissed her in, she thought, an almost brotherly fashion. She could feel that the sensual tension between them had changed into a stimulating elation of another kind. Their relationship had slipped back into its proper place. But Adriana had to say something before they moved on again.

"Thank you Marc. Thank you for understanding... and everything - for giving me this chance and I do realise that it was perhaps... under some duress." She couldn't quite meet his eye.

"It wasn't under duress. You must have realised that and you're very welcome because it was wonderful." He smiled and made her look at him, taking her face between his hands. "But this is something that nobody else can share; truly a doctor's confidence: you're quite OK with that?"

"Absolutely, it never happened."

"Oh yes, it did happen, but not without a very special reason behind it. I shall never forget that; nor should you but you must be prepared for disappointment. These things don't always go according to plan. That's the doctor speaking," he said quietly, looking at her intently, then smiling.

"Arri, it was something amazing; a once only experience which must spoil nothing within our group and must never be mentioned again. I just hope that it will change your life as you wish. I shall never have any feelings of guilt because, if you are lucky enough to have a child, it is my gift; know that it will have been conceived with tenderness and love, although of a different sort – but, and I have to emphasize this - the child will be yours and, without doubt, Julian's. We will all love it and..." he said getting up and looking down at her fondly, "make no mistake - *I shall dance at your wedding* with exceptional exuberance!"

She reached up to kiss him one last time, long and lingering, conveying hope, fulfilment and immense gratitude.

They climbed down to gather up their things; turning around one last time at the door, to look back and to memorise the scene of a magical interlude. Then they stuck the boards back across the entrance and talking companionably, set off on the long walk back to Dromvaar to catch the late returning ferry.

CHAPTER 20

Marc and Adriana arrived back in a high state of euphoria and couldn't wait to relay their news. Guy and Julian were both thrilled that their suspicions about the disused smokehouse on the mainland and inland waterway opposite had proved correct. Both Emma and Alicia were delighted to find Adriana so much happier. The outing and the excitement over their successful observations had visibly done her good. Guy went straight to the sitting room with Julian to call up Alec. They came back out, happy as sand boys thought Alicia, as she watched them walk into the kitchen. Her husband was in his element.

"We are going to get constable MacDonald up to Glencurrie in the morning," Guy told them all.

"I feel it's important to let him take a little of the credit for this, as it will get him back in favour with the D.C.S. and then he'll feel free to update us on an ongoing basis, without causing upset."

"Do we yet know the cause of death?" asked Rose. "I keep thinking of that poor girl and all the awful things she might have suffered."

"No, not yet but Mac hopes to have that by the morning. Then we will have to brief his superiors with our own findings. But tonight let's relax and toast our friends for their admirable bit of sleuthing," Guy said, thoroughly pleased with his day.

"OK – I'm glad that we managed to help. But now I'm going to warm up with a bath," announced Adriana, a bright smile lighting her face. Julian got out his cigarettes, for once also looking just very slightly smug. After all he had been the one to draw attention on the ordnance survey map and consequently they'd hit the jack pot!

"I'm off outside, to freeze my whatsits off whilst having a celebratory smoke," he said.

"Oh Julian, you don't have to go outside for goodness sake – go in the hall or boiler room or something," Emma suggested sympathetically.

"No, no it's quite alright. I'm well trained and it's actually a lovely night," Julian answered unusually cheerful.

Well, Guy thought to himself, it had definitely been a good day all round. After being out in the crisp autumn air, Adriana had a distinctive glow about her and thankfully Julian had also caught the biggest fish of the year, so maybe now things might be better between them.

❄

Molly had returned to her little cottage beside the cafe and so Mary Macquire found herself alone once more in her own immaculate little flat above the Post office. She was fond of Molly but she'd become used to her own space and having everything in order. Molly wasn't a very tidy person. Mary led a very ordered existence and so she spent the few hours, after the business closed, re-arranging things; making up her spare room bed and returning everything to its rightful place. Then she made herself scrambled eggs, listened to the news and weather and retired early to bed.

It was late, about midnight, when Mary was suddenly awakened by an unusual noise. She listened intently. There was no wind, just the gentle surge of the waves breaking on the beach below. Monotonous and calming and she turned over to sleep again reassured; probably just a cat or even a fox at a dustbin. But there it was again, this time there was no mistaking a stone or small hard object striking her windowpane. Someone was certainly trying to attract her attention. Mary wasn't frightened; her husband, Dougie's father, had died many years before. She'd been alone too long to be nervous, just intrigued perhaps. She quickly put on her warm dressing gown and crossed to the window. Opening it wide she leant out to see who it was needing her in the middle of the night.

Miracle of all miracles, it was the boy Sean, his pale face staring desperately up at her. 'Mary, mother of Jesus', his awful Irish mother might have said, thought Mary. She called to him clearly saying that she would be right there, just to stay where he was and to give her a minute to get down.

The boy was wet through, shaking and shivering with cold, unable to speak coherently and merely uttering animal-like noises of distress. Mary quickly looked out to see if there was any movement within her line of vision, where the blackness was illuminated from the bright cottage light. But nothing and nobody emerged from the hidden depths of darkness. She put a protective arm around the young boy and drew him in, shutting and locking the door firmly behind her. Och, what terrible ordeal has the poor child been through now? It was evident that he'd got away from somewhere or someone and likely had needed to swim in the freezing water to escape, she judged by observing his dripping clothes. Mary's warm heart went out to the young boy. She talked to him gently, while she quickly stripped off his wet clothes and wrapped him in her own warm dressing gown. Never mind the sodden, sandy mess on her newly immaculate floor. She half carried the child upstairs and into the bathroom where she ran a warm bath. He was all skin and bones and no weight to bear.

Sean let her bathe his face and poor bruised body. Thankfully Mary noticed that the livid marks were fading and there was no other evidence of further physical violence. His hair smelt of the sea and was matted with salt, so she managed to tip his head back to rinse it with an old tooth mug; not easy but it would have to do. Then she dried and dressed him in an old tracksuit she'd bought for attending the gym in her younger days. She still had her neat little figure so it wasn't that much too big. Then she tucked him up in her own cosy warm bed.

When Mary made to stand up he wouldn't let go of her hand so she bent down again to stroke his forehead.

"Don't you worry now my darling. I'm just going to get you a nice cup of cocoa. It will warm you up inside. I'll be right back." She laid her tender hand against the child's soft cheek, saying again. "I'll be right back, you're quite safe now and I'll only be a couple of minutes."

Whilst making the hot chocolate Mary decided to do nothing more that night. The boy needed rest and quiet. It wasn't even as if he had a caring mother out there at her wits end with worry. Tomorrow would be time enough to alert those who needed to be informed. He was out of harm's way where he was. She felt warm affection and an immense sense of relief that he'd chosen to come to her.

The following morning Mac the local policeman looked out of his kitchen window. The wind had got up and clouds scudded across a troubled sky. The sun emerged fleetingly and with little enthusiasm. He wondered what the day held in store. Mac was a man of routine. He liked to rise early, walk his old dog Donald and start his day ahead of the game. He enjoyed an hour or so to himself before setting off for work and before the various telephones began their frantic noisy intrusion. On boring days, prior to Molly finding the body, he'd been spending most of his time checking gun licences and dealing with petty matters down in the port, wishing for something more exciting to happen. Now he wasn't so sure. The dead girl was little more than a child, not much older than his own daughter in Edinburgh. Such a waste of life and now he also had the young Irish boy to worry about; still no sign of him, or the brutal mother. What was she up to? Where had she gone and to where had the rootless foreigners suddenly vanished? He felt that, in some way, they must all be connected.

At 8.am the telephone rang. It was Mary Macquire asking him to visit her up at the post office. She was insistent, saying that it was important. Mary wouldn't have bothered him without good reason. She was a sensible practical person and, as Dougie's mother, she was a popular person in the village.

Mac heaved himself up from the kitchen chair and, putting aside his rather depressive thoughts, went to refill the kettle for his wife. She'd had a night out with the girls and had a morning off from her work at the mill. She was also a good sort his Elspeth and he was a lucky man. He called out that he was off, patted the old dog on his head, picked up his hat and keys and went quietly out the back door to his car. His mobile rang; it was Guy Hargreaves from the lodge. He needed to see him as soon as possible: he had some interesting information and would like to meet up at Glencurrie. This suited Mac, who liked the Colonel and admired him for the part he'd played in the Iraq war. He was a brave man, no doubt about that and he had a medal to show for it. There was another reason he enjoyed going up the glen; Jean Haddington made the best shortbread biscuits he'd ever tasted. Although this was something he kept to himself. It wouldn't do to let Elspeth think he thought them better than hers.

Constable MacDonald's day was now set. He'd see Mary first and then go on to Colonel Alec's place. He wanted to discuss this immigrant problem further. He wondered whether the retired army officer had any more thoughts on that particular situation. He'd heard that the laird, up at Castle House, had a couple of foreigners working for him and wondered if Colonel Neilsen knew anything about them or even if they were still around. Perhaps they too had moved on. These people usually appeared and disappeared again quite quickly, without settling; like ships that pass in the night, he supposed. Och! It must be terrible to be homeless and in another country.

Nobody liked the laird. He was both rude and arrogant, so the policeman was happy to avoid a meeting up there, if at all possible.

As he drove to the port, Mac thought about his own situation. He considered himself very fortunate. He was still needed in the area it seemed and that was a good feeling, for he'd been at the station nigh on thirty-five years now. He couldn't bear to be considered past his sell-by-date and a burden to the force. It had been his life, helping keep the peace and he dreaded retirement. He parked the car near the post office, settled his hat on his still full head of hair and prepared himself for his meeting with Mary. He liked her very much; she was still an energetic bonny woman. A long time back they'd even gone to school together. As he walked up the path he looked again at the sky. It now looked downright threatening thought Mac, doing up the top button of his uniform.

CHAPTER 21

Alicia knew that Adriana had something to hide. She had an odd slightly uncommunicative look about her and Alicia didn't think that it was just down to the excitement of the findings over at the lighthouse. Every time they were alone and Alicia tried to engage her in conversation, she'd move off as if she had no intention of being questioned further. Her friend had a personal secret, of that Alicia was sure. Adriana had made several telephone calls; privately to London, Alicia guessed. She had a feeling that this was something which she wouldn't approve, however if it was to do with Adriana and Julian's relationship problems Alicia thought that it really wasn't any of her business. Nevertheless, she felt slightly hurt that her friend couldn't tell her: as if she'd been pushed away, just a little.

The men were going over to Glencurrie for a meeting with Alec and Mac, so Alicia decided to try to persuade Adriana into going for a walk with her.

"Actually, I thought I'd stay here with Emma today as Rose wants to go fishing again with the ghillie. She certainly has the bit between her teeth now, doesn't she?" laughed Adriana. "Perhaps another time Ally. Why don't you get your paints out? It's a wonderful sanguine sky today and if the wind keeps the rain off I might take some photos around the house and..." she added conspiratorially... "I think we ought to make Emma have a rest after lunch, don't you?"

"I heard that," Emma walked in. "I'm perfectly fine thank you: I'll put my feet up after we've eaten when we have our coffee. Let's all go for a walk later this afternoon. Jess is going to take Poppy to see those pups again, over at Glencurrie. I have an awful feeling that Uncle Alec's going to give her one!"

"Good!" said Adriana quickly. "I think that a puppy would be a brilliant idea if it's offered: of course you'll cope! Yes, let's all go out later as Rose will be busy fishing this morning and the men are all perfectly happy, caught up in all this latest drama."

Alicia felt even more put out. It was quite clear that, at the moment, Adriana didn't want to do anything alone with her.

Rose was thankful to have had Olly to herself on Skye for a few days. Since then she'd hardly seen him. Now that he too was so involved with all the intrigue surrounding the demise of the poor drowned girl, he didn't seem to have much time for her. But Rose was enjoying trying her hand at the fishing and, after catching her first salmon, she knew herself to be, quite literally, well and truly hooked. So she was quite happy for Oliver and all the men to hobnob with the police. When she wasn't fishing she would rather be with the girls and Poppy. Rose had promised to let her help make drop scones for tea, when the child returned from seeing the puppies. Beth must be due for a bit of free time, so they could have the kitchen to themselves.

Before lunch, in her room, Adriana sat hugging herself in front of the mirror. Her eyes were shining. She would go to the little chapel up on the grouse moor at the weekend, on the next Sunday. Adriana didn't pray often, but she would do anything, anything to make this precious dream come true and become a reality. In ten days time she'd know. She was always on time every month and was at present at her most fertile so her hopes were high. The odd thing was that she didn't feel in the least bit awkward with Emma, and stranger still, nor with Marc either. The lucky thing had been the excitement over the success of their mission, the previous day, as it had covered for them both perfectly. She'd gone up quickly for a bath on their return and she and Julian had even made love again that night which somehow merely reaffirmed their commitment to each other. Her secret liaison with Marc had made no difference; she loved Julian as much as ever. The deviously planned afternoon had been an extremely sensual means to an end. That was how it had to be. Marc had been the soul of discretion ever since. No embarrassing silences or surreptitious glances; for it was over. She told herself he'd only given in because he felt so sorry for them both, but whatever happened – if she was lucky enough to conceive a child, even if it did have dark auburn hair, the child would be Julian's – end of matter. They were all as they had always been – one compatible group of friends, revelling in being together, participating once more in unexpected dramas and, if she and Julian did finally get married, then they would all dance at her wedding.

❄

When the four men arrived at Glencurrie they found not only John, Alec and Mac in the study, but also Dougie Macquire. Mrs H, in her element, had let them all in and, after escorting them to the Colonel, had immediately brought the customary coffee and biscuits.

"Come in, come in, good morning, please make yourselves comfortable," called Alec. His face was lit up with all the excitement and both Mac and Dougie also looked delighted to be there. John stood quietly smiling in the background. As Mrs Haddington firmly closed the door behind her Alec addressed the group.

"There have been further developments," he announced before turning to Dougie.

"Douglas will fill you in. Dougie the floor is yours." Dougie, who had actually put on a tie for the occasion, cleared his throat importantly, put down his coffee cup and told them all of the boy Sean's surprising appearance at his mother's place, in the middle of the night.

Mac then related what he'd heard from forensics. The dead girl had been full of the date rape drug rohipnol and had likely been dropped into the sea, concealed in a sack, semi-conscious and of course unable to move. Literally frozen and drowned - an horrific demise. There were no further signs of violence nor of a struggle, only cuts and abrasions from the rocks. She obviously hadn't just fallen in and whoever had been responsible for wrapping her in a sack and heaving her into the sea hadn't expected the grim evidence to be found. The currents in the area should have taken the body out to sea, but in the rough weather and with an onshore wind at the time, the corpse had been thrown up onto the beach and wedged amongst the rocks.

"Murder in the first degree?" Marc turned to Mac.

"Yes, it looks like it, I'm afraid," replied Mac sadly. "The poor wee thing never stood a chance." There was silence for a moment while they all digested this gruesome information. Then Mac, remembering his duties, continued to enlighten them all as to the present state of the child, now in the care of Mary Macquire.

"He appears to be in a state of shock, blabbing strange things and unsurprisingly isn't making much sense at all. He's been badly frightened and Mary thinks that he escaped from somewhere near the water as he'd been in the sea. The lad needs time, so it's too early to ask questions as yet. Mary would like you to take a look at him, if you would no mind, Dr Neilsen? She's worried that he might have caught his death, what with the water and the cold and the Lord only knows what other trauma the poor mite has endured."

"No, of course not, I'll go straight over," replied Marc preparing to leave. But Alec stepped up and put his hand on his nephew's shoulder.

"Just a minute Marc. There is the question of the boy's safety to consider. Mac and I think that for the moment we should bring the boy here, together with Mary. As far as his vile, uncaring Irish mother is concerned the child will merely have disappeared. They can have the nursery wing. They'll be comfortable there and can have peace and quiet while the little chap recovers. He will need to be interviewed at some point, as his knowledge could prove crucial, but at least here I can see that the timing of the interview is under my control and only when Marc says he's up to it." John came forward smiling. He was delighted to see his brother coming to life again and coping so admirably in dealing with all the traumatic events.

"It's lucky that we have a doctor in the family and a bloody good one at that," he said proudly and then to Marc's embarrassment, patted his son on the back, before continuing, "and, in the past, I've seen my son at work with psychologically traumatized patients. The boy will be in good hands."

"Yes, I know he will John," Alec agreed. "Mac, can you square that with old Dr Wright? I should think he's got enough on his plate at present anyway."

"No problem. The doctor is up to his neck in it, as you say, running around after the forensic team and hobnobbing with all the other medical people down there in the incident room."

"Good, now as far as he is concerned, Mary is the boy's shining knight. At present he trusts no other. I have no doubt that she is the only person to ever have offered him kindness. I've already asked Mrs Haddington to make the nursery wing ready and John is going to collect them later. Dougie, you said that Ailsa is willing to cover for Mary at the post office. As far as everybody else is concerned Mary has gone to see a relative in Edinburgh?"

"Yes, and Mac's wife Elspeth is going to do extra time at the Mill to cover for Ailsa."

"Excellent, well done everybody, we're well organized." Oliver then stepped forward with a question for Mac.

"Rose and I saw loads of police on the way to Skye. What were they up to do you think? It looked like they were looking for someone?" Mac nodded, then answered, addressing them all.

"Yes, they were. When both the Irish woman and the boy vanished into thin air, I suggested putting the word around discreetly within the force. We were all worried for the child after what Mary had told me. Did they stop you?"

"Yes," said Olly. "They asked who we were and where we were going. Very polite they were, but much to my surprise, they even looked in the boot!"

"Good," said Mac nodding, "So they were thorough." Alec winked at Mac then turned to Oliver.

"You see, young man, the police don't hang around up here when something important comes up. Now Guy - over to you. Let's hear about your findings," he suggested, but Guy turned to Marc.

"Marc, it's your story, tell them what you and Adriana discovered up at the old lighthouse yesterday." Marc looked around at his audience.

"Yes, what we found was actually very exciting. There is an internal sea-fed channel, which makes possible a navigable route between the disused smokehouse on this side and the deserted village on Loch Island: and..." he stopped for emphasis, his unusual eyes bright, "both Adriana and I are quite sure of this because we both saw a small dinghy leave from somewhere under the derelict buildings, cut across the upper kyle and disappear up what looked like a concealed, narrow overgrown inland waterway opposite. This I imagine could head up towards your abandoned village."

There was silence as everybody took in this new information. Marc looked across at Julian and caught his eye.

"Even with Guy's binoculars, the entrance is completely hidden from the mainland, by years of untamed undergrowth. You could only find it from the water and of course it's a restricted area anyway, but... it is exactly where Julian said it would be on the ordnance survey map which we looked at last night." Guy moved the coffee tray and once more unrolled the map, spreading it flat for them all to see. Marc leaned across with Mac and Dougie peering over his shoulders.

"Here, right here," he said stabbing his finger on the old smokery buildings and moving it across the water to show the tiny blue line entering the island from the sea.

"Well I'll be damned." murmured Alec.

CHAPTER 22

"The thing is," said Alec as he wound up the meeting, "all this has to go to Mac's superior, the Chief Detective Inspector who will then pass it on to the Chief Constable handling the investigation. Now we have a murder on our hands the top brass will shortly arrive in their hordes. The Criminal Investigation department will send someone, and so will MI5 and because of the Parisian link, MI6. Apart from which, after passing on our information I think it most likely that Special Forces will be called upon. Personnel will be instructed and surveillance put in place. I think a warrant has already gone out for the arrest of Sean's mother. That's correct isn't it Mac?"

"Yes," Mac nodded importantly, "they already have charges pending based on her treatment of the boy."

"OK. Now Douglas, my main aim is to get the child safely settled in here with your mother Mary, before we hand over this information and all hell lets loose."

Dougie and John were dispatched to collect Sean and Mary Macquire. Alec discussed with Mac the best time to set up regular meetings, once their latest information had been passed on. When Mary and the boy were safely installed at Glencurrie, Alec, Guy and Julian would go down with Mac to the incident room which, as there was no police station in the village, had been temporarily set up in Dromvaar town hall.

John Neilsen drove Dougie down to the village and then waited outside Mary Macquire's house for him to return with his mother and the Irish boy. He was worried about any of his son's friends becoming further involved with the on-going drama and was determined to make it his job to keep the girls and Poppy as far away from it all as possible. Thank goodness Ana wasn't with him on this occasion as she had seen enough upset in her life already. For once he was pleased to know that she was safe in their home in the Ionian, looking after his second family. He was truly blessed and felt constantly sad that his brother had lost his wife so early in life. Although Alec had grown-up children, who were all away from home following their own careers, John hoped that perhaps one day he might also find someone else to fill the gap - as he himself had done. Now he was glad to be here to support his brother through unfolding and disturbing events.

❄

Alec knew very well that neither Guy nor Julian would be happy to stand back, particularly after all that they had already discovered. They would want to see the whole thing through, as he would have himself. Oliver, who had been a part of various adventures with the other two men was intelligent, charismatic and a very able sort of person. Guy had told Alec that Olly trained regularly with the TA. Although he was outside now, happily fishing with his young wife Rose, Alec knew he was another person who could be relied upon if required.

Mac left for the port and Marc set off to walk back to the lodge, promising to return to check on Sean once he was safely installed. Alec went to the kitchen to find Mrs H and check the arrangements for the expected new residents in the nursery wing. When he came back he rejoined the two men in the study. He looked across at them for a moment with an experienced and critical eye.

"Do you need permissions for you and Julian to quietly go about your own little bit of detection?"

"Yes sir, we do," answered Julian, "and we have already set that particular ball rolling. Hopefully by this evening we'll have the green light, as tomorrow Guy and I would like to return to the island for some more interesting fishing!"

"Good Lord! You boys don't hang around, do you? And you don't have to call me 'Sir' either; I'm no longer in uniform and you are both close friends of my nephew. My name is Alec."

"Thank you Alec," Guy replied politely. "Now one last thing; the sighting in the Paris night club – we might need Adriana to relate that story directly to whoever is in charge of the investigation. Perhaps we should set that up for this evening after our meeting down there?"

"Yes," replied Alec, a good idea, although they might not want to interview her yet, at least not until the Irish girl turns up again. Now as you are currently employed with, shall I say, the rather more elusive part of our Forces, I would suggest that perhaps you might like to take over the coordination of events from our end."

"No problem," answered Guy. "I've already spoken to a couple of people on the phone and I think it's likely that we may know some of the team coming up anyway, so it will be much easier to work with them. Apart from which, with us here already, they won't have to send such a large group."

"Right, well done, let's just hope that this all ends in the way that we would wish. Keep me up to date won't you."

"But of course Colonel... Alec..., It's good to have someone with your knowledge of the country and experience to talk matters over and I am also delighted not to have to worry further about the boy. I know he will be well looked after here. When he's up to it, they'll want him to see the dead girl's outer clothing, just in case he recognizes it and can give any clue as to her identification. If you wouldn't mind, just make absolutely sure that all those responsible

151

for Sean's care are sworn to secrecy. I would suggest that when Mary and the boy want some air, for the moment they use only the walled garden through the French windows at the back of the house. It would be better at present for them not to put in an appearance at the front of the building." Julian walked across to look out of the window towards the walled garden.

"Does anybody else use that side of the house?"

"No," answered Alec, "only Mrs H and her husband Stuart, both of whom are totally trustworthy."

"Who cleans the house for you?"

"My cleaning lady is at present on holiday in Florida, can you believe and so Dougie's wife Ailsa is helping out a couple of times a week. Like Douglas his wife also is completely reliable." Julian walked back from the window.

"That's fine. But please sir... I mean Alec..., don't have any other people to or in the house until this is all over. There's a post box at the end of the drive isn't there?"

"Yes and deliveries are also left there. Anything needing to be signed for, they ring me first, as it's a long way to come up, if there's no one here. I quite understand what you're saying. I'll have a word now with Mrs H and Stuart. Charlie the ghillie only comes on invitation and nobody else fishes the river without my permission. Equally, there are no imminent visits expected from my rowdy children either. Although no doubt I shall be fielding the telephone calls when all this hits the press."

"Good, that's great," said Guy. "So we've covered everything."

❄

Fergus sent a text message to Beth. *When would she be free again, as he'd like to take her out to supper? He was taking the men to Loch Island early the following day – but he'd be back before dark, or so he imagined, so how about it?*

Beth answered immediately, almost as if she'd been waiting for his message, thought Fergus pleased. She could at least come out for a drink the next evening, even if she was cooking. There was talk of dinner at the Country House Hotel one night and if this happened, Jess would baby sit, she felt sure. Fergus couldn't wait and he was also looking forward to another fishing trip to the island. He knew that the men at the lodge were in some way mixed up in the present investigation underway in the port. The day's work would mean more in his pocket to spend on Beth.

The village was rife with rumour. Police of all sorts were buzzing around everywhere, stopping people and asking questions in the shops and sometimes even requesting the locals to visit the incident room in the Town Hall.

Fergus was surprised when he had a call from Guy Hargreaves asking him to meet him there first thing in the morning.

The Town Hall was a hive of activity. Fergus had never seen so many uniformed police all together in one place. Rather alarming he felt. He'd better get the MOT for his old truck booked in. He didn't want to get had up when Beth was with him; that wouldn't be exactly conducive to romance. Mac was waiting to greet him and Fergus was immediately ushered into a room where he found Guy, Julian and also Oliver deep in conference with two very senior looking police officers, with important looking pips on their shoulders. There were three other minions of the force, busily attending and tapping away on their computers and, just as he walked in, everybody stopped talking and looked up. A pretty young police woman appeared with a tray of coffee and biscuits. All very civilized, the fisherman thought, deciding that perhaps he needn't worry too much about the MOT.

"Hello Fergus," Guy approached him holding out his hand. "Good morning. I'm afraid that as we are going to have to ask you for some further help before this next trip of ours, we need you to sign the Official Secrets Act."

CHAPTER 23

Emma and Marc were alone once more. The men had gone for their meeting with the police. Rose, Alicia and Adriana had gone for a walk with Jessica and Poppy. Beth was in the kitchen seeing to lunch.

"Did Arri confide in you at all while you were at the lighthouse? Did she say anything about the problems she and Julian appear to be having?" Emma asked carefully, "or shouldn't I be asking: doctor's confidentiality and all that?" Marc appeared unfazed.

"I'm not Adriana's doctor but perhaps I'd better let her tell you, if she so wishes."

"OK, but do you think that they'll be alright?"

"I hope so, I very much hope so," Marc replied with feeling. "Now my darling girl enough of other people's problems, what would you like to do today?"

"Nothing much really. I'm feeling lazy and just want to be with you. Shall we have a cup of coffee?"

"Yes, a good idea. Now you put your feet up for a change and I'll go and get it. I'm not sure that all our extra house guests haven't been a bit much for you," he mumbled as he got up.

"I'm not an invalid you know. I'm only having our baby," Emma called after him. Marc stopped at the door and turning around retraced his steps back across to where she sat. He bent down to kiss her, his eyes full of emotion.

"I know there's nothing wrong with you sweetheart, but you are busy performing another little miracle for us." He was staring at her intently.

"I love you more than you can possibly imagine Emma and we are so very lucky to have this happening to us again." Emma promptly burst into tears. Marc took a handkerchief from his pocket and sat down beside her. Putting his arms around her shoulders he held her close.

"Oh dear, the old hormones are acting up again, aren't they?" He kissed her and gently wiped her eyes. "Now the serious decision is... are we going to want to know which it is – a brother or a sister for Poppy?"

"No! Oh no! Definitely not! I want it to be a surprise, don't you?" Emma sniffed and blew her nose loudly.

"Yes I agree, a surprise then it will be for all of us."

"What worries me," said Emma, "is how I can ever love another little person as much as I love Poppy?" He laughed and nuzzled her ear.

"You will darling, we both will, have no fear about that. Now I'll go and get us that coffee."

❄

Rose often found herself feeling just a little out of it when she was with Alicia and Adriana. They were very close and had known each other for ever, or so it seemed. Also, of course, their men were a team in their 'other' world: a world that Olly appeared to slot himself into so easily. He loved his time spent with the Territorial Army and he loved any intrigue. Except when he was with her, he was at his happiest when he was with Julian and Guy. She thought that, now once more, as his two friends became further tied up in the police enquiries surrounding the poor dead girl, Oliver was beginning to consider himself part of that team yet again.

She watched her two friends walking along together in front. There was undoubtedly quite a gap between them and they weren't touching at all as they talked. Rose had the impression that Adriana was withholding something from them all; well perhaps not everybody - not Julian surely? They certainly appeared much happier together; thankfully the immediate strain had lifted, and they seemed to be more at ease with one another. Rose knew that it must be a very private matter. There had to be a reason behind their not getting married: they'd been engaged for ages. She just didn't like being excluded. The little girl called her name and so Rose stopped and waited for Poppy to run up and take her hand. She felt a warm glow flood through her very being. Rose adored this child, her god-daughter who had come into this world after very dramatic beginnings. Alicia and Guy didn't seem to be in a hurry to have children but she had caught the fleeting look of anguish in Adriana's face when she had heard that Emma and Marc were to have another child. Well, thought Rose, why didn't they get married and get on with it? She herself wasn't in any hurry to have children. Her little god-child was more than enough for now.

Alicia and Adriana had walked on some way ahead.

"Won't you tell me what the problem is Arri? Can't I help?" But Adriana was adamant.

"No Ally, you can't help, it's between me and Julian; something we just have to sort out for ourselves."

"Alright but the offer remains. You know that I'm here if you need me."

"I know and I appreciate that, very much, really I do. It will be alright in time, you'll see and so you mustn't worry." She drew closer and tucked her arm through Alicia's. "It's wonderful us all being up here together, isn't it? But I hope that we aren't too much for Emma. We are rather an invasion."

"Yes, we are quite a houseful. I hope that this business, with the poor dead girl, doesn't get blown up into an international incident, because if it does, we won't be seeing much of our men for the rest of this holiday."

"Never mind, guess what, Ally? Julian says that we might have to delay going back home anyway. Wouldn't that be great, we might have another fortnight yet?" Adriana's eyes were sparkling.

"I know. Guy told me. Poor Emma. But what about work?" Alicia was frowning but Adriana only laughed.

"Too bad, it's a police thing, orders from the top. I think that, to a certain extent, we are all embroiled in these goings on, you see. Let's tell Rose. She'll be thrilled: but we might all turn into fish!" They turned around together and waited for Rose and Poppy to catch up.

Thank God, muttered Rose to herself, seeing the two happier faces as she drew closer. No more tricky atmospheres; it's alright again. She squeezed the little girl's hand. "Let's run Poppy. I'll race you, the first one to touch Aunt Alicia wins and..." she looked behind to where Jessica was both picking and eating blackberries and called out – "look, poor Jess is last!"

CHAPTER 24

Fergus was impressed, but he felt sad that he wouldn't be able to enlighten Beth as to what he was about that day. He felt quite important when he left the station in the company of a special task force, seemingly led by Guy. Although he had to admit that he wasn't in the least bit surprised when he'd learnt of his new friends status in the undercover world. He had been impressed at the way both men had handled themselves on that very first sea voyage, totally at home on the boat and adapting without hesitation to his every move. He had also noticed, with interest, that all these men were obviously in peak physical shape.

Oliver had returned to the lodge, to keep an eye on the girls and those up at Glencurrie and to liaise between the two. He was disappointed not to be returning to the island with the others but understood why he was needed elsewhere.

Fergus watched as each man boarded his boat and silently stowed their supplies and equipment. He wasn't introduced; they merely nodded in greeting, already lost in their own isolated clandestine work. Fergus had been told to prepare for another day's fishing, as far as the world was concerned. This he had done and for prying eyes and anybody who saw them leave the harbour, they were merely a group of serious minded fishermen setting off for a day on the water.

They did fish - in the bay, off the Western coast of Loch Island, hidden from the mainland and from the port. The nets were efficiently laid. Once again Fergus couldn't believe that all the men seemed to know what to do. Certainly they'd all had experience on boats and at the end of the day he was delighted to have a full hold. On this occasion there was nothing untoward to see, no sign of the Russian ship and the sea was flat calm. A few grey seals played around the rocks and in the surf at the water's edge at one end of the bay, only distinguishable through binoculars at such a distance. Later a sea mist and light drizzle helped as, under cover of darkness, they set in towards the beach. Then with relays in the dinghy, Fergus ferried his camouflaged human cargo and equipment to dry land. Once they hit the sand they melted silently into the darkness and in a matter of a few seconds were gone. They had everything they needed and good communications, but Fergus had no idea how long they intended to be there. He was told to return to port and to go about normal business until further advised.

The fisherman turned his boat out to sea once more, full of admiration for the professional team that he'd left behind. He'd only been told a little of what they were about, but there was definitely something big on their agenda. An icy shiver ran unexpectedly down the back of his neck, taking him by surprise. The temperature was dropping and there would likely be snow on the hills come morning. He pulled his woollen hat down close over his ears and rearranged his scarf. Fergus never usually felt cold but the thought of a night on that isle, with God alone knew who or what for company, was something he'd not relish. There had been rumours for many a year now regarding the spookiness of the abandoned island; a piece of land where at one time, he imagined, there had been both life and laughter. He turned once more and looked towards the deserted village – perhaps there was something in those rumours after all and it had taken a stranger to act upon it.

Fergus set his bearing for home and put on speed. He had a great catch in the hold, the best for a long time and the thought of Beth's warm comforting arms, later on in the evening, got better by the minute. He was much looking forward to that distraction.

❄

"What time will Julian and Guy be back Olly, do you know? Are you all meeting up at the pub?" Oh bloody hell!

thought Oliver. He really had drawn the short end of the straw. As casually as he could and addressing Alicia in particular, he gave his prepared speech.

"Actually, they might not be back tonight. They could even be away for a couple of days." The girls all swung around to stare at Olly.

"What do you mean?" demanded Emma, slightly cross. "Where have they gone?"

"They're just helping with the investigation, that's all. I don't really know where they are," Olly lied. Oliver looked decidedly uncomfortable, so Alicia swiftly came to his rescue.

"Look everyone, we all know that both Julian and Guy have another job – they are hardly going to let all this murder business go by without lending a helping hand, especially after what Arri and Marc discovered up at the lighthouse." Marc walked in sipping at a glass of whisky.

"I hear my name. What's this about?"

"Guy and Julian it seems, have gone off on other business once more." replied Emma dejectedly. Rose appeared from the kitchen and went to stand by Olly. Marc went to kiss his hormonal wife on the cheek. Oh dear! With this last upset she was near to tears again, poor thing.

"I wouldn't worry darling, just let them get on with whatever they have to do. They'll appear back when they're good and ready. Meanwhile we have plenty going on here to keep us all busy." Alicia and Adriana looked at each other from either end of the sofa and smiled.

"Yes," said Rose looking across at them, "and they are doing what they are best at - right?"

"Yes, right. We are well used to these disappearing acts so we must all get on with our holiday the best way we can." Alicia stood up. "How about another drink before dinner?"

"Good idea. Olly, could you come and help me please?" Marc asked going out of the room, worried for both Alicia and Adriana but deeply admiring of their brave performance. They knew perfectly well that neither of their men would be helping out in the safety of the incident room. They were trained to the very highest level of both physical and mental endurance. Marc had observed them both in action on several occasions. He'd even once seen the two men set forth on a five mile run uphill, appearing back later hardly out of breath. They ran every day, to keep fit, even on holiday. They were game for anything and would never let anybody do a job that they thought they could do better themselves.

The rest of the party settled down to an uneasy evening held together mainly by Alicia and Adriana. Emma went to bed early, clearly upset but trying to hide it. Normally she was strong and staunch but, at present, the baby was making itself felt. The rest of the group played chess and monopoly with relaxed rules and plied with plenty of alcohol. The unspoken condition being that no person should enter into speculation as to what the two missing members of their party might be about.

After dinner was through, Beth came to ask if it was alright for her to go for a nightcap with Fergus. He would come to pick her up. Marc wondered if the fisherman had any news and surreptitiously went out to greet him when he heard the old truck come noisily up the drive. Fergus seemed full of the joys of spring.

"Is all well down in the port?" Marc asked of the fisherman. Fergus quickly answered, holding Marc's meaningful glance.

"Yes, everything seems to be well in control. There is a very efficient team down there now."

"Good," Marc replied and then turned to their smiling cook. "Now go and have some fun Beth and forget about the kitchen for a while. How about Jess, she never seems to want to go out?"

"You don't need to worry about my sister. As you know she's already spoken for. When Poppy is all tucked up Jess is perfectly happy reading and watching the television. Rob rings up every evening and they talk for hours. It's really quite boring," she said grinning delightedly at Fergus. "Mum thinks they'll probably get married." She rolled her sparkling eyes and got into the car as Fergus cheerfully held the door open for her. Marc watched as they drove off down the rough drive. Even the truck seemed to be bouncing along with enthusiasm.

Heavens, these two really are keen on each other, Marc thought as he walked back into the house. How is this one going to end? How much does Fergus know about what's really going on with the investigation? Marc wished he knew how many days Julian and Guy might be away. Olly and he would certainly have their work cut out keeping all the girls happy and he wondered just how long Alicia and the remarkable Adriana would hold up putting a brave face on it all. Adriana really was an exotic creature who positively oozed sex appeal. Dangerous thoughts though, he concluded walking back through the front door with the dogs at his heels; wondering what sort of night her fiancé and Guy were having, wherever they were. It was bloody cold and snow was forecast on the hills. This wasn't exactly the holiday that any of them had planned.

CHAPTER 25

Two days passed and there was no word from Guy or Julian. Those at the lodge seemed suspended in an atmosphere of controlled tension. The group of friends circled around each other with the utmost care. The people with most reason to worry and yet continued to hold it together best, were Alicia and Adriana. Emma shed many private tears but was strong in front of the others. Rose organized distracting entertainment and Marc and Olly did their best to look after the household and keep up a cheerful front at the same time.

On many occasions Marc berated himself for having arranged this holiday with all his friends, but then the present drama was not of their making and unfortunate to say the least. It was all proving a bit much for Emma, but she was sensible and with his comforting reassurance, she accepted and understood that her fragile state was both normal and temporary. Any little thing might have provoked tears at this particular stage in her pregnancy. When she felt the need she just disappeared into her bedroom, from which she would appear later full of energy once more.

On the other hand Adriana remained remarkably stable. Marc hoped, for both Arri and Julian's sakes that their stolen afternoon in the lighthouse would prove fruitful. He still felt not in the least bit guilty. His wish to save his two close friends relationship by far outweighed any sense of guilt for their afternoon of unashamedly intense physical indulgence. What happened was, as far as he was concerned, relegated to the past with no difficulty at all. Adriana was a brave wonderful person with a beautiful body but he had no unsettling longing to repeat their lovemaking. If anything it made him feel even luckier to have what he and Emma had between them. Poppy and the new baby were miracles in their own right. If Adriana conceived a child he just prayed that it would look like its mother and in particular inherit neither his auburn coloured hair nor the unusual fleck in his left eye. The latter was his only real concern about the whole episode. Marc was an excellent doctor and perfectly capable of putting his own feelings to one side whilst dealing with both his patients and anything at all difficult in his own personal life.

❄

Ailsa arranged to take over the running of the Post Office for a couple of hours each afternoon while Mary was on her enforced holiday. A retired teacher was going to do the morning stints when Ailsa was helping with the cleaning up at Glencurrie. She was also happy to join Mary and her mother in the evenings while Dougie was busy in the pub and to help look after Sean if she was needed. Sean soon took to Ailsa, as he had to her mother-in-law, Mary. His little face became less strained and he began to eat some of the delicious snacks that Mrs H so lovingly produced.

Jean Haddington was truly in her element. There hadn't been so much excitement in Dromvaar since the Colonel was away in the Iraq war and returned home to receive his medal. She was so pleased to see Colonel Alec full of life once more, getting on well with his brother and all the young folk and taking such a responsible part in the on-going drama. When she took food and drink up to the nursery she was moved to see that, when her daughter Ailsa was there, the boy was as happy as Larry. She had a natural way with the child. Ailsa had brought some children's books from the library and set about reading to Sean; to take him to lovely, fairy-tale places and away from the hell that he'd been through. They would sit together for hours in the bay window, looking towards the grouse moor, with the boy snuggled into the crook of her arm. The Colonel's nephew Marc had examined Sean thoroughly. Ailsa told her mother that the doctor had been so gentle with the boy and had

166

brought Poppy with him as a comforting distraction. Mrs H told Doctor Neilsen that, in her view, Ailsa was by far the best person to extract information without frightening the child any further. It just wouldn't do to take him down to the incident room. Besides which she had understood it to be of paramount importance that, for the moment, nobody else knew of his whereabouts. Marc agreed whole heartedly and said that he would do his best. Meanwhile, if Ailsa did learn anything of interest, to make sure to let them know immediately as anything significant would have to be passed on.

As Sean's confidence began to return he slowly began to speak again. He lost the sullen sly look about his pinched face reflecting his frightened awareness of his past perilous existence. Little pieces of information began to emerge naturally, so that Ailsa soon managed to get the gist of what might have happened to the boy. She literally felt her own heart contract as she discovered that the awful Irish girl wasn't his mother after all, but a much older sister. She had always bullied him and beat him when he was either cold or hungry and had made a fuss. Ailsa thought that their parents had died some years before as Sean didn't seem, or perhaps want, to remember them. It sounded as if they might have died in suspicious circumstances.

The immigrant people had much to do with the story. Ailsa thought that they were probably responsible for holding Sean prisoner whilst his sister was elsewhere, about God knows what business. It seemed that the night he escaped he was being held somewhere within the old smokehouse. He was locked in a room and had somehow managed to jump out of the window, most probably into the sea and had swum around the building to get to the beach and away. He had then run in the dark, finding his way under the light of the moon, all the way to Mary's house; the one person he knew to be a friend. Sean also began to mention certain young girls - the only people he liked, he said, because they were nice to him and they were so pretty. He thought that his sister helped then in some way and that they came from far-off countries. There was also a posh older man who would come to see them sometimes. But his sister and the strange man always went somewhere so that he couldn't hear what they were talking about. He didn't like the older man, nor did the girls, he could tell, but sometimes they were made to go along with him. His friend Olga hated this man and refused to go anywhere with him. There was a lot of trouble about this and poor Olga had also become very frightened.

This was crucial information. Ailsa relayed it all to the Colonel who then immediately asked constable MacDonald, Oliver and Marc up for another meeting to discuss the implications of this knowledge and to judge best how to handle it, while both Guy and Julian were still away on their mission.

The Detective Chief Superintendent was now insisting on an interview with the ten year old boy, but Guy had suggested that Marc say the child wasn't up to it until he and Julian returned. Unless, of course, they thought there was anything of immediate importance. Mac thought that Guy needed to be told of these latest details before anybody else. They could well be vital information concerning his present venture. Everybody now understood that it had become urgent for the D.C.S to see Sean. It couldn't be put off much longer. But, the Colonel insisted, only if in the presence of either Mary Macquire or Ailsa and accompanied by a qualified policewoman, which Alec knew to be standard procedure.

❄

The first night on the island, the special op's group merely watched as instructed. Surveillance was the name of the game. Everything was tranquil. So discreet were they in their covert movements that even the wildlife remained undisturbed. There were no lights from the deserted village, no faint smell of smoke rose and wafted across on the cold night air; there was no sign of life anywhere. The next day they stealthily scoured the Western side of the island, found the mooring lines, recently in use and the barely disguised evidence of regular comings and goings along the narrow path to the village. Slowly but surely they closed in on the abandoned buildings. As arranged, Guy called in to the incident room twice daily to both give and collect any fresh reports. Neither the Irish girl nor the immigrants had reappeared on the mainland, but the child's information was of immense interest. He agreed that the boy must continue to be protected but should now be sensitively interviewed.

At nightfall, with no more news from either side of the water the group went in.

"I'll go first. Julian, cover me. I'm going to head for the largest and least derelict house, the most likely in use." Guy looked at his luminous watch. "Give me five minutes then follow, but come in, if you can, from behind the building. I should think there'll be a back entrance. Two of you stay and keep watch out here. Any vessel coming in to the bay behind, any movement on the beach, anything untoward - I want to know about it." He signalled to the last members of the party. "You two: I want you to make for the small inland lake, nearest the far side of the village, where it is fed by the sea canal. Conceal yourself there and listen. The first thing you are likely to hear is a small outboard engine, coming from an Easterly direction." He looked up to the sky; the moon was shy, half obscured by cloud, ideal for their purposes. "Anything, anything at all, get back to me pronto. Right everybody? - Go."

The three men moved as mere shadows, flitting silently from side to side, merging with the undergrowth. They stopped from time to time to look, listen and to appraise their surroundings. Then they were gone: disappearing silently into the night gloom. Guy could hear his heart beating loudly. He'd learnt to steady it. He knew that it was partly the adrenalin rush. He stopped to squat under the half tumbled-down garden wall adjoining the house.

The overgrown ivy trailed down, wet and pungent smelling, while the dampness helped to muffle his cautious movements. A mouse or something small in the undergrowth at his feet scuttled away. There was no noise from within the old farmhouse: nothing, but he wasn't sure – just a gut feeling. It looked and sounded empty but there was something. A pile of old sacks with some newish twine lay beside him and an upturned bucket which he needed to avoid. Guy checked his watch. Then, certain that Julian was already in place at the back of the building, cautiously approached the front door. It wasn't locked. He eased it open a crack, then waited just long enough to ascertain that the house wasn't empty. There was just the merest awareness of a veiled energy and a certain smell from within which he knew to be freshly human. Both men moved at the same instant and met in the middle of the room; with protective night-vision goggles they were immediately able to assess the situation. Julian, having come from the back was exactly where he should have been, his gun aimed at a living bundle on the floor. With the lower floor secure; Guy leapt up the stairs two at a time, but there was no threat; nothing surprising; just used bedding and odd items of female clothing and personal effects. Downstairs, the small kitchen was littered with takeaway food packaging and tins of coke. Turning to the bundle on the floor, they soon found that the body was that of an older man tied up and, although filthy dirty and half starved, still just alive. Judging by the trussed man's physical condition, he must have been that way for at least two or three days. The poor wretch was weak and frightened, agitated and mumbling incoherently in a foreign language.

"OK Julian, well done. We need to get this bloke to hospital fast. He's in a right state and delirious. Let's have a closer look at him." Guy leant down to gently untie the man's legs and arms. He was a sorry sight, with wrists and ankles bleeding and raw from struggling to free himself. Guy took out his radio and relayed their findings back to base whilst Julian brought a blanket and tried to make the poor dehydrated victim more comfortable.

"Just the one person," Guy spoke hurriedly, "male, nationality – hard to say as yet but I would think one of the Russian speaking countries. About sixty-five, badly dehydrated, malnourished, a couple of lesions to the head; probably inflicted by a boot, and I'd say from the position he's lying in, a broken left hip. No identification whatsoever... Come in... say again?" He listened for only a moment, "Affirmative, in other situations I'd ask for a helicopter but, as is, I'd rather have a boat meet us on the Western side of the island. I don't want to advertise our being here more than necessary at this time. Tell Fergus same place as before, where we disembarked and to get a move on as this man's in a bad way. I'll have two men stretcher the patient to the beach now. I only have the basics but he'll be wrapped in a thermal blanket and I will have given him a shot for the pain. Make sure to have an ambulance meet the boat in the port." He then called up his surveillance team waiting outside the village and told them to get to him fast. The victim was now beginning to show less confused signs of life and was moaning continually with pain.

"Hello there, if you can understand me just nod your head." The man's face was creased up in agony but he managed the slightest nod. "Good, so you speak English. We are part of the British army. We have to get you out of here as soon as possible. We'll rig up a stretcher and try to make you more comfortable. I have a pain killer which will suffice until we get you to hospital. You'll be alright, OK?" Guy took out his medical kit to prepare the shot.

The man was trying to speak; he seemed to be asking a question or was he whispering a name? "Olga. I think he's asking for someone called Olga," Julian said, holding the man's head to dribble a little rehydration fluid into his mouth, then leaning in closer, the better to hear the frail words.

"OK remember that; careful he doesn't choke on that drink. Now let's give him the morphine. There's a folding combat stretcher in my back pack, also a thermal blanket. Perhaps you can get that assembled, Julian. We'll need to tie him securely as it will be a bumpy ride to the sea; but luckily he'll soon be away with the fairies and won't remember this particular journey. The others will be here at any minute now. Then I want all the other buildings checked. We'll be down to four of us until the men get back from the beach."

CHAPTER 26

Constable MacDonald appeared at Glencurrie accompanied by the Detective Chief Superintendent and by a well meaning policewoman, along with someone from forensics looking rather more formidable in his work uniform. Alec was all ready to meet them and Mrs H had organised tea and her best shortbread to make the meeting with Sean as easy as possible. They were all worried for the child. Nobody wanted the boy further upset after what he'd already been through. The visitors walked in to the nursery where Ailsa was sitting quietly playing dominoes with Sean.

Forensics had a bright blue piece of clothing to show him. The boy reacted as soon as he caught sight of it in the impersonal, see-through plastic bag. Startled he looked from one to the other of the group. The severe looking forensics man stepped forward, after a signal from the D.C.S and took the creased coat out of the bag, holding it up for him to see.

"Olga - that's Olga's," he cried in amazement, pointing, then with excitement, "is she here...? in the house...? I want to see her!" He looked at the strange men's faces for reassurance that she was somewhere close, but none of them said a word. They just looked grim, although the policewoman moved forward ready to console the child. Sean instantly picked up on the tension within the room. He pushed her away and ran across the room to grab the coat. Then he held it to his face and beginning to sob went back to Ailsa, where she sat on the sofa, holding out her arms.

"Where's Olga? Where is she, I want her?" he whispered desperately into her neck. Ailsa held him tight; she couldn't bear to see the child's distress.

"It's alright darling, it's alright. Perhaps she just lost her coat?" She gathered him into her arms and looked up hopefully at the Inspector who silently shook his head. She met the man's eyes and knew then that the blue coat belonged to the murdered girl who, most likely, had been Sean's only friend in the whole sad business. Ailsa could but hope that he couldn't sense what she was feeling and become aware that something terrible had happened to his friend. It was too soon - far too soon for him to cope with such an horrific revelation. Alec turned to the senior policeman.

"I think that'll have to do for today Chief Superintendent, don't you? Shall I show you out?" The policewoman and forensics man retrieved the coat with some difficulty from the sobbing child and turned towards the door. Alec could see that the D.C.S was disappointed and had wanted more information, but the man had no choice but to follow the other two out of the room. Outside the front door, by the police car, Alec made his apologies.

"I'm sorry Chief Superintendent, but as you can see the boy is still in a traumatized state so we'll just have to take it very slowly. My nephew, Doctor Marc Neilsen, said that the boy must have no further upset. In his case recovery is reliant on security and nourishment of both the physical and mental kind. In short, a good dose of tender loving care is what's needed for the moment. Meanwhile we will of course relay anything relevant that comes to our notice."

"I understand." The D.C.S sighed. "It's a pity, but you're right, we'll just have to wait a bit. At least to a degree we have identification of the coat. However the situation isn't as bad as the last case I was on when the only witness happened to be a dog." Alec laughed. This stern man had a sense of humour after all.

"That must have been extremely tricky, what happened?"

"I'm afraid," answered the detective with a wry smile, "the case, although on-going at present, is most likely to join a long list of other unsolved crimes in the archives of the criminal records office."

"Well," said Alec, "I sincerely hope that, given time, things will soon become clear for you here."

"Yes, Colonel Neilsen, thank you, I'm sure they will. I would like to see the boy again as soon as you think fit. Meanwhile we have plenty else to keep us busy at the moment, so we'll leave you in peace."

Alec watched the car retreat down the drive. The occupants had spent a disappointing mere twenty minutes in the house. Alec was well aware that the detective had intended to question Sean intensely. But they should have kept the coat out of sight and produced it last. Insensitive, heavy handed - and nobody's fault, except their own, the Colonel thought grimly.

After the men had gone and Sean appeared to have accepted Ailsa's explanation that Olga had decided to go home for a little while and had perhaps left her coat behind, Ailsa left him with Mrs H who produced hot chocolate before going to find Colonel Neilsen. There was something else which had come to light this very morning and she wanted to tell Colonel Alec, for he would know best what to do. She knocked on his study door and waited, holding her breath while she listened for his invitation to enter. Ailsa didn't often feel nervous but on this occasion she did because she knew that the information she had to impart was of grave importance. She was so glad that she hadn't told that thoughtless policeman first.

"Come in. Ah! Hello Ailsa. Do come and sit down. That poor child, I'm so glad that unpleasant ordeal is over. You handled it very well and you're quite right, it's far too quick to tell him that his friend, the girl Olga, is dead. They must be certain it's her. Someone will have to be found to identify the body properly and it certainly won't be Sean. I can assure you of that."

"Yes," agreed Ailsa determinedly. "That would be over my dead body, Colonel Neilsen. It can't possibly be the boy. I'm very fond of the wee bairn and he's been through far too much already. I should think that would finish him off. He'd never recover. Can you make sure of that Colonel Alec? They must have stipulations about underage children identifying bodies?"

"I should think so. Yes, almost certainly, although there may be special exceptions made when there is nobody but a child to do the deed. This whole thing will blow at any minute now and then hopefully there should be others who can perform that particularly distasteful job."

"Good. There's something else that I think you need to know and which I have only just discovered. It is something very delicate, very delicate indeed, but could just possibly have some bearing on all this horror." Alec, realising that this could be serious, turned his desk chair around to face Ailsa better.

"Alright Ailsa. I'm all ears. Fire ahead."

"You know about the two immigrant people who seem to do odd jobs up at Castle House?" Alec nodded as Ailsa, now red in the face, looked down at her hands wondering how to continue.

"Go on," The Colonel said encouragingly.

"Well, you see, this involves the laird. I know the lady who sometimes 'does' for Lady Strathkellan."

"Ah, that would be Lorna Doon as we used to call her on the odd occasion that Caroline and I were forced to dine there. The only good thing about the whole evening was Lorna's cooking. She was a wonderful cook."

"Yes, and she still is, Colonel Neilsen. Anyway Lorna tells me that when his wife is away Lord Strathkellan often tells her not to come. Lorna says this state of affairs has been going on for some time now. She thinks it odd as, apart from the housekeeping side of things, she always used to see to his midday meal when he was alone. He can't cook, seldom goes out and usually gets stuck into a bottle of whisky. One day last week she looked in the dustbin to see if there was evidence of what he'd been eating. She found something else...." Alec was riveted, especially as he thoroughly disliked Alistair Strathkellan and also felt very sorry for his lovely wife Finola. God alone only knew why she hadn't left him years before.

"Go on please Ailsa. What did Lorna find?" Ailsa looked up, now bright red in the face. She took a deep breath.

"She told me that there was a black plastic bag, tied up tightly with string separate from the usual rubbish which normally he'd never bother to seal. For some reason she felt that she needed to see inside and so she undid the tie..." Alec cleared his throat.

"Alright Ailsa. Tell me exactly what was in that bag?" Ailsa, sitting bolt upright said it all in a rush:

"There were young girl's skimpy under garments; certain pornographic equipment and what looked like the packaging from some sort of a drug. She thought that it was the one they call the date rape drug, the one that's also used medically." Alec remained silent for a minute while he considered these implications. Ailsa burst out again:

"Poor Lady Strathkellan! That dreadful man has been luring young girls up there, I dread to think what for, every time she's gone away."

"Yes," Alec replied thoughtfully, "it looks very much like it. Where is this bag of horror now then? Do you know?"

"I think Lorna gave it to the Polish boy who does odd jobs in the garden, to get rid of."

"OK, now Ailsa this is important. Do you know anything about this Polish boy and where I might find him?"

"Well, I don't know where he lives exactly, maybe Lorna does. She says he's a nice boy. He doesn't work there on a regular basis as he does plumbing jobs elsewhere. Dougie has mentioned him visiting the pub occasionally. The other man working sometimes up at Castle House is a nasty piece of work. He's Albanian and cruel, according to Lorna. She doesn't like the laird either, never has. She only stays on for his wife. She's very fond of Lady Strathkellan and she says that between them, both her husband and the Albanian bully poor Javek all the time. That's about all." Ailsa said, "but I can find out more." Alec sat quite still, considering a course of action.

"Right Ailsa. Now what I'd like you to do is find out where Lorna lives. I'd also like to know where we can find the Polish boy."

"That's easy. Lorna has the cottage behind the mill. It belongs to the laird. Lorna's a widow and her husband used to work in the Castle garden. Also, she is the most likely person to know where to find Javek. When he has time off he sometimes goes to her cottage for a meal."

"Good. That's excellent Ailsa. Now I want you to keep all this strictly to yourself. One of us will go to visit Lorna Finlay." Poor Ailsa looked thoroughly uncomfortable with this idea. Alec leant towards her and covered her hand kindly with his.

"You were absolutely right to come to tell me about this. A murder has been committed. If the laird also has been up to no good, we have to get to the bottom of it all, as there could well be a link. At present the police are very busy investigating the murder and, you never know, all this might help. You mustn't distress yourself Ailsa. I'll be very circumspect in approaching Lorna. She may even be desperate to talk to someone in authority about her fears. By now most of the village will have heard the news of the dead girl. Someone, somewhere has to know something that will help tie up the loose ends and it could just be this information. You have done a wonderful job gaining the confidence of that pitiful child up there in the nursery and looking after him is the best thing that you can do for now. Are you quite comfortable here? Have you everything you need?"

"Yes thank you Colonel Neilsen. If you don't mind I'd like to stay here with the bairn. What will happen to Sean when this is all over? He can't go back to that dreadful Irish girl."

"No, no of course not. But don't worry your head about all that for now. I'll keep you up to date as much as I can with what goes on. Please thank your husband Dougie for letting us keep you here, helping for so long. He must be missing his wife! But remember not a word of this to anyone!" Ailsa smiled.

"I understand Colonel Neilsen and I feel relieved to have got it off my chest. I'm sure that you'll know what to do."

Alec got up from his chair. "Yes I do, so you mustn't concern yourself anymore. Now I'm going to go along to the lodge and have a chat with my nephew and his friend Oliver."

Guy was still away, but Alec knew that this latest news was too important to leave. He didn't want to alert the police as yet; there was still a certain amount of private surveillance that they could do themselves. He just wished that he could communicate directly with Guy.

CHAPTER 27

"I'll go," Oliver said without hesitation. "Nobody knows me up there and I've done this sort of work before. I'll borrow Beth's car, visit with Lorna, Mrs Finlay - first and try to find out where the Polish man is likely to be found; then I can take it from there."

"Alright, I think that's a good plan." Alec would have preferred to go himself but he'd be recognized, which could ruin the whole manoeuvre. Apart from which he wasn't sure that he could be held responsible for his actions, should he come across the laird. Oliver was young and frequently worked out with the Territorial Army. He was capable, fit, intelligent and now in full mission mode.

"Someone must be both here and up at Glencurrie to answer the telephone at all times, just in case a message comes in from Guy's people. If it does, it's important that he gets to hear all this latest information. Alec, do you think there is any way of getting an update to him through constable MacDonald perhaps, via the incident room? He may not be using an ordinary mobile. I can try a text but I'm sure the investigative team would be a better bet as he's bound to touch base every so often."

"Probably. I'll certainly give it a shot. Presumably they have some modern, high-tech, airwave version of the walkie talkie. But you go, as Lorna will be home by now. Let's just hope that she's not gone visiting. Just be careful and expect the lady to be upset. She's a nice woman and it's a nasty business."

❄

Oliver was thrilled to be doing something useful again. He'd sent a message to Guy asking him to get in contact urgently but he had no idea if it would or could be picked up. Then he'd spoken with Mac, after which he set off for Mrs Finlay's house behind the mill, closed now, with only security lights surrounding the yard and buildings. He found the cottage easily and sure enough there was a light on inside but it looked like there was a second car parked outside. She had a visitor: he hadn't bargained for that. The car was a very old Mercedes with plenty of dents and a tyre looking as if it needed air. Oliver wondered whether he should wait until the person left, so he parked around the corner. Then he returned to the courtyard and stood in a doorway opposite the cottage out of sight - and waited.

Even from a distance he couldn't help but hear wails of distress coming from inside the cottage. Someone was extremely unhappy but it didn't sound like a child or a woman. He heard a woman's raised voice, trying to calm things down, then more animal-like cries of pure misery. Just as he had decided to go and knock on the door it opened and a young man came stumbling out, sobbing. Oliver shrunk back into the shadows to watch. An agitated female - it must have been Lorna - called after her distraught visitor.

"Javek, Javek come back, don't go, come and stay here with me, dear. You could be wrong, it mightn't be her." But the dishevelled young man just waved one hand without turning around and kept going until he reached his car. He got in, stalled it and finally drove off unsteadily up the hill in the direction of Castle House. The woman went slowly back inside, shutting the front door behind her. Right, thought Oliver - my cue.

He strode across the yard and knocked on the door. It opened again almost immediately. A fleeting look of relief promptly leaving her face, the woman stepped back with astonishment.

"Goodness me, who are you? And where the devil have you come from?"

"I've come to help," said Oliver without hesitation looking at her intently and with his most disarming smile. "May I come in?" Lorna stared at the good looking man in front of her and made her decision. She was at her wit's end, she didn't know what to do, she did need help and this good samaritan just happened to be standing on her doorstep. If he were a rapist or kidnapper too bad, she'd still let him in.

"Come in, do. But I must be telling you that I don't usually invite strangers into my house and this time it's only because of the extremely stressful circumstances...."

"Then I must re-assure you quickly, Mrs Finlay. My name's Oliver and I am a great friend of Colonel Neilsen's son Marc. The Colonel has asked me to come to see you."

"That's alright then, if the Colonel's behind the visit. I'll make us a pot of tea and I shall be having a wee dram in mine. You can be sure of that."

They sat either side of the little fire place, sipping strong tea laced with a dash of whisky, while Oliver told Lorna all that he knew and asked what he needed to know. As he spoke he appraised the lady. She was about sixty five to eight years of age, he thought, with grey hair and piercing blue eyes that most likely missed nothing. She was neatly dressed in a rather old-fashioned bright blue twinset, with a single row of pearls around her pale birdlike neck. In fact he considered she was rather like a brave little bird with brightly coloured plumage. Now she fluffed up her feathers, gave a small shake and launched forth.

"The boy you saw leaving in a right old state; that's Javek; he's Polish and he's a good boy. He came here to the UK with his girlfriend Olga about three months ago. He has plumbing qualifications and so found work quite quickly. Olga is beautiful. I told her that she would have no trouble finding employment. She has stayed here with me, on and off, when she's not with Javek or her new friends. But she's disappeared, off the face of the map, and now what with this murder...," her voice trailed off and Oliver finished the sentence for her.

"Javek thinks that this dead girl might be her?"

"Yes, he's convinced of it and he can't bear the thought of even offering to identify the body... in case it is Olga. I have said that I would do it if necessary. But that's not all. He also has a story to tell regarding the laird up at the house here," she indicated with her hand, pointing in the vague direction that Javek had taken. "I've told him that he has to tell the police; he's got some evidence in the boot of his car but he's hell bent on revenge and taking the laird down with it. That's what worries me most. In the sort of mood he's in he could do both the laird and himself some mischief." The story was beginning to make sense, thought Oliver.

"Mrs Finlay... now whereabouts...,"

"Call me Lorna, everyone does," she interrupted.

"Alright Lorna, where does Javek live?"

"The laird has a small lodge at the end of his drive – he's there when he's not with Olga and that's where he'll have gone now, to lick his wounds poor boy. He'll be alone as the Albanian monster he lives with is away, praise be to God."

"Good." Replied Oliver with relief; understanding to whom she was referring.

"Is the laird presently at home?"

"Yes, when his lady wife's away he's usually in residence; busy organizing his unsuspecting visitors and their filthy entertainment, but the house is a good three-quarters of a mile away from the lodge. He won't be seeing you and I believe that Lady Strathkellan is due back this evening anyway, so he will have been cleaning up." She looked hard at Oliver.

"You're a nice young man, I can tell, but I can assure you that Lord Strathkellan is a wicked person and his wife has a terrible time of it. That's why she's away so often. She can't stick it. I know some of it. Lady Strathkellan tells me. He's up to everything you can possibly imagine... and worse," Lorna, finished grimly.

"Right." Olly stood up. "I'll be on my way up there then. Thank you for the tea. Now if you are worried, or need anything, ring the Colonel at Glencurrie, the phone will always be answered. This is my mobile number which I will also have with me at all times." Oliver handed over the scrap of paper on which he'd already written the numbers.

Lorna saw him out, gave him the directions and waved until he was out of sight. Then the staunch little woman took a great big breath of refreshing cold night air and looked up to the sky.

"Pray to God the dead girl isn't Olga and that the laird gets his comeuppance," she muttered to herself with feeling "and as for that young man Oliver... they don't make many like that anymore."

She watched the retreating tail-lights disappear up the hill and stayed for as long as she could hear the car. Her heart had steadied its erratic beat and she felt better than she'd felt for a long time. Lorna knew that she should have called Mac earlier in the day and told him everything as soon as she had become suspicious. But if she was honest she couldn't face finding out about the girl and causing Javek more distress. But now she wouldn't have to worry. Help had arrived in another form: thank the Lord. She pulled her cardigan tight around her thin shoulders and turned to go inside. It was cold, very cold, there'd be another frost tonight and she must soon get Javek to put her tubs, full of herbs, into the little greenhouse in her back garden.

Oliver continued on up the road until he came to a pair of impressive gate posts, just as Lorna had described. There was a small grey Victorian lodge at the drive entrance. This must be it - yes there was a sign pointing up the drive to 'Castle House'. It was an old board certainly, as you could still just see, underneath and in smaller letters, 'Beware Small Children and Dogs'. There didn't appear to be any light on in the building but the old car was parked in a curved bay beside the lodge. There was no point in trying to be quiet and this was bound to be difficult, so Oliver also parked in the parking place, got out and listened. An owl flew out of a tree almost in his face, making him jump. The movement of its great wings made an eerie whooshing noise as they beat and stirred the air. Spooky on such a night. Olly watched as it flew away through the trees and disappeared to hunt.

He wondered how Guy and Julian were progressing. He guessed that they too were hunting, but most likely on the island and their quarry would be of a different sort - human. Oliver checked his mobile hoping for news from someone. Nothing. They must still be incognito and busy with their task. The temperature had dropped dramatically in the last few days. He felt the hairs on the back of his neck prickle - but not from the cold – premonition. Not a good feeling and he didn't relish this next visit. There was still no sign of life. The young man inside must have heard the car, but he'd obviously gone to ground hoping that whoever it was would give up and go away. Oliver wasn't about to give up; he had a job to do and he knew that Marc's uncle and his friends would all be relying on him. He approached the front porch and knocked loudly on the solid oak door.

CHAPTER 28

"All the other buildings are empty. No sign of life at all."
Julian shut the door and took off his padded jacket.

"Good," said Guy, "then we wait." He looked around the
living room. There was nothing much to see; just newspapers, dirty
coffee cups and some outdoor clothing hanging on hooks by the
door. Then he spied a sheet of paper weighted with a stone on the
mantelpiece.

"What's this?" They both scanned the sheet with the torch.

"Looks like a timetable, with something... a name... written
in... Russian I think here... down the bottom." Guy looked closer.

"Yes, shipping details; ETA. Also estimated time of departure
by the looks of it." They heard approaching steps, killed the torch
and shrank into the shadows; three knocks, pause and one more. It
was the men back from the beach.

"Alright, secure. Come in. Now you're back I'm going to
have a proper look upstairs. Anything you touch replace exactly
as it was. Make yourselves a hot drink while the going is good.
There's no electricity but a calor gas camping stove. Be careful not
to damage evidence. The place is littered with the remains of both
abusive substances and happy pills."

Upstairs Guy found more unsettling evidence of foreign,
teenage girls' clothing. There was nothing to suggest that the place
had merely been used to house the odd shepherd in summertime.
He brought a bundle down with him to inspect the tags inside.

"These clothes, I would think, were used for travel and then
discarded on arrival here. Have a look and see if you can make out
the country of origin then return them upstairs. It's as I thought.

My findings so far are that young girls have been brought here, most likely ferried over by ships from middle European countries. They probably would land on the West of the island where we came in and where, as a matter of interest, Julian and I have seen a Russian ship lurking. This deserted island, I think, has been used as a half-way house before their prey was moved on to God knows where in Europe. Paris we know about, this is where the last group were taken and I imagine, groomed and re-clothed before they were sent on to their miserable fate. These girls will have been promised the world to get them here. They may have come willingly but it's unlikely that they had any idea what they were in for. Perhaps the girl that was murdered found out and reneged to her cost. Who knows? But hopefully we will be able to find out." One of the men handed around the tea and they sipped their hot drinks, while Guy talked.

"First, we have to prepare for the return of the Irish woman and those helping her here. They will come from the East, from the direction of the old smokehouse on the mainland. They will cross the channel and enter the inland waterway which comes into the small loch on the East of the village here. We will hear them before we see them and have confirmation from our other two group members in position where the small canal meets the inland lake. Second, there has to be someone on the mainland in or around Dromvaar helping these people. We need to find out who that is. It will be somebody with money and influence. But for now - be prepared for the return of these callous people. Remember the Irish woman will be alert because of the disappearance of the child. Make sure that everything is as it was left. They will likely sense our presence so we'll have to be quick. Have your vests on; they may well be armed. Now I'm just going to call in to base."

The night wore on. News came in that the Irish girl had been seen in the pub. Guy and Julian remained in the house co-ordinating matters, while the four others changed places at two hourly intervals. It was bitterly cold and the wind had got up again. At dawn Guy received the awaited information on his two way radio. A boat engine had been heard at the entrance to the narrow canal. Everything was ready. They would relay the details once the occupants came into sight.

Once again both Julian, Guy and their team experienced a heightening of tension. Adrenalin surged through their veins, lifting their spirits and relegating tiredness to the past, as they waited with every sense finely tuned for action and the outcome of the operation.

Javek was desperate and let Oliver in as soon as he understood that Olly had come from Lorna and was there to help. The Polish boy, already in a terrible state, sank into a chair and completely broke down. He sat wringing his hands and weeping with misery. Then he'd take a deep breath and ramble on in Polish for so long that it took Oliver most of the night to calm the poor young man down and persuade him to speak in English. Olly managed to send a text to both Rose and Alec so that they knew he was alright. Then he set about getting to the bottom of the whole sorry tale. Finally he managed to make sense of it all.

Olga and Javek had grown up together in Poland and went to the same college. There they had fallen in love and decided that they would come to England when they'd finished their studies. He had his qualifications and Olga was so beautiful, he said, that she would have no trouble finding work. They travelled overland to Hamburg and picked up a Russian ship bound for Scotland. On the ship Olga had made friends with an illegal party of equally beautiful young women travelling to Scotland. They didn't like the men escorting them but the girls had been promised passports and a dream-like new life. Finally Olga had agreed to join them.

"Do you have a proper passport Javek?"

"Of course, Olga as well and I think that's one of the reasons the men were trying to persuade her to join the group, because she was already legal. They had drugs on board and I wasn't happy about these men becoming responsible for my Olga so I stayed very close." When the ship arrived off Scotland we were all offloaded and brought to Loch Island. The living arrangements were terrible there, no electricity even, so the next day I insisted that Olga come with me to the mainland." Javek took out a cigarette and lit it with a shaking hand.

"And Mrs Finlay took her in?"

"Yes, I found work up at Castle House, thanks to Lorna and Lady Strathkellan. I love gardening. The laird lets me stay here, in the gatehouse, with the odd job man who is Albanian and one of the cruellest people I've ever come across. I hate him and as for the laird, he's just as bad." Javek's black eyes were now flashing with hatred; the tears had dried.

"Where is this Albanian man now?" asked Oliver trying to keep him talking.

"I don't know. He goes off at regular intervals, for which I thank my God in heaven."

"And Lord Strathkellan: what does he get up to?" At this Javek jumped up and moved across to the window, twitched the curtain and looked out. There were stars somewhere up there but here, where the trees encroached, the night was black.

"He is the wickedest of all," he announced with feeling, then turned around to face Oliver once more. "I have evidence of his wrong doing and if he is responsible for the disappearance of my Olga, I shall kill him."

Trying hard not to show too much reaction Oliver continued his questioning calmly.

"What does the laird do Javek?"

"Huh! What doesn't he do? The Albanian brings him young girls to play with when his wife is away. He drugs them so that he can do whatever he wishes. Then they are taken away again."

"And Lorna says you have this bag of evidence?"

"Yes."

"When did you last see Olga?"

"Over a week ago: two days before I heard about the body on the beach. She said she was going to meet her friends somewhere near Dromvaar. She said..." he started to get emotional again, so Olly took him over to the old sofa and sat down beside him.

"What did Olga say?" Oliver prompted. Javek stubbed out his cigarette and got out another one, lighting it unsteadily.

"She said that her friends had been found jobs and that they were all going away. She wanted to see them before they left." Then he disintegrated once more.

"I told her not to go... it's her, I know it's her, my Olga is dead. We love each other... we were going to be married and now... she's gone."

"Javek you have to try and keep yourself together. You can help me and I promise you that, whether she is dead or alive, we will find Olga. We will go together to identify the body; you have to be brave about that."

"I can't... I can't do that."

"Yes, you can, I will be right there beside you. We have to know if it's Olga or not Javek and the police will need her full name. The worst thing is the not knowing. Do you understand?" He nodded miserably.

"Now, is Lady Stratkellan at home yet?" He nodded again.

"Yes, her car came by just after I arrived back here. She waved. She's nice."

"What about the Albanian? Did he say how long he'd be gone for?"

"He left last night for two or three days or so he said."

"And when are you next expected at work here?"

"Tomorrow is my day off. I was going to spend it looking for Olga."

"OK. Now this is what we are going to do. Whatever the outcome we'll find Olga together. We'll leave here, in my car, as soon as it's light. I want you to come with me to see Colonel Neilsen. We'll take the bag of evidence with us. You will be quite safe and you needn't worry anymore about the Albanian. Now try and get some sleep, OK?"

"OK. Thank you. Dziękuję bardzo." The exhausted young man muttered meekly.

Oliver was awash with tea and mentally exhausted. He sat back and considered his difficult evening's work. Javek's revelations had tied up a lot of the loose ends. He wished someone would contact him. He needed to get all this to Guy somehow as, wherever he was, it was vital to their mission.

He looked across at Javek on the sofa, wrapped in a blanket. The sad thing was that the dead girl was almost certainly Olga. Sean had already identified the bright blue coat. He checked his mobile again – good finally there was a message, but from Alec. *'Guy has received latest, go carefully, Alec.'* Olly quickly texted him back: *'There is much more. See you later, Olly'.*

CHAPTER 29

Guy put his hand-held radio to his ear, raising his arm to indicate silence while he listened and repeated the conversation so the others could hear.

"Three adults - one a woman – walking - no obvious armoury – five, seven mins at most... Affirmative, loud and clear... OK follow with caution, see you shortly - Out." All four men inside the cottage melted into the shadows exactly as planned. Guy checked his watch once more. "Two minutes. Wait till all are inside. Take one each, as discussed. Julian, cover us all."

This was one of the best moments in life as far as Guy and Julian were concerned. All senses were finely tuned and alert. This was what they were trained to do and this was what they'd been waiting for. A flickering light showed through the window first, then they heard the voices just before the shuffling footsteps approached the cottage.

The door was flung open and two people came in, but not the third. There was a slight scuffling and grunting just outside as the man undid his trouser zip and urinated against the wall.

"Jesus what a stench! Let's hope the old eejit's gone," hissed the girl, sweeping the torch light around the floor to where a bundle in the shape of a man lay silent and still. She kicked the solid prone mass which Guy and Julian had expertly rearranged. There was no reaction at all.

"He's gone, the aul git. Dead as a door-nail. One less to worry about. Maybe my bealin brother has buggered off for good too, or even better drowned; he never was much of a swimmer, afraid of the water; silly bastard. Feckin stupid to let him go like that though. You two are bloody liabilities when you're fluthered. Make some tea, then you'd better go drop this good for nothing bag of filth in the water, nice and deep and well weighted, out on the loch... and be sure to shut the feckin door you dosser ..." the third man, irritated, came in mumbling curses in a foreign language and banged the door shut.

Blinding light instantly illuminated the scene. Shouts of alarm and brilliant flashes of movement as powerful bodies hurled themselves, around the room, with lightning speed! The door crashed open once more and it was all over in a matter of seconds without a single shot being fired. The young woman fought like a cat, swearing obscenities that even Guy was surprised to hear spat from a female mouth, let alone from the same chic individual he'd seen fleetingly in the Parisian nightclub.

"Shut the bitch up until she calms down," he ordered. A neck tie was forced over the woman's mouth and tied firmly at the back of her head. The two other foreign men appeared dazed and disorientated. For the moment they seemed to be in a state of shock and incapable of speech. Once all three were securely immobilized they were shoved inelegantly onto chairs and warned not to move or to speak. The girl went on kicking, her face purple with rage, so both ankles were then expertly tied to the chair legs. At that she gave up, but hatred, not fright, blazed from her cold black eyes. The two men sat in shocked disbelief, with terror etched clearly on both their dim faces, as they stared up at the menacing group in their dark camouflage gear and intimidating night vision goggles.

Guy moved away into the kitchen, with his walkie-talkie. The others heard him sending his report.

"Affirmative, yes all secure, as expected – the Irish woman and two men – come in... not sure of nationality as yet but almost certainly middle European. Send the boat back please, again no helicopter until we wind up the rest on the main land. Anything else yet from Oliver...? Negative..? Alright then we'll be on the beach, ready to embark in..." he again checked his watch. "One hour five... about the same time as it takes the boat to get there. Thank you... and out."

Julian fished for his cigarettes, looking at Guy as he lit up. He took a long drag and smiled. Guy grinned back and looked at the other four men standing around their incapacitated prisoners.

"Job well done. Very well done everybody."

❄

Oliver shook Javek awake.

"Javek! wake up, wake up. Does the Albanian have a motorbike?" The young man was immediately attentive and listening. They could hear a motorcycle approaching.

"Yes, that's him. I'd know that bike anywhere. But he was supposed to be away at least until tomorrow!"

"Well, he's back and about to arrive. OK now - keep calm. Get up! Quickly! and be getting yourself a drink. Make out that you have a girl from the village upstairs and say that's her car outside. He won't spot that it's rented in the dark." Javek appeared almost struck dumb with terror.

"I'm going to hide, now don't let me down. It'll be alright. Hurry now and make it look good!" The motorbike was slowing down to turn into the parking place. The burly thug barged into the house oblivious that his housemate might have been asleep. By the dim side light the Albanian saw a dishevelled looking Javek lying back on the sofa drinking a beer.

"Whose wheels?" he growled, looking around as he unsteadily approached the sofa. The Polish boy didn't answer but shakily put down his drink, looked up and offered a weak grin.

"What've you been up to then laddie?" With one hand the huge man grabbed the boy roughly by the shirt collar and hauled him up to stare into Javek's pale frightened face. With bloodshot eyes and foul, alcohol soaked breath the Albanian bent even closer coughing.

Javek, gagging, turned his face away then quickly remembered what he must do.

"You said you'd be away so I've got a girl up there," he answered, struggling to get out of the clinch and wondering what on earth Oliver planned to do. They were in a precarious situation. The Albanian had been drinking heavily, he was big and strong and Javek had seen him half kill a man in a brawl. Surely Oliver would be no match in strength and when he was found out Javek dreaded to think what might happen.

"You're a moron bringing her back here; you'll get us in trouble; or is it one of the lairds cast-offs, eh? She's out of it is she? You little bastard, been having a good time while I've been away have you, eh?" Javek nodded as best he could, the man turned his head to spit and Javek took the opportunity to wriggle out from under his clutches. "In that case I'll take a look myself. No doubt the little whore could do with a real man." He started to take off his belt in preparation and began up the stairs. Oliver moved out of his hiding place as soon as the man had gone and relocated, shrinking back into the shadows once more. There was a bellow from upstairs and thunderous footsteps coming back down.

"You fucking little liar. What's all this about then?" Javek was shaking uncontrollably. He'd been beaten up before by this giant of a man and now that the Albanian had found himself tricked he was even angrier.

As the man launched himself at Javek, Oliver appeared like a bullet out of nowhere, knocking the huge man off his feet and to the ground with an almighty crash. As he fell, the Albanian whacked his head hard on an old pine table, splitting the wood in two with the force. The crumpled man lay on the splintered debris without moving; just a long sigh exhaled from his ugly, open mouth. Like a deflating balloon, thought Javek as he stood unbelieving, staring down as if mesmerized at his hated adversary now motionless. But Olly had other concerns. He bent to feel for the big man's pulse then began to check for weaponry.

"Javek! He's not dead! Quick now; get a grip, he won't be out for long. Find me some rope or something and hurry up about it!"

"He carries a knife - at the back in his belt." The young man answered, pulling himself together.

"I've a tow rope in the car, I'll get it." Javek ran outside. It was getting light. He'd been in such a state when he arrived he hadn't locked it. But there was a hard frost, his hands were trembling and the boot wouldn't open. He kicked it once, twice - then it flew open. He ran back in, trailing the rope behind him.

They tied the Albanian securely and left him where he was, still unconscious on the floor. Olly noticed Javek couldn't resist giving the solid disgusting mass of humanity a good kick as they left the room. They retrieved the black sack from the Polish boy's Mercedes, then leapt into Beth's little car and headed down the hill at speed.

"Could we stop at Mrs Finlay's do you think? I feel badly about her and she's been kind to me and Olga."

"Yes alright," replied Olly, "but just a quick visit. I'll make my calls from there."

Lorna Finlay was already up and about although it was only six-thirty in the morning. She saw the car approaching and watched the two dishevelled looking men get out and head for her door. She had it open as they approached. "Good morning, the kettle's on, come right in. I'm that pleased to see you," she said, as if this was a perfectly normal and expected social visit, so early in the day. Lorna turned towards the kitchen smiling. She knew she'd been right to trust the young man Oliver. Her instincts about people had, so far, never let her down.

❋ ❋ ❋

CHAPTER 30

Douglas Macquire also was awake early and hoping for a call from Mac. Last evening he'd recognised the tough little Irish girl as soon as she'd walked through the door with the two foreign men. He'd quickly made sure that he served them himself. As he took their orders he'd had the chance to have a good look at all three. They were all, without doubt, a rough lot. Then, after he'd seen them settled, he'd gone into the back and rung Mac.

Ailsa had stayed another night over at Glencurrie. Dougie was a bit worried about that situation. She was becoming very fond of the Irish child. He was a nice lad and Dougie could see how well the boy was responding to care and kindness: he'd never had a chance before. But what on earth was going to happen when the poor bairn was handed over to the social services and how was that going to affect his wife?

As Dougie lay alone in his bed he couldn't help wondering whether, when all this was over, if it might be possible to foster or even adopt the boy; he thought it unlikely as both he and Ailsa, at forty-five and fifty, were bound to be considered too old. Ridiculous the way these things were done these days. He felt quite sure that a couple of lesbian pop singers would be thought more suitable. If Caroline the Colonel's wife had lived she would, Dougie thought, have managed to sort something out. She'd been a very special woman and had understood the ways of the world. Well, there was no harm in asking Colonel Alec about it at an appropriate moment and when Ailsa was out of the way. That's just what he'd do.

This decided, Dougie turned on his back and considered his day ahead. Fergus had brought in a great catch two days earlier, now safely in the freezer, so the pub had an excellent fish menu to offer. Ginger the chef was in his element. He'd be acting like the French before long and wanting rosettes or stars in recognition of his culinary skills. The pub seemed to be full to bursting most days, what with the influx of so many strangers dealing with the investigation. Life down in the port was going to be a bit dull for the rest of the winter when they'd all gone home. But hopefully there would still be plenty of business coming from the shooting lodges as had happened for the last few years. Christmas and the Hogmanay weren't long away. As it was, the quiet season never seemed long enough to get all the repair work done.

Douglas liked Colonel Alec's relations and his nephew's friends. They were a good crowd of fun, decent people. It didn't surprise him at all to hear that two of the party had official status within the special services branch of the army. Nobody had seen Guy, nor Julian, for a couple of days now; not since they'd gone out on that fishing trip with Fergus. The fisherman was saying nothing: he must have had been sworn to secrecy, just as he and Ailsa had been. This made Dougie feel quite important. Mac told him all that he could, but even so there was something bigger going on that deeply involved that Irish bitch who'd been so inhumane to the little boy. He was sure of it. He'd give a lot to know what she was up to. Still, he thought, Mac will ring when he can. I'd best get on. Dougie rolled out of bed, found the old worn slippers which always felt good to shuffle onto his feet first thing in the morning, then pulled on a thick Shetland cardigan, knitted by his mother and went downstairs to make a cup of tea.

❄

Back in the incident room, which was manned all through the night, constable MacDonald was having a hard time getting any information at all. He'd arrived back just after sun up and was sure that something had happened, but the senior people he knew either weren't around or seemed to have clammed up. He had tried to ensure that his news last night had been passed on to Guy. Mac felt it to be important for Guy to hear that the Irish girl was back and even about the young boy's short encounter with the D.C.S. It was becoming clear to him that she was in some way implicated in the young girl's murder, but for what motive they still had to find out. This was hard core stuff and Guy Hargreaves, wherever he was, needed to know what he was up against.

Mac decided to report to Colonel Neilsen again at eight o'clock. The Colonel had said that he was an early riser and to come at any time. Mac preferred to be at Glencurrie where he was treated with more respect. Also Mrs H made the best cup of tea, usually served with her famous biscuits. Then he received a phone call from Oliver which decided everything. He and a team were needed immediately up at Castle House lodge.

Marc was having a hard time, as well, trying to keep the girls happy. Last night they'd all gone to bed in an unsettled state; hardly surprising really. He also would have liked to get out of the lodge for a change of scene and to visit his uncle. But he felt it necessary to stay by the phone until all the girls were down. Alicia and Adriana were already up and sipping tea while they caught up on the early morning news. They wanted to see if there was anything about the murder. The other two weren't up yet, but he could hear Rose moving around, while Emma was having a lie in. Jess was looking after Poppy and giving her breakfast with Beth, in the kitchen. Five minutes later Rose appeared downstairs. Marc looked up as she walked into the snuggery where he was reading the paper, or pretending to.

"Hello Rose. Good morning. Anything more from Olly then?"

"Hello Mark. Yes, another text, just saying he's fine and on his way to Glencurrie,"

"What time did that come in?" Rose looked again at the mobile she was carrying.

"Quite early actually: about six forty-five this morning."

"Good Lord, the poor man must be exhausted." Marc got up having decided that he could now go.

"Why, has he had no sleep? Where has he been, Marc, do you know? I thought perhaps that he'd spent the night over at Glencurrie?"

"Yes, perhaps he did." Marc answered quickly. "I think I'll go over there too, if you're alright here?"

"Yes, we're fine. I'd just like some news from Guy and Julian." She dropped her voice. "I know Olly has only spent most of the night chatting up an old lady but Adriana and Alicia must be out of their minds worrying about Guy and Julian. Although, I must admit, they are both very good at hiding their real feelings."

"They're used to it," replied Marc going out. "They're in the sitting room watching the television. Go and have some breakfast."

Thankfully Rose had no idea what Olly had really been doing. Alec had kept Marc up to date and sent a message asking him to come over when the girls were down and he felt able to leave the lodge. Marc had been itching for Rose to come downstairs, so that he could go over to his uncle's house, as Olly also should be there by now. Mac would probably have arrived also and the policeman might have some more news from the incident room about how the others were faring.

Marc called to Alicia, to tell her where he was going and that he wouldn't be long, then grabbing a coat and scarf and much relieved, went out followed by the dogs who were asking longingly for a walk. He gave in and took them around the garden before letting them back into the house. It was a bracing morning, minus five on the thermometer on the wall beside the greenhouse. The bushes were all covered in a hoar frost and the bird bath was completely frozen over; he broke the ice with a loose stone. My

God, thought Marc, it must have been bloody cold if his two friends had spent these last nights on the deserted island, even if they were togged out in thermal gear.

They must be incredibly tough to survive unscathed in such conditions. Winter came early so far North.

Adriana had awoken early, her first thought was of her fiancé: where on earth were they? She had got up, drawn the curtains and looked out across the garden, over the moor and towards the sea. She was sure that they'd gone out on an operation. They would have at least rung in if they'd merely been helping coordinate things in the incident room. Perhaps they'd gone back to Paris. This was now the third day they'd been away. It was always the same: the first two days, with no word were OK, but after that she found it difficult to carry on normally or to concentrate on anything for long. She went to have a bath determined not to let worry get the better of her.

Lying in the warm scented soothing water Adriana considered her body. She'd slept surprisingly well and felt good. She missed Julian yet strangely enough was pleased to have had these last couple of nights to herself, just to revel in the possibility of something wonderful. She placed her hand on her stomach. Was there life there, as yet unconfirmed? Could she imagine a vague tingling sensation in her breasts? Were they just a tiny bit tender? She had no feelings of grouchiness before her period, due the next day, just an extreme longing for a miracle, but she had to calmly wait it out. Only time would tell.

Alicia regarded her friend as she sipped her tea in front of the television. Adriana looked surprisingly rested and peaceful considering their present situation. There was something about her that was different. Arri was definitely hiding something. Suddenly Alicia had it. Perhaps Adriana was pregnant. Perhaps the telephone calls had been to her doctor in the South, and they'd been having treatment. Wouldn't that be just something? Up here when they were all together? But she couldn't say anything. She'd just have to bite her tongue and not let Adriana know that she might have guessed her secret. No: surely she would have told her? After all they were really the closest of friends.

"Do you realise Arri, that we have been here ten days already?"

Adriana turned to look at Alicia. The news had finished, with nothing more from Scotland. There had probably been a curb on information for the time being while there was action taking place and now the weather man was doing his thing.

"Yes and with any luck, when the men arrive back we might all be able to get back on holiday for the next ten!"

"Three whole weeks. We never expected that did we?"

"No and if it hadn't been for that poor girl we wouldn't have even been given the extra week."

"Perhaps we should go to Skye for a few days to give Emma a break. Rose says it's beautiful and you've always wanted to go."

"Yes, I have." Adriana's face lit up. "If the men are busy here, all of us girls could go on our own. That would be even better for Emma: Poppy is fine here with Jess and Beth and of course with her father. What do you think?"

"Um, good idea. Actually it's an excellent idea and another thing: just to prolong things a bit more, I'd also quite like to stop in the Lake District for a night on the way South." There was no question about it, thought Alicia, Adriana looked completely different and she'd never looked so pink cheeked and healthy. She knew her friend so well; they'd been through much together. But is it possible to tell these things even before the result was known to be positive? Although perhaps it was something else altogether and the problem had now happily been resolved. Oh well, thought Alicia, hope springs eternal.

Rose walked in munching on an apple and holding a mug of coffee.

"We have a plan," Adriana announced. "As soon as the men are safely returned to us we think that we should leave them to it and all of us girls go across to Skye. What do you think?" Rose bit into her apple.

"Brilliant. I know where to stay. It's a lovely little hotel right on the water and I can show you everything. Olly and I didn't really have time to explore much. There's loads to see. We never got as far as the mountains and they're beautiful. Do you think Emma will come?"

"I think so." Alicia replied. "It would do her good as quite understandably she's been upset by all this murder business."

"It will be perfect, just the four of us. Let's just hope that the situation here has been sorted and that the men will merely be busy winding up the details. Then we'll be able to leave with peace of mind."

Adriana was thrilled with the plan as it was just what she needed also: to get away while she prayed for confirmation of a small miracle. First of all she'd go by herself up to the little chapel on the moor and say some prayers for real.

CHAPTER 31

Marc was just setting off to Glencurrie, when Fergus's old truck came roaring up the drive with his two passengers. The girls had all rushed to the window and then had spilled out onto the drive to welcome home both Julian and Guy. The men looked weary and none to pristine, but they seemed to be in high spirits due, apparently, to the successful outcome of their mission, although they soon made it clear that they weren't intending to hang around for long at the lodge; a quick shower, a change of clothes and they would go to join the others up at the house.

Alicia was sitting in the armchair by the window of their bedroom, silent in thought, while her husband made himself human once more. Guy stepped out of the shower, wrapped a towel around his waist and went into their bedroom. He knew she'd be there. Ever sensitive to his struggle in changing gear between mission mode and normal life, she never hurried or worried him, but just quietly waited. As he approached she looked up and smiled.

"By the look on your face, everything went according to plan, I imagine?"

"Yes." He said and held open his arms.

"You must be exhausted," Alicia whispered, savouring his hard lean body and wishing that they could disappear from sight for an hour or two, "and I know you have to go."

"Yes," he repeated, "but the adrenalin's still on the run so it won't take long and a small delay won't hurt." He scooped her up in his arms and carried her to their bed.

Adriana sat watching from their bed as Julian got dressed. He was still somewhere else and hadn't returned to her. The job needed finishing and he wouldn't relax enough to let her in until the operation was fully accomplished. Hopefully, by this evening things would be different. She hated this time, when after the initial relief of their safe return, it took a while for them to get back onto an even keel once more. However hard she tried to understand, Adriana still felt totally excluded and hurt because of it. She broke the silence.

"I know that you will be going off to Glencurrie shortly and that it will still take some time to conclude things, but Alicia and I thought that we'd get out of your hair while you do that and perhaps take a trip to Skye. Emma will come. It would be a good break for her and Rose knows the ropes because she's already been there."

Julian looked up from lacing his boots. She saw his face flicker as his thoughts returned just long enough to take in what she'd just said. Not as patient as Alicia, Adriana pushed the point.

"What do you think? Might that not be a good idea?" Julian crossed to the window, opened it and lit a cigarette. He knew he should give it up but it always gave him that kick start when he most needed it. He looked across to where Adriana lay. She was such a distraction because she had such sex appeal. He'd take her away and have her all to himself for a bit when this was all over, but for now he mustn't let his thoughts wander - it wasn't their time again - yet.

"Yes, it is a good idea. I need to concentrate still and it would be fun for you after all the worry we've put you through. Olly says it's a beautiful island and you could suss out the fishing for me!" Julian smiled, back with her for a fleeting moment and then turned to look from the window once more. He took a long, last drag of the cigarette and leant out of the window to stub it, half smoked, on the grey stone. He crossed to the bed. Adriana smiled and held her breath. Would he or wouldn't he?

"Come my darling, let's go down. There'll be time for us later." Adriana sighed, took his hand and together they went to join the others.

Alec, Olly and Javek were holed up in the study when the others arrived at Glencurrie. Mrs H was her usual bustling self and delightedly showed them in, as she informed them that the nice Polish boy thought her biscuits the best he'd ever eaten.

News was exchanged and Guy wanted to hear Javek's story again but at first hand. The young man had managed to pull himself together after the horrendous night which he and Olly had just shared. But he remained adamant that he wouldn't identify the young woman's body. As he knew about Sean's identification of Olga's bright blue coat, he was beginning to come to terms with the prospect that the murdered girl was, in all likelihood, his Olga.

The marine authorities and the Coast Guard had all been alerted and asked to pass on any information regarding Russian or other unusual shipping in the area. The Albanian, who had been brought in by a team led by constable MacDonald, was in police custody being intensively interviewed. For Guy and Julian another trip to Paris was on the cards, but how to deal with the laird was the next immediate problem. Lord Strathkellan appeared to have gone to Edinburgh on business for a couple of days, leaving his poor wife in a miserable state of confused worry. Eileen Mcloughlin her long time friend, who owned the mill and who hated Finola's husband, went up to Castle House to keep her company and to commiserate.

Airports and departure stations of all kinds had been circulated with the laird's description. Guy wondered if the Scottish lord might make a dash for France. Inverness was probably the easiest and the nearest way across the water from Dromvaar. The man had plenty of money and many wealthy contacts. Guy hoped that the authorities had been quick enough. The last thing anybody wanted was for the wretched man to disappear and, if the truth be told, he'd really like to find the vile man himself.

Olly took Javek over to Mrs Finlay's cottage where he was to stay until further instructed. Guy and Julian went once more down to the incident room where Oliver would meet them. Lady Strathkellan was about to arrive for an interview, escorted by her good friend and protector.

*

Life at the lodge was quieter and returned to a semblance of normality over the weekend. The men rested while they had the opportunity before their next foray and the girls made their own plans for the following week. They booked rooms at the hotel Rose had suggested for two or perhaps three nights and planned to set off early on the Monday morning with Alicia driving the 4x4. The men were sad to see them leave, but at the same time relieved: Julian and Guy because they wanted to finish their job unencumbered; Oliver because he hoped to be included in the wind-up program; and Marc as he thought it a very good thing for his wife to be away from all the drama for a few days. This holiday had not turned out as anybody had expected.

It was a clear crisp morning and the journey through beautiful mountainous country of the Highlands to the Kyle of Lochalsh didn't take long. They stopped for a snack in a pub at lunch-time, feeling almost as if they'd been let out of school. As Alicia drove across the spectacular bridge to Skye all their spirits lifted. It was great to leave all the problems and anxiety behind and, thought Adriana, by the time they returned she would be well past her due date.

The little hotel, on the water, was just as Rose had described. It was the most perfect location. The rooms they were given, separate from the main part of the house, were all four looking out across the beautiful Sound towards the Isle of Ornsay, with its lighthouse proudly advertising the island to all passing sea traffic. In the far distance a range of mountains graced the horizon, glowing pink in the afternoon light. These were the distant Knoydart Hills, Rose announced, who, now considered herself extremely knowledgeable. That evening the girls were all in their element. Everybody felt this hotel to be something special, a haven of peace in which to hide away and as far as Emma and Adriana were concerned – just what the doctor ordered. The restaurant had delicious food and charming staff. The sitting area was arranged into cosy little nooks to snuggle into both before and after dinner. Bookshelves held an assortment of interesting reading: after dinner, Rose found the enchanting little book that she'd already read about the otters. She handed it to Emma.

"Olly and I went down to see them one evening when the water was calm and the weather gentle. So we must all go to see them together."

"That's a lovely idea. Let's get the forecast for tomorrow. I'll go and ask at reception," Adriana replied with enthusiasm and got up to leave the room.

"If it's not raining tomorrow – it does apparently rain a lot here – I vote we walk to this other hotel Olly and I found, for lunch. We had tea there. The owner is a renowned chef, who sometimes holds cookery classes, so of course the food is wonderful. It's about a two hour excursion. What do you think?" asked Rose thoroughly excited about the whole trip.

"That's a great idea, but what about you Emma? Do you think that might be a bit much for you?" asked Alicia characteristically thoughtful.

"Absolutely not," Emma answered quickly, "as long as we go fairly slow and if I don't want to trudge back, I can always rest while you all walk home. Then you can come and collect me with the car." Adriana re-appeared brandishing a printed sheet. She looked at all the expectant faces.

"Guess what? Tomorrow the sun is actually coming out to visit for most of the day! How about that?"

"How brilliant, I can't believe our luck. What a happy thing!" Rose, all pink in the face from the wine at dinner, was grinning from ear to ear.

"Yes, it is, and I'm going to have an early night? I'm more than ready for my bed. What time shall we meet for breakfast?"

"Let's be lazy – nine to nine-fifteen perhaps, if that's alright. I take a while to get going in the morning I'm afraid." Emma said.

"Good, OK sleep tight everybody." Adriana yawned and went to retrieve her coat. Rose immediately followed suit, for once worn out by her own enthusiasm, leaving Emma and Alicia sitting together studying the little book about the otters.

"That's the first time that I've known Adriana be the one to suggest going to bed," Alicia laughed, silently wondering once more.

"Maybe she and Julian overdid it last night," Emma answered.

"Yes maybe, I hope so." Alicia agreed thinking otherwise. One of the staff appeared to ask if they wanted anything more to drink. Emma turned to the smiling woman, her eyes sparkling.

"Do you know something?" she asked. "I have never ever felt so cosy comfortable and happy in any other hotel as I do here with you."

"My friend is right," Alicia agreed. "We feel we're in another world. Your hotel is nothing short of magical."

The woman laughed.

"Well, please come back, you are most welcome," she said, "but you are right, of course. We all love being here. Even when the rain and mist comes down, there's still a mystical allure and many stories just waiting to be told!" she smiled again. "Now what may I bring you?"

❄

A little later, Alicia and Emma stepped out into the cool night together and walked down to the edge of the water near their rooms.

"What a lovely place this is. Perhaps it really is enchanted. You can definitely feel the ages past. Do you think there's a friendly ghost?" Emma whispered, taking a deep breath. Alicia stood still beside her, in the quiet night air, peering out across the Sound. Not a breath of wind stirred and the water hardly rippled.

"Yes, I wouldn't be at all surprised and I'd like to hear the legends. It's so romantic; even the stars seem to sparkle brighter here than I've seen anywhere else."

"Quite honestly, everything seems brighter now we're away from all that horrible drama and we are a long way North. I really do feel peace of mind for once."

"I agree and I have never felt so sleepy. It's the sea air."

"Me too," Emma responded, "but that's just the baby." Alicia turned to Emma, her blue eyes gleaming in the light of the moon.

"Let's make a wish, here and now, just the two of us?"

"OK," replied Emma yawning, "then let's go to bed and sleep for two days! You go first."

Alicia wished with all her heart that, when they all returned here together, Adriana would have a child as well as a husband and Emma wished to come back with Marc and two children after the safe arrival of a little boy.

Adriana lay in her warm bed snuggled up with the hot water bottle that Rose had cleverly insisted they all bring. She experienced no usual premenstrual symptoms; just a sense of calm, contented relief. First and foremost, Julian was through another mission which seemed to have had a successful outcome, as far as she could tell. Also she felt strong feelings of kinship with Emma. How could that be, after what she'd done? The strange thing was that in her heart she thought that Emma might even have understood her desperation and possibly even forgiven her, had she known of the betrayal.

Adriana made two decisions, in her mind. One was that, if she hadn't conceived a child ten days before, then that was it – her one and only opportunity. There must never be another, at least not with the same lover. The second was that, should she be lucky enough to be pregnant, she would determinedly consider the baby to be Julian's and never more dwell upon that stolen afternoon. They had been told not to give up hope and that there was an outside chance. So that was how it must be, for all their sakes. A settled, all enveloping tiredness overwhelmed her and even before her other two friends came across to their rooms, with an arm cradling her stomach protectively, Adriana was soon fast asleep.

CHAPTER 32

The Irish girl proved a hard nut to crack, as were her sidekicks, all of whom, although under secure guard, seemed almost relieved to be fed and watered in relative comfort, compared to the facilities they had endured on Loch Island. But, with a translator by his side, the frail elderly Ukranian recovered enough in hospital to haltingly croak out a few of the crucial details, filling in the group's most recent movements and that of the laird. He was also able to describe both the Albanian ogre and the girl Olga. Although all the girls from the last intake appeared to be beautiful, dark and of similar height; there was no doubt about Lord Strathkellan's identity. There was no word from any of the various authorities involved as to the man's whereabouts, but at his wife Finola's interview she had said that lately her elusive husband often went to France. In all likelihood the errant lord had slipped the net. So Guy and Julian set out for Paris convinced that, with highly capable contacts and colleagues there, this was where he was likely to be found. Their French counterparts were hot on the girl trafficking racket between European countries: there was an ongoing operation already in progress. Shared intelligence had numerous likely suspects under surveillance, including the two Asian dealers seen on that previous occasion in the nightclub. The laird was already on the list of known acquaintances. The French were delighted with the extra input and help from Scotland.

"We'll visit that club again tonight. It should be organized," Guy said as they flew, with two other agents, across the channel in a small aircraft arranged by their army superiors. He turned his head to see the other two men on the far side of the plane, also deep in conversation.

"Good, let's just hope that the bloody Scot has headed in the same direction and not made his escape further afield," answered Julian gloomily.

"Yes, but it may take several visits to the club, before he shows himself. He may well lie low for a bit."

"We'll need some English speaking women with us then: as a cover."

"I'll ask for that also, but hopefully they should have thought of it by now, anyway."

"Did you speak to Alicia last night?"

"Yes, they're all fine and pleased to be on Skye and away from all of this, I think. How are things with Adriana?"

"Better. Arri has always wanted to go 'Over the Sea to Skye'. Remember what she said when we first planned this trip, in your club, in London?" Guy nodded, thinking that little did they know then what an unexpected and traumatic holiday it would turn out to be. "She's much happier and seems to have accepted our rather uncertain future."

"I doubt it." Guy replied. "She just doesn't want you distracted at the moment. You're an idiot; marry her anyway, before someone else does. Adriana is fun and sexy. She's gorgeous. She'll be snapped up by somebody else if you delay much longer."

"I hear what you say. I know you're right but I'm still thinking about it, wondering if it would be fair on her though. You know the children thing. But look, I don't want to talk about it now. We're about to land." The steward appeared with their jackets then went to sit with the rest of the crew.

"Very well." Answered Guy, "but don't say I didn't warn you. That girl is a knockout. She turns heads wherever she goes and, God alone knows why, she actually loves you!" He dug Julian in the ribs and was grinning good naturedly, easing the tension. "And, by the way, I meant what I said – you really are an idiot!" Julian also was laughing as he fastened his seat belt.

The little plane landed smoothly, taxied away from the main airport and came to a standstill the far side of a huge covered hangar where a large, dark, unmarked car was waiting to meet them. They were taken to the headquarters for French external security, in the twentieth arrondissement, where meetings were lined up with people from both interior and exterior intelligence agencies. The two agents accompanying them on the plane, were also to work with the French team, providing backup during each evening's manoeuvre. The surveillance team, already in place, had further useful knowledge of the activities of suspect club members.

The plan was set for that very evening. The French had done a good job and had produced two attractive English speaking women agents for company. Dinner at a restaurant near the club would mark the beginning of the operation. Meanwhile Guy and Julian were to go to their hotel to rest, consolidate info and to prepare for whatever was to happen next.

❄

Luckily, breakfast was a moveable feast as both Emma and Adriana overslept. Rose and Alicia were already in the restaurant tucking in to cereal and fruit juice when they finally appeared.

"Hello you two - you must have slept really well!" Alicia, evidently, was full of joie de vivre this morning. "The kitchen was about to close so I thought you'd like scrambled eggs Emma. I ordered kippers for you Arri, I know you love them. Come and sit down."

"Yuck! No thank you very much, not this morning. I don't think I could cope with fish... not after all that wine last night," Adriana answered quickly, grinning self-consciously. She would never have thought she'd be glad to feel slightly queasy but perhaps it was just psychological.

"You didn't have that much, did you?" Alicia caught an unusual look flick fleetingly across Adriana's face. She was embarrassed and Alicia's suspicions were becoming more apparent. "Oh never mind, I'll eat them," interrupted Emma quickly. "I'm well past that awful sickness stage. You can have my scrambled eggs, Arri. We all need sustenance before we set out on this marathon trek."

The four young women walked at a leisurely pace. They could already make out their goal, the larger hotel at the far end of the Loch na Dal. The track made easy walking: the turf was surprisingly green and springy. The vivid scenery was perfection. The water in the sound was ultramarine blue except where, nearer the shore, it reflected all the bright autumnal colourings from the trees and flowers on the bank edge; orange, yellows and red. As they walked alongside the loch where it crept inland, away from the main sound of Sleat, the water beside them became ever stiller; the reflections were so clear that you couldn't be sure which had the best clarity: the real thing or the mirror image. An occasional fish rose, with a sudden splash, the droplets sparkling as they caught the light, the disturbed water expanding into rippling circles before settling to merge and vanish from sight. The distant Cuillin hills to the West appeared, in perspective, to be set layered in different colours, pink then deepening purple to a final misty charcoal. There was no sign of habitation except for the hotel ahead and the odd far-away little white croft house. A few sheep grazed amongst the heather, their wool coats thicker than any seen in the South.

"I wish we'd brought the dogs," remarked Adriana, "I miss Fudge and he would have loved all this." She waved her hand around indicating all the space.

"I know, but it was nice for Poppy to have them at the lodge while we're away and he probably would have chased the sheep, disgraced himself and got us into a lot of trouble," Emma replied, stopping to shade her eyes against the glare and scanning the vast empty countryside. "Do you think the red deer ever come as low as this?"

"Yes, possibly, I should think they come down at certain times of the year, to forage for food, when the Cullin hills are covered in snow. Most likely now they'd still be higher up, where there are no people at all," answered Adriana. "Come on, I'm hungry and you must be too Emma. After all, you're eating for two."

"Thanks," replied Emma "But I don't want to get too huge too quickly. Poppy was big enough."

❉

Lunch was scrumptious - especially good after all the exercise. The hotel was smart and the staff ultra efficient. Their waitress, the girls decided, was one of the most beautiful girls they'd ever seen. None of them could work out where she came from, so Adriana couldn't resist asking her. The girl laughingly told them, in very reasonable English, that she was Polish.

"How long have you been here?" Adriana asked.

"Oh, not very long," the young girl said moving quickly away. She obviously didn't want to be questioned further.

"Adriana, you are so nosy; you've frightened her off," Emma reprimanded quietly. "Poor girl; it's none of our business!"

"No, but why would a beautiful girl like that be working as a waitress miles from anywhere?"

"Because she probably likes being here on this lovely island," Alicia said, taking the wine bottle from the ice bucket and refilling their glasses.

"She could have a wonderful job modelling in London or Paris," continued Adriana determinedly.

"But she might not want to do that!" argued Rose. "For heaven's sake Arri, you're like a dog with a bone."

"OK, OK let's have pudding. I'm still hungry." Magically, the girl reappeared with the menus.

Emma didn't want to walk back, so Adriana said she'd stay to keep her company and wait for the others to return with the car. They sat in a bay window and watched Alicia and Rose setting off once more across the well tended garden. The light was already changing as the day slipped gently on towards dusk. Their two friends waved as they went out of sight and Adriana ordered more coffee. She turned to glance at Emma who looked the picture of health. Her lovely long dark hair shone and her clear skin needed no makeup. Adriana felt warm and contented! 'Sleek as a cat' came to mind and she longed for this feeling of well-being to continue. She smiled across at Emma, wishing she could share her thoughts. Emma returned the smile.

"It seems so far away here from all that hideous trouble, doesn't it? I just don't know how you and Alicia can remain so calm when the men are out on a mission."

"Well, I suppose we're used to it. It's a bit like being an army wife although not as bad. After all, they could be months away in Afghanistan. As it is, when they go off it's not usually for more than a week at most. I think that their main task is dealing with emergencies of one kind or another."

"Don't they ever talk about it?"

"No, not much. It's not allowed and I prefer it that way as I'd rather not know when the operation is dangerous and they're in the middle of it. As we all work in London, sometimes Alicia and I stay with each other, if we feel the need, but we're usually alright and just try to get on with our lives the best way we can. Now, with this murder up here having upset everything, I'm just glad that we are all together."

"Well, I think that you are both rather wonderful," Emma said, smiling at the waitress, who was hovering with the new pot of coffee.

"Let's move and sit beside the fire. Is that alright?" she asked of the girl, who seemed a little distracted.

"Yes, of course, please follow me." She settled them by the fire and poured the coffee. She lingered for a minute afterwards as if wanting to ask something.

"Excuse me, but are you from around this area?"

"No, no," replied Emma." We are all from the South of England but we are staying with friends near the village of Dromvaar. I don't expect you know it as it's quite a long way away from here." The young girl let out a tiny gasp. Then seemed quickly to collect herself.

"Oh yes, I have heard of it. I hear it's a lovely area. I'm going off now so I hope you have a good time on Skye. Please come and see us again." She smiled rather nervously and turned to go. Once she was out of earshot Adriana leaned forward.

"There's something about that girl: I don't know what it is and I can't quite put my finger on it."

"What on earth do you mean, Arri?"

"Did you see the way she reacted when you said we came from Dromvaar? She couldn't wait to escape!"

"Yes, but maybe she's heard about the murder. The news must have reached Skye by now, surely. She probably didn't want to say anything for fear of spoiling our day. Anyway, I've got to disappear for a minute. I won't be long."

The ladies room was spotless with a small arrangement of roses on a side table and very up-market liquid soap and hand cream. It was a stylish hotel, well run and comfortable thought Emma, judging by all these special little luxuries. She left the wash room and went for a quick explore of the rest of the hotel. She picked up a brochure, with some leaflets advertising the cookery classes, which on another visit might prove tempting. Luckily the small hotel shop was shut, but Emma could see through the glass door some appetising looking treats and presents to buy. The barman was busy tidying up the area while the Maitre d'hôtel was seeing off the last of his lunch customers. The dining room was already being made up for dinner. The interior furnishings were elegant and tasteful, with tartan carpets adding to the very Scottish atmosphere. Everywhere was immaculate and the flower arrangements were as good as any Emma had ever seen.

As she finished her full ground floor tour, Emma bumped into their lovely waitress by a side door, just as she was leaving for her afternoon off.

"Hello again," said Emma, "thank you so much for looking after us all. I hope that you have a bit of a rest now as it must be such hard work."

"Oh no, it's not hard work at all. I love being here. The people are all so nice to me. It's very different from where I was before."

"Good," replied Emma determined not to overdo it and ask where exactly she had come from. "That's great to hear. What is your name?"

"Oh, it's... it's Eva, Eva is my name." Her eyes were startled. The girl was uncomfortable about being asked her name and she seemed to have to think for a second, almost as if she were going to say something quite different. There was no doubt about it.

"Well Eva, good luck. Perhaps we'll come to visit you once more before we go back to Dromvaar."

"Oh yes, please do come back. Er...," Eva looked quickly around, to see if anyone was around and listening, Emma noticed.

"Excuse me, but we heard about the dreadful murder in Dromvaar – you don't by any chance know who it was do you?" Eva appeared for a moment almost frightened. "You see, it didn't say on the news; they just said a... a body was found...," surprised by the question, Emma watched the lovely face as she answered.

"Yes, I think it was the body of a quite young person. A very pretty girl in fact." Eva let out an involuntary cry of horror; her face looked stricken as her hand flew to her mouth.

"How sad. Oh how terribly sad!" she gasped, her eyes staring in her white face. She was clearly upset. Emma put out her hand and touched her arm kindly.

"You mustn't take it to heart Eva, these horrible things do happen from time to time and, I do agree, it is especially awful when it's a young person." They were both distracted by a voice calling from outside.

"Oh! Oh, that's just my friend, she also works here. We're going to catch the bus to the town," Eva said pulling herself together. "Goodbye and thank you." Emma held open the door.

"Now go and have fun: think of nice things; goodbye." Eva smiled politely and ran out.

"Come on Olga," the friend called once more, "hurry up, for goodness sake. We're late." Eva glanced back uncertainly, or perhaps almost pleadingly thought Emma, who merely returned the wave as if she hadn't heard and went back in.

The door swung shut and Emma stood for a minute contemplating and re-enacting the last few minutes. This was slightly odd – Eva, Olga? Or perhaps both? Or even a second or maybe a nick-name? Had she misheard? Heavens, thought Emma I'm beginning to behave just like Adriana who always jumps at the slightest suspicion of intrigue. Nonetheless it was a bit strange and worth discussing with her friend.

But when Emma returned to their sitting place Adriana was fast asleep by the fire. It was unlike Arri to sleep in the daytime and she didn't like to disturb her.

When the others arrived with the car, there was much hilarity, as they made their arrangements for the evening. So Emma soon forgot all about her interesting meeting with their waitress - until very much later, that is.

❄ ❄ ❄

CHAPTER 33

Guy and Julian decided to walk to the restaurant.

"I have to say, this is the first time in this job we've gone on a blind date." Julian stopped in a doorway and stooped to light another cigarette. There might not be another opportunity this evening. Guy stopped also and waited while Julian cupped his hands around the lighter. They walked on, matching their stride. It was a fine evening, no rain, cool but not bracing like Scotland and with just a gentle breeze. They hadn't even bothered with overcoats; they'd be too cumbersome if they had to move swiftly. Julian, as usual, had complained about wearing a tie, but Guy had insisted it to be necessary. He didn't want any bother at the club later. They had to blend with all the select company, be ever watchful, and at the same time appear to be enjoying themselves with their long time girlfriends who they would only just have met.

"I'm mightily relieved to have had to sign the Official Secrets Act, way back at the beginning," Guy replied with a chuckle, "as I should hate to feel it necessary to tell Alicia of an excellent dinner eaten in one of the best restaurants in Paris with two attractive French girls for company."

"I know what you mean, but I might add that I'm not too keen to be relying on woman for this particular assignment."

"I don't think we need worry. I have been assured that they are the best and that they are well briefed," Guy answered. He was really looking forward to finishing this job. However if, as they had thought, the rot had spread further afield and several more countries were involved, then it could well take much longer than expected. Thankfully their women were perfectly happy where they were. He had encouraged them to stay a fourth night on Skye.

They were all so lucky to have the lodge to return to and not to be renting some other place at vast expense, as had first been planned.

"Alright, we have arrived. The table is booked, I should think we're first, but the girls should be here soon." They were meeting late, on purpose, so that it wouldn't be too long before moving on to the club. The restaurant was full and buzzing. It was one of the most popular eating places for all age groups. Their table was inconspicuously in the corner facing the door from where it would be easy to recognize the French agents as they came in. The head waiter escorted the two men to their table. Guy immediately asked for the wine waiter and ordered a bottle of Sauvignon. It had only just been poured when he looked up to see the arrival of the two women.

"There they are, on time and both very well turned out."

"Christ! They look quite different," muttered Julian, slightly awed and leaning forward to get a better look.

"Of course they do. They've done their hair, made up their faces and dressed the part for the evening. B'Jesus, they've certainly done us proud," Guy finished under his breath, getting up as he prepared to welcome the two young women who were being escorted towards them between the tables.

"Yes, but I'd rather they weren't quite so attractive," mumbled Julian dubiously, also jumping up.

"Well they are what they are - so make the best of it. I certainly shall," replied Guy firmly as the two agents approached.

"Bonsoir Monique," said Guy to the blonde and, "hello darling," as he kissed the redhead with feigned affection, only just missing her lips. Julian stepped forward, also kissing Monique perfunctorily on both cheeks and smiling at Hélen. He was naturally a shy man with the opposite sex and slightly tongue-tied in front of these two chic, confident, French women. All dressed up, they just weren't the same two rather insignificant girls he'd met earlier at head-quarters. They all sat down and the waiter poured two more glasses of the Sauvignon.

"And how was your day?" Guy turned to Hélen, raising his glass.

"Tres bon, very good thank you Guy." She had a particularly seductive way of pronouncing Guy's name, using a hard G and an 'i' instead of a 'u' as only the French can, shortening his name even further, Julian noticed, as he studied the two women. Monique was petite with short blond hair. She was extraordinarily curvaceous for one so little. How on earth did such a small person get through the tough physical training to hold down this type of job, he couldn't help thinking? But she had to be a lot stronger than she looked. She had tiny hands with perfect, long, deep pink finger nails. She wore a tight fitting black dress with very high heels; to make up for what she lacked in height. Also there was something he'd worried about earlier at the office: Monique was very young. Far too young for this sort of work, Julian considered, feeling rather protective. Hélen was older, tall and slim with beautiful thick, long red-gold hair. She had surprisingly dark eyes, which made Julian wonder if her lovely head of hair was actually dyed. If so it was extremely well done. When they'd met before she'd worn it swept back in a pony tail, now it was over her shoulders hanging loose in all its gleaming glory. Hélen wore a dark red silk dress with a wide black patent leather belt and shoes. Both were expertly made up and, as intended, seemed completely different out of their practical work clothes.

The four well trained and expertly briefed agents settled into an evening which, to all intent and purpose, alien eyes could only have seen as a perfectly normal social occasion between friends talking a well used mix of English and French. The food was good, the company both attractive and enjoyable and Julian soon realised that there was much more to the little Monique than he had at first thought. At the appropriate time they moved on to the night club. Entrance had already been arranged and another table booked, in Guy's name, which would be held for the entire evening. A French agent, in disguise, had been taken on as a waiter with all the necessary qualifications. He would act as liaison with the team outside: his job was to look after them during the evening.

The noise level was acceptable and the music tasteful as Guy and Julian had found at their last visit. This club was the elite new in place. Paris never sleeps so, even though it was eleven o'clock, there were still empty tables. All four professional people, now in well rehearsed work mode knew that they could be in for a very long wait which could, quite possibly, run into days. As yet, there was no way of knowing.

❄

Oliver and Marc went to the pub. It had been a busy day. Olly had spent much of it down at the incident room with Javek. The Polish boy had seen his Olga's coat and he was now convinced that his girlfriend was dead. Oliver took him back to stay with Lorna Finlay as the distraught young man didn't want to be on his own. As she saw Olly out to his car, Lorna told him that she was quite prepared to identify the body herself, as Javek had continued to refuse and was in no fit state to do it. But Mac had said that as Mrs Finlay had heart problems the Detective Chief Inspector was hoping that the Ukranian would help when he was a little more recovered and released from hospital. He'd obviously also been very fond of Olga.

The Irish woman had continued to remain stubbornly silent but the Albanian had sung like a canary. The captive group had now been moved to a secure location within Barlinnie prison on the outskirts of Glasgow and were undergoing intense interrogation. The brains behind the whole girl racket seemed to be based in Paris with, it was thought, lesser branches of the sinister dealings in Belgium and the Netherlands. Except for continuing surveillance of shipping in the North Western coastal region of Scotland, intelligence concentration now moved away from Dromvaar to both London and the continent. The various international agencies involved were hoping to track down the bosses, Lord Strathkellan and as many of the unfortunate girls as possible.

Fergus was at the bar when Marc and Oliver walked in. They sat with him and discussed everything except the drama that they'd all been living through. Mac also appeared, off duty, to join them. The local policeman was pleased as punch for having successfully brought the Albanian in to custody. Dougie was in his element with the restaurant as busy as ever.

"So Fergus, how are things going with our lovely cook?" asked Marc teasingly when there was a pause in the conversation. Dougie, carefully pouring a whisky for a customer over the far side of the bar, answered for him.

"The man's smitten, don't you know?" The customer, a regular, turned to wink at Fergus who laughed good-naturedly.

"Beth's special," said Fergus, not rising, grinning then taking a large gulp of his own beer completely un-fazed.

"What are you going to do when we all go home?" Oliver asked concerned for him. These two people really seemed to have something worthwhile going on between them.

"Get her up here for her holidays, all being well," he answered determinedly: "but we'll see. The lassie has a mind of her own!" he chuckled.

"Well, good luck to you and for what it's worth, I think that Dougie's right Fergus. Beth is smitten," said Marc, picking up his drink and getting to his feet. Then he leaned towards the fisherman, placing his free hand on Fergus's shoulder.

"We're going to have dinner here, so Beth is free this evening, if you want to collect her up for a drink!"

"It's already arranged, thank you" replied Fergus with twinkling eyes. He looked at his watch. "At the moment she's helping Jess highlight her hair, or some such thing!"

They said goodnight to both the fisherman and the policeman and went to their table in the corner of the restaurant, as far away as possible from all the noise around the bar.

"This is a treat, what with one thing and another," Olly said, feeling more relaxed for a change.

"Yes, some holiday it's turned into. Where the hell do you think Julian and Guy have got to now?"

"God alone knows. Anyway, the girls are alright and all together. You've certainly done your bit, so let's have a decent bottle of wine while the goings good!"

Later that evening, up at Glencurrie, Ailsa sat talking to her mother. Something was bothering her daughter and Mrs H thought she knew what it was. It was Sean. Ailsa was worried sick about what was going to happen to him when this drama was all over. Mary Macquire and Jean Haddington had already discussed the situation. Jean was going to talk to the Colonel to see if, with all his contacts, he could help. It was quite apparent that, as the child had no relatives except for the dreadful Irish sister, for whom Sean had never once asked and who would surely be going to prison, Ailsa and Douglas should be allowed to adopt the child. Mrs H and Mary were going to do everything in their power to see that happen.

✳ ✳ ✳

CHAPTER 34

"Let's go to visit Dunvegan Castle," Alicia suggested two days later at breakfast. "We've seen your otters Rose and explored the black and red Cuillin Hills. Here, at the hotel, they say that Dunvegan is the best of all the Scottish castles."

"Good idea," said Adriana, "I'm on for it and it's a lovely day again." As far as Adriana was concerned, after passing her due date, every day following was getting progressively better and she was happy to do whatever the others wanted. She was beginning to feel on the top of the world as she had never ever been this late. She wondered whether it was still too early to buy a pregnancy test. She thought that you needed to wait a fortnight, so perhaps she would give it a bit longer.

"How about you Emma – how do you feel?" Emma was looking pensive.

"I've just remembered something. I can't believe how forgetful I've become with this," she answered patting her stomach then looking up at Adriana.

"What? What did you forget?"

"You remember the pretty Polish girl who waited on us at the smart hotel, where we had lunch on our first day and you Arri thought there was something not quite right about her being there?"

"Yes," said Adriana, "I do, but what about her?"

"Well, after Alicia and Rose left, we had some more coffee and then I went to the ladies' room. On my way back to where we were sitting, I went on a bit of an explore of the rest of the hotel and I bumped into our lovely waitress again, just as she was leaving...."

"And?" prompted Adriana interrupting and sitting up.

"I asked her name and she hesitated before saying it was Eva, then repeating it, almost as if she'd had to think about it. That was one thing, but the really odd thing was that she had a friend outside, waiting for her, who called out clearly, 'Olga! Come on Olga, or we'll miss the bus'... don't you think that's a bit strange?" There was silence all around the table. They all stared at Emma. Then Rose piped up.

"And they think that the murdered girl, although not yet identified, was not only beautiful but middle European and also possibly called Olga?"

"Mary mother of everybody! Are you sure about that?"

"Yes, I overheard Olly talking to Julian."

"Bloody Hell! That's a bit too much of a coincidence, isn't it?" breathed Adriana.

"Yes, it is. Why did you think there was something not quite right about her Arri?" asked Alicia, her eyes narrowing in concentration.

"Because Eva or Olga, whichever she is, was shocked that we'd come from Dromvaar, almost as if she knew the place well, but didn't want to let on. She hasn't been at this hotel for long. The girl is a fish out of water. I felt that she had something to hide and that it was really troubling her." At this Rose looked thoroughly excited.

"Right! Well in that case, I think we should leave the castle for today and go to find Olga, Eva, or whatever she's called and have another chat. What do you think Alicia?"

"I think that first Rose should ring Olly and make sure about the name being the same."

"OK, I'll do it now," replied Rose with enthusiasm, jumping up. Can you order some more coffee...? And some hot milk. I won't be long."

Rose was back in just a few minutes, looking thoroughly pleased with herself.

"I spoke to Olly. The word has it that the murdered girl was called Olga because the body was clothed in a distinctive bright blue coat which has, apparently, been identified as belonging to an Olga whoever... he says it could be interesting although more likely a mere coincidence; by all means talk to the girl again, but to go carefully and whatever we do not to frighten her off. If necessary he'll come."

"Well, bye bye Bonnie Prince Charlie and Dunvegan Castle and hello to another fattening meal," Alicia announced holding in her stomach. Rose giggled.

"This is what I call good, stimulating fun."

"Yes, but please do remember there's been a murder and the men have done their darnedest to keep us all away from it." cautioned Emma doubtfully.

"The thing is," Adriana stood up, "we haven't been poking our noses in looking for trouble. This particular enigma appears to have come to us."

"And, of course, there may be nothing in it at all. It could be pure chance, although Olga is quite an unusual name, I would have thought, especially up here." Alicia pushed her cup away and also stood.

"Well, let's go and see shall we? I'll go to reception and ask them if they'll book another table for us. Are we going to walk?"

"No," replied Adriana adamantly. "It's too far. I shall arrive all hot and bothered. Let's drive, take our boots and anybody who wants to walk back can do just that, but I shan't."

❄

233

The waitress didn't put in an appearance until their meal had begun. She'd gone into town to run an errand for the manager, she told them later and the bus had broken down with a puncture on the rough road. Another bus was supposed to come to the rescue but she and her friend hadn't waited: they'd accepted a lift from a local person they knew, so that they wouldn't be too late for work. Adriana had been so disappointed when there'd been no sign of Eva, yet her face had lit up when the girl suddenly arrived with an offering of bread during their first course. They all agreed that, after lunch, they shouldn't approach the Polish girl en masse. It was decided that Emma and Adriana should stay as before while the others set off to walk back. They could be picked up at the half way point where the road crossed the track.

Emma bided her time. Arri seemed to be nodding off again on a sofa a little distance away and Emma sat in an armchair by the window. Eva was collecting coffee cups when Emma called her over. She told her how much they had all really enjoyed their lunch. Then, as Eva leant across to pick up her empty cup, Emma smiled up at her and trying to put the girl at ease, put her hand on her outstretched arm before asking quietly,

"Eva, my name is Emma. Is your real name actually Olga?" Eva let out a half strangled sob. Her hand flew to her neck and her cheeks flamed.

"You heard?"

"Yes, I heard and bearing in mind that we have come from Dromvaar, I need to talk to you as I think it could be important, both for you and a lot of other people." Olga, or Eva, stared while she tried to decide what to do. The young English woman steadily held her gaze. Emma was having a baby, her other arm was protectively around the soft mound. She had a kind face. This decent looking young woman just might understand. There was no one else she could talk to. But could she put her trust in a complete stranger?

"Not here!" Eva looked around desperately to make sure that nobody was watching, but everybody else had now left. Nearby there was only Adriana, listening as she 'slept' in her chair. It was a Wednesday, low season and hardly anybody was around, neither guests nor staff.

"I can't talk to you here, but outside; after I finish in half an hour, by your car in the parking area."

"OK Olga, but make sure you come. It really is essential that you do."

"I'll come. I need to know things too – thank you for finding me. You are so kind," she whispered as with shaking hands, she removed the rest of the used china, picked up the tray and almost dropping it, set off in the direction of the kitchen.

Emma got up and went to sit by the fire next to Adriana.

"Did you hear any of that?"

"Most of it," she said. "But I think we are going to need Olly. We don't know enough of what's going on."

"I think that we'll soon be discovering more for ourselves, without bothering the men." Adriana frowned.

"I wonder if we should wait around outside in case she runs?"

"She won't," said Emma. "Olga needs to know things and we are her only hope."

"How can you be so certain?"

"I think she's sweet but a very frightened and lonely girl, at present. She also badly needs a friend who might be able to help."

When they went outside Olga was already standing by the car.

"Hello Olga, this is Adriana." Then Emma raised her voice, for the benefit of a passing member of staff. "We are going to town if you'd like a lift?"

Olga waved at the barman heading for his motor bike and answered loudly.

"Thank you so much, that's very kind. There might be no bus yet."

❄

They sat in the car up a track and out of sight of the road. The young Polish girl was sad and vulnerable and because they were kind the whole story spilled out in an emotional rush. She told of her journey with Javek from Poland, about her meeting up with the other girls on a Russian ship and their subsequent arrival and transfer to Loch Island. She and Javek soon left and went to stay together on the mainland, but when the other model girls were to leave for other places, Olga had gone across once more to the island to see them all and to say goodbye. There was an Irish woman in charge who was dominating and cruel. They all hated her. The woman had a little brother who was also terrified of her. The little boy and an older Ukranian man became her friends. The other men, supposedly in charge of them, were terrible people. She started to cry when she told of how she wasn't allowed to go back to Javek on the mainland. They were kept as prisoners and the conditions over there were dreadful with little warmth and no electricity. They were assured that they would only be on the island for a short time as they would all be moving to exciting new destinations. Olga was the only one who didn't believe blindly in the rosy future being planned for them all with a 'wonderful new life'. She soon discovered that all the others had forged passports; hers was the only legal one, which seemed to make her more important.

One night an evil, aristocratic man came and tried to make her and her friend Eva go with him across the water to his house. Olga wouldn't give in, no matter what he promised. She knew that there were drugs around and she was suspicious, but her friend was

236

eventually persuaded to go. Olga gave her friend her warm, bright blue coat as it was cold and Eva loved that coat. She never came back and Olga hadn't ever heard from her again.

The following evening, when the others were all being given their instructions for leaving the next day, she had gone to bed upstairs. The kind Ukranian, who seemed to have taken a fatherly shine to her, told her to escape: to leave secretly, if she could. He said that he'd left a rusty old ladder up against the wall, underneath the bedroom window. Olga must use it to get away that night before it was too late. She borrowed a dark jacket and boots, stuffed a change of clothes into a small bag and climbed out of the window. Those downstairs were too busy to hear anything or to see her dark crouching shadow run silently from the house to the nearby bushes and on and away to freedom.

There was a path leading back to the beach along which they'd come when they had first arrived off the ship. It was a fine clear night and she could see by the light of the moon. Olga told them that she had run as fast as she could until she no longer felt she could be seen or followed. She stopped to listen once in a while, but there was nothing; just the occasional disturbed animal and the frightened thudding of her own heart, magnified in her ears. When she reached the sea she found the dinghy tied up to some rocks and covered in vegetation. Javek had taught her to sail on a river at home, so Olga understood boats. She managed to push it into deeper water, walk it round the hazardous stones and jump in without getting too wet. Then she rowed for hours close in, avoiding the rocks, and on down the coast. With the currents helping her she soon found herself many miles South of her island prison. Luckily, it was a still night and the sea was oily calm. In the early hours of the morning she had been given a tow by a fishing boat going in to the Kyle of Lochalsh. The fisherman thought she'd just come out from one of the nearby coves. She tied up alongside the quay, hopped out and walked into the post office, where she saw an advert for a waitress in the hotel on the road to Sleat.

"Why didn't you get in touch with Javek?" Adriana asked.

"I didn't dare when I heard of the murder. I thought it was safer for Javek if I stayed away and I thought they'd come after me for escaping. I was too frightened and I feared that it might have been my friend Eva who had been killed. I just couldn't bear to know. But now I'm certain it was her." She burst into tears again. Emma put her arm around her.

"It's alright, you're safe now. We have professional people in our life who will know what to do. But I think that Javek needs to know that you are OK, don't you? Also you'll be pleased to hear that the little boy Sean also managed to escape."

"Oh that's wonderful, that poor little boy has endured so much. It must have been terrible for Javek too. He must wish we'd never left home."

"When are you next off duty Olga?" asked Adriana.

"Tomorrow evening. Then I'm off until the weekend."

"Well, I suggest that you come to stay with us at our hotel tomorrow night and we'll decide what to do then, don't you think?" Adriana looked across at Emma who nodded in agreement.

"OK... if you're sure? I have some money. Thank you so much, it's such a relief. You have no idea." She smiled weakly.

"Now, where would you like to go?"

"I think back to my room," she said shyly, sniffing and dabbing at her nose. "If you don't mind?"

"Yes, that's fine. You must be exhausted. We'll drop you back and then go on to pick up our friends. But first I'll write down our telephone numbers for you, both the hotel and my mobile. What time do you finish tomorrow?"

"At six o'clock, after tea and when I've laid up for dinner."

"Alright, we'll be there to pick you up, in the car park."

When they said goodbye after more tears, Emma was

rewarded with a blinding smile. Olga really was a beautiful girl. Then she ran in through the side entrance, turned once more to wave and disappeared through the doorway.

Later that evening, after more discussion over tea back in their own hotel, Rose went once more to ring Oliver.

"Olly, it's me. Olly darling I'm sorry but I think we do rather need you here after all."

CHAPTER 35

Nothing at all, of any interest, had happened on the first two nights in the Parisian nightclub. Although always on the 'qui vive' in case the situation was suddenly to change, the four young agents spent a relatively peaceful time getting to know each other. Guy always needing a project, took the whole thing in his stride and when they were all together found the opportunity to update his French. But Julian found dancing up close with Monique two nights running decidedly unnerving. She was obviously an experienced girl in every way and he found he was uncomfortable with the feeling that, although so very young and good looking, in her work she was most likely his equal. Guy couldn't resist teasing his friend and colleague when they parted company each night in the early hours of the morning. But Julian found the whole situation unamusing and seemed to be getting through ever more packets of cigarettes.

During the daytime the men went for an early morning run along the Seine, followed by coffee and a croissant in a small cafe, after which they remained in their rather insignificant hotel, which was mainly inhabited by business men and was not far from headquarters. Everybody had their own lives to attend to and nobody took any notice of a couple of unassuming Englishmen speaking Franglais. Guy kept in close touch with the incident team back in Dromvaar who also liaised with Oliver each day. During these operations there was usually no contact with the girls, but in this instance Oliver was able to send them a text from time to time, giving out no information as to what the men were about or their location, but merely to reassure them that all was well.

While they were relaxing, Julian gave much thought to his predicament with Adriana and the difficult decision he must make.

He wanted to marry her so much, but the knowledge that it was unlikely that he could ever give her a child hung heavily on his shoulders. This unwelcome news, only learnt from their doctor just before they came away, had rocked his confidence. Their relationship had always, without question, been great - until now. If they did marry, surely in time she would regret her decision and their relationship would disintegrate? He couldn't bear the thought of that.

Guy thought of nothing except the job ahead with all its possible ramifications. Alicia, who he adored, was another world away: out of sight and out of mind. His concentration, so finely tuned during a mission, was absolute. He was very aware of his colleague's problem at home. When they set out from the hotel each evening he made sure that his friend left these unsettling anxieties behind in his room. This type of distraction had no place in their tough line of work.

The third night looked like ending in the same way, until at about eleven thirty, when their 'waiter' came across. An associate, on the street outside, had just sent word that they should be informed that three people of interest were about to arrive.

At last, this could be what they'd been waiting for. Both men felt the immediate adrenalin rush; the excitement both enhancing their mental state and boosting their bodily strength.

The trio in question came in, following a small group of noisy young people. They walked straight past the incognito agents' table, on past the dance floor and through a door in the wall at the back of the room, only discernible from the dim light filtering through as it was opened. The first man was an Asian who Guy had never seen before. The second Oriental was one of the two he recognized from the previous visit and the third, even though the man was dishevelled and unshaven, was undoubtedly the elusive laird. Although the pictures Guy had been shown had been taken at a younger age, there was no mistaking him. Guy raised his hand once to their waiter colleague standing nearby anticipating instruction. The man nodded and momentarily disappeared behind the bar to call up the other agents outside, confirming positive identification. The trap was now sprung.

Three quarters of an hour went by before the door at the back opened once more. The two Asian men came out with a very young dark skinned girl with an incredible figure. She must have already been there or come in from the back. They walked over to sit at the same corner table, at which Adriana had recognised the Irish girl on their previous visit, where a reserved card had been placed. A few minutes later the Scotsman re-appeared with a good looking blonde woman, most likely in her mid-forties. They were laughing politely as they also went to the booked table. It was quite clear that a business negotiation had taken place between the blonde woman and the three men and that a transaction was almost concluded. The young girl sat quiet and shy without speaking, ignored for the moment, while the others wound up their meeting. Another few minutes passed, then the whole group sat back smiling. The deal was closed, they all shook hands and another bottle of champagne was ordered.

"What nationality is that one?" asked Monique, indicating the girl with the amazing body. Guy thought for a minute surreptitiously studying the facial features of the good looking youngster and tapping into his knowledge of the many Arab countries.

"Middle Eastern certainly - probably about thirteen or fourteen." He hesitated then added with assurance, "and most likely, given the world situation at present, Syrian I should think. War and unrest in a country helps rackets like this one."

"Mon Dieu," exclaimed the French woman "and so young."

"I'm afraid so," replied Guy. "A new country, a different coloured skin and a young girl as yet completely unspoilt by men. This one, by the jewellery and the way she is dressed, is probably from a well to do family. She'll be worth a lot of money."

"Quelle abomination!" Monique and Hélen looked at each other, disgust and determination both sliding fleetingly across their faces. They talked softly and with lowered eyes, as they continued to observe their quarry.

The blonde woman drank a glass of champagne and then left. She seemed in a hurry. Guy signalled to their waiter who immediately turned away to use his personalized mobile. There was time; the woman had a coat to collect and she had also stopped to talk politely to someone she knew on her way out.

"Julian, I think it's time for you two to do your bit on the dance floor. Now, please."

Monique stood up, drained her glass and taking Julian's hand they set off between the tables towards the centre of the dance floor. She was totally focused and knew exactly what she was doing. Guy followed their progress. People were already looking at the alluring Monique with interest.

Hélen picked up her drink and turned her head just in time to observe one of the Asian men lean across the dark girl, cup her chin in his hand and kiss her hard, full on the lips. Hélen quickly nudged Guy with her foot and they both saw the older man, on the young girl's other side, surreptitiously drop something into her glass before he quickly topped it up with newly arrived champagne. Unaware, the poor girl sat back taken aback by the aggressive kiss. Yet she still managed to smile shyly, both resigned and subservient in her predicament. The laird laughed loudly and looked over towards the dance floor. The young woman took up her glass and continued to sip her champagne little knowing that in a relatively short time she would be powerless.

"Bastards!" Hélen muttered, looking away. "How did this girl ever get herself into such a situation?" Guy also had to quell a rising sense of rage. In this job he felt vulnerable only where women and children were concerned. "I just hope we get this lot and put them where they belong."

"Oui," agreed Hélen grimly. "I hope so too, but don't forget we've been onto this one for a long time. Everybody is ready. We have every chance. Monique's good, isn't she?"

"She certainly is, but she's too sexy for her own good and I don't really like someone so young being used in this way."

"Pas de problème, don't worry," Hélen calmly reassured him. "I've seen her in action on many diverse operations and there is very much more to Monique than you can possibly imagine. You will see. She is very able."

Monique was dancing like a professional stripper, with her back to the group under surveillance, gyrating her hips in an almost obscene way. The Scotsman's attention was caught and Guy could tell that he was longing for her to turn around. Even Guy was riveted by her dancing. She was amazingly supple. When she did turn around Lord Strathkellan simply couldn't take his eyes off her. He leant back and said something to the others and they all stopped talking to watch. Julian saw Guy raise his glass and the play acting began. Julian deftly instigated a jealous row, supposedly, as far as all the onlookers were concerned, because of the promiscuous way his girlfriend was dancing. It worked perfectly, people at first were amused then embarrassed; then some edged away, putting a little distance between themselves and this mesmeric sexual performance. Finally Julian threw up his hands and flounced off towards the gents and the indignant Monique went to sit by herself at the bar smiling with satisfaction. No man in the room could help but react to this stunning animal magnetism.

Guy sat watching, wondering how long it would take the laird to make his move.

"Come on darling, let's dance," Guy said, standing up and taking Hélen's hand. It was a slow one, they moved around the floor and as they passed Monique he pulled Hélen close towards him and said in her ear, loud enough also for Monique to hear,

"Watch your drink, my darling." Monique inclined her head just so he knew that she'd heard and Guy and Hélen continued on around the room. As the music changed and more couples got up to dance, he saw the Scotsman get off his chair and start threading his way through the dancers across to an empty bar seat beside the beautiful French girl. The man introduced himself immediately and Guy saw Monique smile in a most tempting way whilst, holding out her glass to the barman for a top up.

Julian returned to their table supposedly in a huff and sat grumpily sipping his wine. Guy, catching their waiter's eye, again excused himself to Hélen and crossed the room to where the young man was standing. As they passed he whispered quickly,

"The dark girl is drugged, they'll be leaving shortly, please alert those outside – two Asian men and the young dark girl. Red dress and I think I could see a light coloured fur jacket. Also watch Monique's drink carefully. I don't want her out of action."

"D'accord, yes alright, don't worry, I understand." He had to raise his voice to be heard against the beat of the music which had become suddenly louder. "I'm about to take over from one of the barman now anyway." he turned away, putting his mobile to his ear.

A few minutes later, the young dark girl seemed to be needing air and the group started to leave. The laird saw them move and waved goodbye, with a lewd grin on his face and a thumbs up sign to his Asian friends. He knew exactly what the beautiful Syrian girl was in for. The very thought only heightened his determination to have this young French girl for himself. He had everything ready back in his hotel room. He then turned back to Monique and mistakenly knocked over her spiked glass which she had carefully placed by his elbow. Pretending to be slightly drunk, she asked for another. The meticulous barman quickly handed her a glass of fresh champagne. The slick Scot had failed once but Guy knew he'd try again.

Guy, Julian and Hélen had seen the minor commotion.

"She really is good." Julian was impressed. "I wonder what's going on outside?"

"It will be fine." Hélen was confident. "Our people are also well prepared, although they'll not make a move right outside the club. They won't want to upset what we have going on in here. The man returning with their car will be parked around the corner." These two girls really were quite something thought Julian. How could he ever have doubted them? God, he was looking forward to a cigarette when this was all over and he would have liked to smack the Scot in the face right now. Guy leaned over sensing Julian's tension.

"I think that you should go up and ask Monique if she's going to come home with you now. It's about the right time. But don't lay it on too thick." Julian got to his feet and ran his fingers through his hair, his usual gesture.

"Alright, see you in a minute." He disappeared through a throng of newly arrived people. Guy turned to his blonde companion.

"Come me-darling let's dance again and see how Monique is doing. I can't quite see from here any longer, too many people in the way now."

It was quite evident that Alistair Strathkellan was trying to persuade Monique to go with him. She appeared to be thinking about it. In fact she was well aware that the others had only just left. She must bide her time a little longer.

Julian sauntered over pretending to be rather nonchalant. He circled the dance floor and came to a halt beside Monique.

"Bonsoir, excusez-moi," he said rather rudely turning away from the laird, who had his hand up Monique's skirt, stroking her thigh, whilst smiling at her conspiratorially. For all the world to see, the Scotsman thought himself in control of the situation. Julian continued with their agreed plan of action, feeling a wave of anticipation.

"Maintenant, Monique. I've had enough of your behaviour. I'm going back to the hotel in a few minutes. Are you coming or not?" Monique smiled naughtily at the Scot, ignoring Julian.

"Perhaps... not!" she said giggling.

"Come on now. Stop being so ridiculous. You've drunk far too much. It's time to go."

"Non, no I am not coming," she said determinedly. Strathkellan interrupted.

"She doesn't have to go if she doesn't want to, she's over age you know," he said confident that he was winning. "Don't worry young man," he said patronizingly, "in due course, I shall make sure she gets a taxi or I shall see her home myself." Julian turned towards his adversary.

"So you are English." He stared at the corrupt man in front of him who sounded so convincing. He could once have been good looking, but now looked unhealthy and was running to fat. An excess of illegal substances, Julian decided. He'd seen it all before.

"No, I am actually a Scot through and through. Alistair is my name, so Monique, I can assure you, will be in very good hands." Julian fixed Monique with a furious scowl.

"Well stay then, have it your way, I really don't care. Quite honestly I've had enough. You shouldn't have been let out of kindergarten... or been given such a good dinner," he muttered grumpily as he locked eyes with the barman. "Make sure, if this man has gone to his bed, that the silly child gets a taxi home would you? And don't go on filling her glass either. She's already had far too much." He handed over a generous tip. "Merci bien et bonsoir." As soon as he turned to walk away Monique dissolved into giggles and snuggled up to the laird.

"You'll look after me, won't you Alistair?"

"I certainly will and I shall also take you home with me when you are ready to leave," he whispered. She put her hand on his knee and squeezed hard. He ran his free hand right up underneath the skirt of her dress.

"Let's go when I've finished this drink, shall we?"

Julian went back to the table.

"Alright, that worked well. I'll be outside exactly as planned. Another few minutes I should think - then they'll go."

"Monique has a coat to collect also," Hélen reminded them.

"OK, we'll follow in five then." Guy picked up his innocuous looking personal hand held. "Use yours if there's anything to report outside."

Fifteen minutes later Monique and Strathkellan came out into the cool night air. Monique played her part perfectly. She stood, wobbling slightly on her high heels, staring up at the stars saying,

"Shall we walk a bit Alistair? I think there's a taxi rank down the next street."

"Whatever you like 'ma cherie', as the rest of the night is on me. You'll stay with me? Yes?"

"Mais oui, but of course and I shall keep you busy for a very long time." She said licking her lips in anticipation.

"And I shall do things to you that you have never before experienced, I can promise you that."

"Ha, come let's walk and find our taxi!"

They walked around the corner. Monique stopped again, turned and went into his arms raising her face up to him.

"I don't think I can wait," she breathed, pulling him into a darkened doorway and letting him kiss her, undoing his overcoat buttons and worming her way in through the layers to his body. His hands were all over her. He pulled up her skirt and started to tear at her underclothes. Desire was heightened by the excesses of his indulgent evening. Nothing else mattered now. The big Scotsman never saw the three men approaching, placing themselves in strategic positions. He was far too busy with this beautiful young girl who seemed so willing. He would soon have her unconscious back in his room and totally within his power. He would be able to do everything he wished. He was obsessed with every perverted sexual act, oblivious of the consequences to these young girls, one of whom had already died. Fuelled with a constant supply of both alcohol and drugs, this was what he now lived for and he couldn't wait to get started with this one. Monique was not part of his business dealings. This little French girl was an added bonus and she was all his.

Suddenly she was out of his arms and thrusting him away. The frustration was intense as he was about to have her there and then. Then he sensed something untoward. 'What the hell was going on?' Bodies were hurling themselves around him. "Fuck! We're being mugged!"

It all happened so fast, but it wasn't until Guy and Julian calmly stepped out of the shadows with extra armed backup beside them, that Lord Strathkellan realized it was all over. His criminal activities had finally caught up with him. He should have taken up the offer of a fully paid trip to the Far East when it had first been offered.

CHAPTER 36

The dead girl remained unidentified. Interpol had failed to find a match with any missing young person from Poland, the Czech Republic, or Slovakia. They were now searching further afield in Hungary, Bulgaria, Romania and even the Ukraine. A translator had been found and the elderly Ukranian victim had now recovered enough to relay useful information and to identify the body himself; so Oliver decided that it would be a good idea to take both Lorna Finlay and Javek with him to Skye. They were both going to be greatly upset waiting for the results of the identification, so he thought it best that they were well out of the way.

Olly didn't know quite what to make of Rose's excitable and rather garbled story. But it certainly looked as if the girl at the hotel in Skye could possibly be one of the group's unfortunate young girls. He thought it very doubtful that this one could possibly be Javek's poor girlfriend, arisen from the dead, so to speak. Although he supposed that one of them might have managed to escape from the Irish girl's clutches and could be hiding out under an alias. For obvious reasons he had decided to tell the young Polish man none of this. There was no point in raising his hopes when they were about to be dashed with the identification results. Javek had already accepted that, in all likely-hood, the dead girl was his Olga.

❄

Emma and Adriana went to fetch the beautiful waitress at the appointed time, when she had finished at the hotel the following day. She seemed so pleased to see them and readily jumped into the car with a small overnight bag on her shoulder. That evening she joined them for dinner in their hotel and told them the story of her childhood. Her father had died at an early age and she had lived with her mother and grandmother in a village near Gdansk and close to Javek's family. As children they had grown up together, everybody had been happy for them when they had set off on their travelling adventure. Olga had kept in touch with post cards. Neither of their families had any idea of the predicament in which they had found themselves once that had reached Scotland. Her mother believed the British Isles to be a safe wonderful country for her daughter to visit and she had Javek to look after her. The knowledge of what had actually happened would have created horror within both families and the shock, she said, would have certainly killed her failing grandmother.

At their hotel that night the set dinner was grilled local fish or roast venison with a variety of appetising starters. They all chose smoked salmon to begin, followed by the roast, then finished with an ice cream made with blackberries. It turned out to be a happy evening, in so much as Olga obviously felt safe, with the burden which she carried considerably lightened. The four young women had decided not to tell her that Olly was bringing Javek and Lorna the next day. Let it be a memorable and miraculous surprise for them both. Rose realised that Olly had much more information than they had and he was disbelieving of her tale regarding Olga, so he would have no intention of telling Javek of any possibility of finding her alive. Adriana and Emma, having heard the story directly, were in no doubt at all and decided to set up the meeting in the best possible way. Alicia said she'd move in with Adriana for the night so that Olga could have one of the four rooms, facing out across the water, to herself. She must need some space after all that had happened. It was the most romantic and calming setting imaginable. The four English women all went to bed that night happy in the knowledge that the lovers were soon to be reunited.

Half an hour after they had all gone to their rooms Emma, who was reading in her bed, heard a tap on her door. She knew who it would be. Olga tearful again, appeared before her dressed in her warm pyjamas. She was distraught. Their well intentioned kindness to her had been almost too much. Emma, understanding, sat her down on the sofa in the little downstairs sitting area of her suite and gently took her hand.

"What's wrong Olga? Tell me!"

"It's Eva, I know now she's dead and... we were really good friends... I'm so sad... and what if Javek doesn't want me anymore?" It all came out in a rush. Emma felt thoroughly maternal.

"Oh Olga, of course he'll want you. He's going to get the surprise of his life, but it will also be like a miracle to him."

"You think so?"

"I'm sure so, and you know you are just going to have to accept that your friend is dead. It's dreadful, I know, but there is nothing that any of us can do for her now. Let's just hope for her sake that it was quick and she knew nothing about it because most likely she was drugged unconscious. You'll just have to hang on to that. You and Javek have your whole life ahead of you. You are so young and have been so brave, Olga, but now you must concentrate on your own future together. Would you like to stay in here with me tonight?"

"Yes please, if you really wouldn't mind."

"Of course not, you can tuck up on the sofa which makes into a bed and I've seen plenty of extra blankets upstairs in my cupboard."

They had a cup of hot chocolate together and then Emma saw Olga, go peacefully to her bed. It was understandable that the poor girl was apprehensive. She had run away, but by doing that, she had most likely saved her life. When Emma kissed her goodnight she realized that really Olga was little more than a child as yet, but at the same time, an exceptionally bright and courageous one. She just hoped that the hapless dead friend had died quickly and hadn't suffered too much at the end. If she had, Emma hoped very much that Olga would never find out about it.

"Don't worry," Emma said gently as she turned out the light, "trust me. It will be alright."

"I know and I do trust you. Thank you, I'm so lucky to have met you all. May your dreams and those of your little one be sweet and refreshing. Goodnight."

"How lovely," whispered Emma also feeling quite emotional. "What a beautiful saying."

Oliver was awake and up early the following morning. He knew that Lorna and Javek would be out of their beds, so after letting the dogs out and re-settling them by the aga in the kitchen, he left a note for Marc on the table and then quietly left the lodge.

Breakfast with Lorna Finlay was a treat as she had porridge, with thick cream and brown sugar, followed by homemade drop scones, cooked on a griddle. By the time they set off Oliver felt both well nourished and enthusiastic about getting away from Dromvaar and its rather depressive atmosphere. He remembered the route well. Javek was fascinated by the scenery and for Lorna it was a journey she had long wanted to make. When they finally came to the Kyle of Lochalsh they had to stop to admire the spectacular view across the bridge to Skye. The sun lit the unusually flat water with seductive molten silver and the autumnal colourings on the land above seemed bathed in gold. Further in the distance they could clearly see the famous red and black Cuillin hills. The beautiful vista raised everybody's spirits, and Lorna in the back, sang 'Speed Bonnie Boat' in a melodic gentle voice.

Oliver had enlightened Lorna as to the reason for this journey, but as far as Javek was concerned this was just a day out to join Oliver's wife and friends while getting away from all the horror for a while. When they arrived at the little hotel, exactly as expected, they went into the main reception hall and were soon shown into the sitting area. There they found the girl's seated together in a big bay window where they had been watching for Olly in a suppressed state of excitement. Lorna went to the ladies room quickly and Javek shyly shook hands with them all. When Lorna reappeared and had been introduced, Emma suggested that she and Javek might like to walk out to the water's edge, by their rooms in the other building, to see the stunning view of the island and lighthouse from there. Javek jumped at the chance to be out in the air and nearer the water. The others stood quietly together in front of the window, so as to watch. "What's going on?" asked Olly intrigued.

"Don't speak darling, just observe," whispered Rose with shining eyes, "because if we are right, this could be the most romantic meeting you will ever see." Oliver did as he was told and went to stand by his young wife.

Lorna and Javek appeared together and began to walk slowly across the gravel and down towards the Sound. Lorna, with her arm tucked into his, suddenly stopped. She had seen a familiar figure appear from behind the building to their right and walk across to sit on the bench by the water's edge immediately in front of them.

"You go on dear, I'll come in a minute," she said gently, her voice little more than a croak. Javek had seen the girl too. He turned to look at Lorna, his eyes filling with tears as a look of total disbelief swept across his face. She gave him a little push.

"Go on my dear! Go on!" He made a little choking sound and continued unsteadily across the gravel by himself. When he reached the strip of grass between them, Olga rose, turned and slowly began to walk towards him. Both were absolutely speechless. Javek opened his arms and Olga ran towards him, her hair flying out behind her, tears pouring down her cheeks and a blinding smile lighting her radiant face. That smile could be seen from the hotel and could have lit the entire island. As the lovers met and were clasped once more in each other's arms the onlookers all turned away, to afford the couple the privacy they deserved. Lorna tactfully walked off in another direction.

Emma and Adriana sat down and got out their handkerchiefs. Alicia was staring into space remembering another time and another place and Rose dashed into Olly's arms. No one spoke until Oliver first recovered himself and announced in a wobbly voice,

"I think this definitely calls for a celebration drink. I'll order it, then go and rescue Lorna."

CHAPTER 37

While most of the young people were engaged elsewhere, life became quiet again at both the lodge and Glencurrie. The Colonel's brother, John, had gone South to see friends in Yorkshire. Oliver had gone to Skye and Marc had been working full time at the medical centre, filling in for one of the doctors who was away on a course. After all the recent drama, Alec was finding life just a little too peaceful. The weather was clement and he had taken it upon himself to teach Sean to fish from the river bank in front of the house. It was his own fishing so nobody else came there without his permission. He gave the young boy an old trout rod with which to learn. The excitement when the child both hooked and landed his first fish was something to see. Mrs Haddington's husband, Stuart, stood beside him, giving instruction as he reeled the fish in and Alec, who'd been watching from the window and saw the line go taut then bend, rushed out with a landing net. When they all went back to the house and Sean was busy with Stuart, practicing the art of cleaning the fish without cutting himself, Mrs H decided that it was as good a time as any to approach the Colonel about the boy's future. She knocked on his study door.

"Come in, come in Jean." He was smiling as she entered. "Yes after all these years I do recognize your knock, you know! Sit down do. Now wasn't that fun, did you see the child's face? The sheer joy in it?"

"Yes I did," she answered, "I heard you shout, Colonel, and I watched from the kitchen window. It certainly was a sight to see. Now I'll come straight to the point if I may?"

"Go ahead Mrs H," said Alec chuckling, "you always do and I have a pretty good idea what you have come about too!"

"Oh you do, do you Colonel Neilsen?" she laughed, "well then, you won't be surprised when I say I've come about the boy's future? You see, I was wondering if you thought there might just be a chance that Ailsa and Douglas might be able to adopt the child and what we can do to get things going in the right direction."

"And I have been wondering about that very same thing," he said. "Now I have already spoken to a lawyer friend in Edinburgh. She has much to do with the social services' head-quarters there and happens also to know the person who runs the adoption centre in Edinburgh. So, Mrs H the wheels are already turning, as you might say."

"Oh my goodness Colonel, that's great. Should I mention this to Ailsa, do you think?"

"By all means talk to Ailsa and Dougie. But make sure they know that they will have to be formally assessed, and that there will be interviews and searches and paperwork like you wouldn't believe. The whole process is bound to take longer than you can possibly imagine, ridiculous I know, but I think that until such a time has passed, Sean will be allowed to stay here with us and carry on as we are. So keep your fingers crossed and I promise you that I will do everything in my power to see this happen, provided, that is, you are absolutely sure that this is what both Ailsa and Douglas would want? It is a big responsibility to take on and it won't always be easy. Sean will come with a lot of what I think nowadays is called extra baggage!"

"I am one hundred percent certain, Colonel Neilsen, that this is exactly what my daughter and her husband would want. Sean has had a terrible childhood so far. I am well aware that much of this will have rubbed off so to speak, but he will have a good life from now on, surrounded by a loving family who will teach him right from wrong - and we are all very fond of him as you know."

"Good," Alec responded, "as am I, Mrs H, and I shall make it my task to teach him to be the best fisherman in the whole of Scotland.

Now let's go and see how they are getting on with cleaning that first catch of his, shall we?"

❄

Marc dropped in to Glencurrie, in the evening on the way back from the surgery, just as Oliver rang in with the good news from Skye.

"Goodness what a day it has been." Alec sighed happily when he finally put the telephone down, "let's sit by the fire in the study and have a whisky together, then I'll tell you about the conversation which I've just had with your friend Oliver. It has to be one of the most romantic of stories I've ever heard. But would you like to stay for dinner Marc? I'm on my own and would enjoy the company."

"Yes, thanks Alec that would be lovely if Mrs H has enough, do you think?"

"Have no fear Jean Haddington always has enough! But perhaps you'd just ask her to lay another place?"

"OK, but I'll just go first and ring Beth and Jess, to tell them what I'm doing, if that's alright? I can't wait to hear all the latest – have you also news of Guy and Julian?"

"I certainly have," Alec replied with a grin, "but go and do that telephone call then I'll fill you in with it all. Oh! Don't forget to see Mrs Haddington on the way back."

Mrs H had already laid another place for dinner and was humming merrily to herself as she prepared another piece of steak, when Marc put his head around the kitchen door.

"Away with you, back to your uncle. It's all organized laddie," she said before he could speak as she whacked the steak with a tenderizing hammer. Marc had seldom seen her in such good humour. Perhaps it was all about having a child in the house.

They all seemed to have taken on a new lease of life since Sean had arrived.

❄

Fergus had heard from Mac that the boys, as he called them, would soon be returning and, as far as Mac could tell, everything that they had hoped for had been achieved. He needed to see Beth again while everyone was still away and she wasn't too busy. He had been wondering if perhaps she might be pursuaded to return next summer to help with the cooking in the restaurant of the pub. During the tourist season, Dougie had already told him that Ginger would be needing another well qualified person as an assistant. Fergus thought that he might have mentioned it to him on purpose, so he was going to see what Beth's reaction to this idea might be. He really couldn't accept the thought of their having to say goodbye so soon without having made another plan. Of course there was also Christmas to think about and 'Hogmanay'. She might be persuaded to come up again for the festive season. He felt quite nervous in his stomach. What if she said no? Then he would know that they had no future, but that just didn't bear thinking about either. They were good together and made each other laugh.

He sent a text which was soon answered: *yes, she'd love to see him later, for supper, after she'd helped Jess put Poppy to bed.* Fergus decided to take her to a small restaurant in the next town. He didn't want Dougie looking down the back of his neck, listening to what he said, or witnessing his possible rejection.

❄

Oliver left the following morning via the hotel where Olga worked. He was going to see the manager with her to see what could be done about letting her go without much notice. Javek was desperate never to let her out of his sight again, but Olga said she'd leave when she could, but that the management had been kind, taking her on without references in the first place. She wouldn't let them down and would work as long as she had to. Mrs Finlay went with them after thanking the girls and saying that she'd just had the time of her life! Luckily now that the busy summer season was over, the hotel had found her a room with a wonderful view over the loch and Oliver had paid for them all.

The girls decided to stay on one more night. The men weren't due back until the next day and anyway would be occupied again in the incident room for a while. Adriana in particular wanted to give Julian a bit longer to wind down. It was now over a fortnight since her day spent with Marc and she definitely felt different. Perhaps she could soon buy a test kit from the chemist.

"Do you realize that we have been away from home for nearly three weeks?"

"Yes, and Lord knows when we'll have another chance, so we have to go to Dunvegan Castle before we leave here," Rose declared with enthusiasm. "I've read up about it. I want to see the Fairy Flag and go out in the boat to see the seals, 'up close and personal'. Some may even have pups." Rose was dancing around the others her eyes sparkling.

"Rose you really are so funny: you definitely have a thing about otters and seals!" exclaimed Alicia laughing. "What exactly is this Fairy flag that you keep talking about?"

"I shan't tell you anymore until we go there," Rose answered grinning annoyingly. Alicia held her hands up.

"Okay. Alright let's go then if everybody agrees, that is. It will be fun." The others all nodded unable to hide their laughter. Rose, on occasion, was still little more than a child.

"Good, that's settled then."

"And I'll find out where we can have lunch," Adriana announced, getting up and marching off towards the reception with a purpose.

"I have never known Arri so keen about food," Emma said, sitting back on the sofa and smiling contentedly, when Adriana was out of earshot. "She's just like me, but I'm having a baby... you don't suppose... I mean you don't think that she might also...?" Emma stopped. They were all staring at her.

Rose's hand flew to her mouth.

"Oh my God! Perhaps she is!"

Alicia waved her hands around trying to quieten her friends.

"Sh... Sh... I agree, it is possible, but for goodness sake don't anybody say anything yet - just pray." Adriana was coming back and caught the last couple of words.

"What are we praying for?" Arri asked. Alicia was the quickest.

"We are praying that Olga's hotel let her go."

Rose carried it on smoothly.

"Yes but, if she has to stay a bit, I did wonder whether they might have given Javek something to do there also, perhaps in the garden. He's such a polite, good looking person and says he loves gardening."

"What, so you mean he'd stay as well?" Emma joined in.

"Actually that's a good idea," replied Adriana completely unaware of what they had really been discussing. "After all, the hotel is smart and must make a mint of money. I'm sure he'd be happy chopping wood or anything really as long as he and Olga are together. Anyway, I have found out about lunch. There is a cafe, but we are going to take a picnic and have it in the grounds of Dunvegan. We are lucky as there's no rain forecast today and no chill wind either. I've also got a map of Skye." She held it up for them to see.

My friend looks almost smug, thought Alicia wondering once more about Adriana's physical state.

"Good," Emma began to get up. "I shall be starving again soon so let's go!"

"I shall be too," agreed Adriana. "It must be all the romance and the sea air." Alicia raised an eye brow at Emma and the others busied themselves picking up their things and getting ready to go across to their rooms.

CHAPTER 38

"So, what do you think of the castle?" asked Rose, with shining eyes.

"I think it's wonderful. Stunning." Alicia replied without hesitation.

"And it's got incredible atmosphere," Emma added. "I suppose that's because the family are here for part of the year. It doesn't have that unlived in, fusty musty feel to it."

Adriana had a faraway mystic look in her eyes.

"I can just visualise what it must have been like in ancient times though; when the Macleod and MacDonald clans were all fighting. The place has such character with so much information impregnated in its walls and, just imagine, even Flora MacDonald was here when she was helping Bonnie Prince Charlie to escape."

They all sat gazing up at the castle from a bench in the lovely sheltered gardens, huddled up, eating the picnic that the hotel had made up for them. After lunch they planned to go out in the little boat with the ghillie to see the seals.

"Oh look, here's the lovely lady who was at the entrance when we arrived. She said she'd come to find us when she took her break and here she is." Rose waved enthusiastically.

"Let's ask her to tell us more about the legends surrounding the Fairy Wrap," Adriana suggested with renewed interest.

"Hello!" they all chorused.

"We are so pleased to see you," piped the irrepressible Rose, "as there is so much that we are desperate to know about the intriguing Fairy Flag. We are all completely hooked." Morna walked up to them smiling broadly.

"Good, I'm delighted, that's just what we like to hear and it's my pleasure as I love to talk about the Fairy Cloth." Alicia moved to sit on a flat stone nearby to make room for their new friend, who sank down thankfully in her place.

"I'd be out on my feet by now, if I were you; what with all that standing and smiling at complete strangers. I don't know how you do it," Emma said with feeling.

"Och no, I love my job and meeting interested people, like yourselves, is just great," she said settling herself and carefully giving Emma enough room beside her.

"Will you tell us then about the legends?" Adriana couldn't wait to hear about the ancient myths.

"Of course. Well now; the Fairy Flag sometimes called the Fairy Wrap, Banner or even Cloth. I'll start with the three most important facts. The first is that the Fairy Flag was almost certainly brought originally from the Holy Land. The second is that it has magical powers and the third is that it is believed to contain a force strong enough to win battles."

"Is that why it has to be protected now behind glass," asked Rose, "because a few mindless people try to snip off little pieces to take home?"

"Sadly, once in a while in the past, yes. But also because the cloth is so old that the fresh air and atmosphere were helping it to disintegrate."

She went on to tell them of the various legends born around the time of the Crusades. But her favourite she kept until last and the way she described the magical event had them all spellbound.

"It was at the time when the Fifteenth Chieftain here was a mere baby. The child was in his cot, asleep in the fairy tower, which you have just seen." They all looked to the castle tower where she was pointing. "The wee bairn was being watched over by a young girl while celebrations were taking place over on the other side of the castle. The piper was playing and guests were dancing. For a young maid this must have been irresistible. After a while she knew that she just had to have a peep. So, making sure that her charge was tucked up and away with his dreams, she ran out of the tower and across the hall to a place where she could spy on the gathering without being seen." The storyteller's hand fluttered in front of them as she described the young person running in bare feet across the castle hallways.

"Well now, the music and the dancing was so beguiling that the girl stayed far too long. Suddenly, with horror, she remembered her responsibilities and she raced back in a flash to the tower, her heart beating fast with worry and guilt." Morna paused for effect, holding her hands up to her face.

"The young maid came to the open door and, looking in, couldn't believe her eyes. The babe had indeed kicked off his warm blankets. But there he was cosy and safe, wrapped in the Fairy Cloth with the fairy sitting at the end of his cot, singing a lullaby as she kept watch. And, to this day the lullaby is still sung by mothers to their babes on this island and of course here at Dunvegan."

There was silence for a moment as the gentle woman looked at the entranced faces of her rapt audience. Emma spoke first.

"What an absolutely lovely story."

"You see, I knew there was something extra special about this castle." Rose declared knowingly. Alicia laughed.

"Morna, you have no idea just how much we have been bullied into coming here."

"Well I'm so glad we did," replied Adriana. "As I knew once we were inside, that Dunvegan has an atmosphere that is totally unique."

"And I," said Morna "am just thrilled that you have all enjoyed your visit so much. Now I hope that you will go to see our seals. The men down there will look after you and will be delighted to take you out in the boat. You'll come back with more information about the local bird, fish and animal life than you can

267

possibly imagine. Now I must be getting back to my post for this afternoon. As you know we have stayed open later than usual this year and we have a large group booking expected."

They all thanked their new friend and, promising to return, said their farewells. After clearing up their picnic debris they then set off down the winding path to find the men with the boat.

The seals, 'up close and personal', as Rose would put it, was a fitting finale to the day. The water was choppy and they were all asked to put on life jackets, 'just to be on the safe side' insisted the welcoming ticket man. The ghillie took them out around and in between all the little islands on Loch Dunvegan. He took trouble to explain the different habits of both the common and shyer grey seals. Some were swimming but most were lying lazily relaxing on the rocks or half submerged in the water. Rose was insistent that they were all smiling, whereupon the boatman explained that their sanctuary was indeed a haven, inhabited by the seals, fish and birdlife alone, so that the beautiful creatures did in fact have plenty to smile about.

In the early evening, as the sun faded over the horizon, the four friends returned to their hotel tired and happy, all with stored memories of a truly golden day spent at Dunvegan. Alicia drove, Rose prattled away, reliving the best parts of their day and both Adriana and Emma went fast asleep in the back. Rose, pausing to look over her shoulder remarked,

"And we didn't even have to sing the lullaby." Alicia chuckled and was even more convinced about Adriana's condition.

※

When the girls finally arrived back at the lodge the next day, all the men including Alec were there drinking tea by the fire. Poppy was obviously entertaining everybody as laughter could be heard throughout the entire house. The little girl was thrilled with the soft baby seal which Rose had brought back from the Dunvegan Castle tourist shop. She'd spent ages choosing one with the nicest face!

The men looked relaxed and seemed to have managed to slip back into holiday mode again remarkably well. Beth had planned a delicious dinner for their return and the mood from there on was nothing short of festive.

Guy said that both he and Julian had decided to take another week to make up for all the time lost working. The girls had no problem either. Adriana had brought a couple of manuscripts with her to read for her literary company and Alicia said she would ring her journalistic work place in the morning. She was sure that they would like a travel article on Skye, as well as the West coast which she had already started to write on her computer. She would title it: 'Over the Sea to Skye'. Rose spoke to her friend and partner in the interior decorating business they shared. All their present projects were on course and surprisingly most of their bills had been paid, so she was happy to continue covering for Rose with the help of their very efficient and energetic young assistant.

Oliver posed the only possible problem. Would his company in the city be happy about this much extended holiday? It turned out that the city firm had been reading their newspapers with interest. The story, in its entirety, had just hit the press all over the UK in a big way and as Olly had been part of the enigmatic operation his bosses seemed to be secretly delighted with the extra publicity that would follow him back. It was, they said, a good talking point and excellent PR for the firm.

※

Fergus took them all out for a day's deep sea fishing off Loch Island. The girls wanted to see where so much of the drama had taken place. They weren't allowed to disembark because of the continuing investigation. Even the beach was now cordoned off, but Guy was able to point out where the dinghy had been and the beginning of the tracks leading to both Julian's loch and, in the opposite direction, to the abandoned village which hadn't been deserted at all. In calm water and with blue skies above they trolled for mackerel and even Adriana became excited by the immediate results.

"This is more the sort of fishing I like," she enthused, hauling in another heavily loaded wriggling line of slippery silver fish.

Fergus was helping, standing ready to unhook the fish quickly, expertly knock them on the head, then throw them into the waiting bucket. Rose was watching with interest. This was a seriously cold-blooded business. She thought the whole easy procedure far too predictable and said she preferred to wait and hope for a while, whilst appreciating the surrounding scenery and gentle atmosphere of the river. When the fish was finally hooked it was far more rewarding she felt and better for the soul. Marc was amused by the differences in their characters. He studied Adriana surreptitiously, wondering how she really was. His friends would soon have been at the lodge for a whole month. Time had flown, but it was now three weeks since their liaison. Adriana looked well, content and confident, he thought. She must be well and truly late for her monthly cycle by now and she did appear radiant; so he felt that the situation must be very much more than hopeful. He then concentrated on his wife. Emma was sitting aft with Olly, laughing. She looked absolutely blooming today. They'd been teasing Alicia who, with Fergus's hat perched nonchalantly on her head, was at the helm under Guy's instruction. Beth was arranging the picnic at the table behind them. What a very happy group they made. This was what he called a golden day to remember. An exceptional day, given what had happened.

"Beth, you're a girl after me own heart!" Fergus, confident in the helmsman, had come in to the cockpit, kissed her on the cheek and was eyeing the food. Beth had the good grace to blush.

"This is my job," she said, pleased with the stir her picnic would cause. With Emma's permission she had really gone to town for what she felt to be another special occasion. There was cream of vegetable soup, crab sandwiches, hard boiled eggs and homemade chicken with ham pies, cheese, celery and apples, plus her speciality to finish with - individual chocolate mousses.

"A feast for a king", Fergus pronounced, washing his hands thoroughly, while Beth held out a towel.

The fisherman was over the moon as Beth had agreed to come up again at Christmas and would ask for a job at the pub for the new season. Although to start with, she had told him firmly, she would only accept if Dougie offered a room with the work. Fergus already knew that a room went with the job.

Beth's sister Jessica wasn't keen on boats of any sort so she and Poppy spent that day with Alec, Sean, Ailsa and Mrs Haddington who had again cooked one of her memorable meals, which they all enjoyed in the kitchen. Alec said that they should do it more often as the kitchen was cosy and warm and in winter it would save heating up the dining room all the time.

❄

Two days later, social services came to Glencurrie to see Dougie and Ailsa together with Sean. Alec had insisted on a senior person coming for the first interview and also wished to be present himself. The woman, a Mrs Rawlings, was charming, very thorough and took a sensible view of the whole situation. Constable MacDonald, at the police station, in the next village had already filled her in with the details regarding the boy's sister, his only known family member. Sean was well and happy where he was for the moment and she was quite agreeable for him to stay on at Glencurrie. But of course, while all the searches and paperwork were being attended to, she would need to see their living quarters at the pub before a final decision could be made. She had to make sure that Sean would have his own room and wouldn't be camping in the bar, she had said, smiling encouragingly. When Mrs

Rawlings suggested to Sean that he might like to live with Ailsa and Dougie, the boy flew into Ailsa's arms his eyes bright and his face red with excitement. Ailsa looked at her husband over his head and smiled through her tears. She might at last have a child she could call her own. The social services woman explained that there had to be enquiries made to make certain that there really were no close relatives in Ireland who might lay claim to the boy and immigration issues to be addressed. She said that in her experience she thought it was doubtful they'd find anybody over in Ireland wanting another mouth to feed. Sean didn't seem to remember any other family member except for the dreadful elder sister who was in custody, with the others, waiting to be charged.

In Paris, the laird, the Asian men and the blonde woman were all being held in a high security establishment, along with various other members of the group from further afield. There were many who had been under surveillance that night. A list of over a hundred and fifty girls was being trawled through methodically in the hope that most could be traced and returned to their families and homes. For all of the unfortunate innocent young people, the promise of a golden future had become nothing short of a terrifying ordeal with no possible means of escape. A few would never be found; some, now with drug related problems, would need hospitalization rehab and therapy before being relocated to their home countries. It was hoped that the dead Polish girl, Eva, would be the only enduring tragedy.

Javek and Olga were working together at her smart hotel on Skye for the time being, although Olga was required to give statements and to be interviewed, at police convenience. For the future they were offered full time work at Castle House and Lady Strathkellan said that they could have the cottage at the end of the drive on their return. But first she wanted it cleared out, cleaned professionally and then completely re-decorated. Javek could have a piece of land in which to make a garden. They deserved a fresh start, she said and she intended to oversee the project herself. It would be fun.

The Dromvaar people all hoped that Finola might now also enjoy a better life with her evil husband out of the way for good. Marc imagined that she and Alec might now see a bit more of each other again. They had always been good friends - until Alistair Strathkellan had come along to spoil it all.

CHAPTER 39

The salmon fishing season was coming to an end and Rose decided that she'd love a day's hind stalking, which had recently begun, if she dare to ask Alec. Olly, amused and much to Rose's indignation telling her that she should have been born a man, asked Alec for her. Alec, delighted that Rose seemed to love all the sporting pursuits offered by Scotland, said that he would arrange it with his stalker and announced that he and John would walk with them at the beginning of the day. Oliver wasn't too certain about the plan at all. He loved seeing the deer in the wild, had never been stalking and wasn't too sure about shooting them. It was the time of the rut and he'd heard the stags sometimes, when the window was open on a quiet night, far away in the distance across the moor. They simply roared their heads off; an incredible and curiously uplifting noise. Alec explained that although telescopic sights were now compulsory to ensure a clean kill, man still had to pit his wits against weather and beast, which were exceptionally canny. After a long and arduous stalk it was considered a fairly even match, he said. Culling of the old and weaker hinds was essential to the future of the red deer apart from which their numbers had to be regulated. This explanation made Oliver feel much better.

The day dawned damp, raw and cold with a slight frost and a shifting mist almost obscuring the mountains as they were caught in an occasional glint of sunlight showing the early snow on their tops. After two or three miles, as the track became smaller and the ground steeper, Alec and John turned back towards the house, leaving Rose and Oliver in the capable hands of Hamish the stalker. Olly rather wished that he could have gone with the older men to join the others by the fire. His heart wasn't in this organized pursuit and it was a murky old day to be walking or crawling across the moors, as he believed was likely. He thought that there'd been quite enough excitement and turmoil for this particular holiday. But his young wife was trudging on uphill along a rough path, enthusiastically keeping up with the stalker. There was nothing for it but to follow; at least it was good exercise and in lovely country. There were headed, he knew, for the wilder moorland where the beasts were known to be feeding.

They walked in silence, taking in the spectacular surrounding scenery, listening to the constant squelch of their feet as they covered the boggy ground, while concentrating hard not to leave a boot behind in the more marshy places. Grouse and the odd ptarmigan, disturbed by their progress, periodically flew noisily and low over their heads. Hamish led them on up to the very top of the hill where he could spy out the land below. He took out his binoculars and studied the huge view in front of them. Rose was excited; her heart was racing. The scenery for once seemed untouched by the human hand, as it must have been for generations. There was a small loch below them and when the sun broke through the mist, the land glowed rich in colour but, however hard they tried, neither Rose nor Olly could see any sign of deer. It was dead quiet with no wind. Rose could almost hear the blood pulsating through her veins as she lay on her stomach scanning the moorland. Their breath was visible in the cold air. It was so good to be alive and out in this huge empty area of wild beauty.

Hamish was deep in concentration, his eyes screwed up against the hazy light. He was now peering through his telescope. She wondered what Olly was thinking. Rose knew that he thought her blood-thirsty and was only here beside her because he felt he must. She glanced at his still profile. No, she was wrong. He was as entranced as was she by the stunning wide open space spread out before them. He was enjoying being out here, in this natural place and away from the rest of the world.

Hamish suddenly grunted and slowly shifted along until he could hand over the binoculars. He put his finger to his mouth and pointed. Rose adjusted the vision and raised the glasses to her eyes, concentrating on where he was pointing. Sure enough beside the loch, almost hidden by boulders and blending with their surroundings, there was a small herd of deer. The three observers waited, silently watching, until the descending mist enveloped the hill again, then they scrambled cautiously on down towards the water.

When the mist next lifted, they were half way to their quarry. There was now a slight breeze, but they were downwind of the deer, which were still unaware of their presence, as they hid carefully behind some rocks. The moving shrouds of low cloud made way for patches of weak, glimmering sunshine, so the only thing to do was to continue crawling along, out of sight, down beside a winding, craggy stream which flowed into the loch. Soon they were only yards away. Olly could see that Hamish was heading for a deep bank covered in heather and set back from the burn, which would give relatively dry, good cover and the chance of a fair shot. The stalker whispered that if the deer were disturbed they'd head for the gully to their right. Olly could even smell the deer now that they were so close. He found himself excited by the thrill of this stealthy pursuit. The elements were on their side, they were still downwind. Hamish had judged the stalk perfectly. There were three stags: a large mature beast with at least eleven points to his antlers and two younger stags, with smaller heads, on the edge of the group, weighing up their chances for moving in and taking the hinds from a much bigger and heavier adversary. The majestic stag, already in possession of the half dozen hinds, was warily standing his ground, periodically snorting and stamping a foot daring the others to come any nearer. Once he let out a deep throated roar; warning off his opponents. The stalker readied the rifle and gently handed it to Rose. She'd been out shooting pheasants in the South, a completely different sport, but she had never considered killing a creature as big or as impressive as one of these.

"Now aim for the heart of the oldest biggest hind on the left of the group, standing a little on her own. You have a clean shot," Hamish whispered, "and remember once shot the beast will know nothing but she'll still run. We just have to hope that she won't get as far as the gully before she drops."

Rose raised the rifle to her eye. Olly held his breath. The animal suddenly stopped feeding and looked up; seemingly to stare straight at them. Had she sensed them in spite of their furtive approach? Rose felt the old hind was looking only at her, fearless. She took aim just behind the shoulder as she'd been told. Just a split second before she fired a covey of grouse flew noisily up from the heather between them, making their unusual cry 'get back, get back' and alerting the deer. The big old hind leapt to one side, with surprising speed and the shot went wide. The herd took off as one. They ran until they disappeared over the edge of the gully into their own safe haven.

"I missed," announced Rose.

"Och no, you didn't miss, the darned grouse got up just before you fired. It was not your fault," Hamish reassured, although definitely disappointed.

"Even if you'd got her clean, likely or not she would have made it to the gully. The beasts know they're safe down there and it's not possible to drag anything out of that deep hollow."

It was time to turn back. As they began the return climb up the hill, with Hamish ahead, Rose turned and said quietly to Olly over her shoulder.

"I missed on purpose Olly: I couldn't do it. I couldn't shoot that magnificent creature, even though I know it has to be done."

Olly chuckled.

"Well, I have to say that I'm glad you missed too. But don't, whatever you do, let on to Hamish."

❄

That evening Alec rang to say that Hamish had asked if he could take 'Miss Rose' out again the next day, after some grouse. The stalker had told him that Rose knew what she was doing and had just had a bit of bad luck with the deer. Rose jumped at the invitation and once more Olly felt that he should go with her. After his earlier reservations before they'd set out, he was glad to have had his day out on the hill. The stalk had been exhilarating and he now understood exactly what Alec had meant when he'd said that you had to pit your wits against the weather and the canny beasts. At the end of the day it had been an even match and, on this occasion, the deer had shown they'd held the upper hand.

❄

The next afternoon Hamish took them into lower country where he said the grouse were most plentiful. The stalker had a dog with him this time and explained that he would lead them to a suitable spot and then he would walk away some distance over to their right. From there he and his dog would try to drive any birds back towards them. Rose felt much more confident. She was a good shot but knew that grouse were both faster and lower flying than the larger pheasant. She and Olly stayed in position for fifteen minutes while Hamish set off. At the agreed time Olly took up his binoculars to see the stalker far off in the distance standing on a small mound. His arm was thrust high above his head with his hat on the end of his stick. Olly, making sure that he was also clearly visible and taking his cap off his head raised his own arm in response. Then he gave his wife a peck on the cheek and stepped well back behind her.

"Good luck", he whispered.

"Thanks!" replied Rose. "I'll need it!"

The adrenalin rush took over. Rose took a firm stance, loaded the gun and immediately became completely concentrated. A few minutes of silence passed. Olly could see Rose's out-going breaths circulating in the cold air then disappear, only to be followed by another. He became almost mesmerized by the regularity of her breathing. She was steady and still. He scanned the distance for sign of movement hardly daring to turn his head. Then the dog, in advance of Hamish, flushed out a covey of grouse. But they flew away quick and low out of range sending their eerie startled call up into the raw atmosphere above.

"Damn," muttered Rose, "too far."

A few minutes more passed while they could hear the stalker giving instruction to his dog, then a single grouse emerged with a flurry into the air. Rose's reaction was too slow; she still hadn't quite got her eye in. She could just see Hamish now out of the corner of her eye approaching from her right. He was making a lot of commotion and waving his stick with a plastic flag attached to the end. Rose took a deep breath, exhaled, and then readied her gun once more. Just as she'd regained her balance three more birds suddenly and noisily rose out of the heather just to the right of her. This time she was ready. They flew straight past her; a perfect right and left and both grouse plummeted to the ground.

Hamish gave a victorious salute, waited for Oliver's response, then sent his dog to find the birds. Olly hurried to the side of his ecstatic wife exclaiming,

"Oh my God Rose! Is there no end to your talents?"

"Of course not!" she responded with elation. "Well, I think that honour is satisfied so far as Hamish is concerned, don't you?" Rose made the gun safe and stood grinning from ear to ear. "I didn't want him to have to tell Alec that I'd missed everything today as well!"

"No! That wouldn't do at all," replied Olly. "But I had no idea you were such a good shot. That was brilliant," he said his eyes shining with pride.

The eagle eyed stalker had seen the birds fall and the dog had no trouble retrieving them. Rose could see even from a distance how pleased the man was as they walked to meet him.

"Well done, Miss Rose," he said. "The Colonel will be delighted." Smiling happily Hamish took the gun from Rose, then with the brace of grouse safely stowed in the game bag slung over his shoulder, he called the dog to heel and they turned for home. The sun was low and it was a beautiful soft misty evening.

"What a day it has been," sighed Olly taking his wife's hand where the path widened.

"Yes, it has been an amazing day. Thank you for coming again Olly and I'm so glad that I couldn't shoot that vulnerable creature yesterday."

"So am I," agreed Olly, "so am I."

Hamish must have rung Alec on his mobile as he and John came to meet them again where they rejoined the main track back to the house. As they approached, the stalker indicated towards Rose then took the birds from the bag, holding them high for the men to see. Alec winked at Hamish and said, "well done Hamish, I see you've shot a brace."

"Och no Colonel! It was Miss Rose. She's a fine shot. Indeed, it was a right and left, you see."

"Congratulations are definitely in order Rose. Very well done; grouse aren't easy. You have to be completely focused and extremely quick."

The triumphant, pink cheeked Rose was silent, for once. Grinning happily she nodded politely in answer to Alec's praise and bent to stroke the dog before turning to the stalker.

"Thank you Hamish, thank you very much indeed for making it all possible." Hamish touched his hat with old fashioned courtesy.

"You're very welcome Miss Rose. It was very well done indeed." Olly was almost jumping up and down with delight!

❄ ❄ ❄

CHAPTER 40

Adriana finally got to visit the chapel, up on the moor, the day before they went home. It was a Sunday and open for a small service that evening. She went with Julian for a last walk by themselves. They came to a fork in the path. 'To the Chapel' it said, pointing one way, on an old fashioned wood sign.

"Let's go and look," she said, taking his hand, "there's something I want to talk to you about."

"Alright... actually there's also something that I want to say."

"But can it just wait until we've seen the church which I've been longing to visit?"

"Yes, alright, come on then or we'll be late for lunch at the pub."

"It doesn't matter," Adriana replied, feeling just a little shaky, "they'll wait for us and this is more important."

The little chapel was very old indeed. It was set in a hidden valley beside a stream. The tracks leading from each direction looked well worn. The board outside informed them that the services were held there once a month. Inside it was a rare treat to find nothing locked or hidden away. The church, although small, was beautiful in its simplicity and would benefit from the sun all day long. As it was, a golden light streamed in through the stained glass windows from the East, creating the illusion of a warm, multi-coloured rainbow. There were cream flowers on the altar and on the font in preparation for the evening's service and the stripped wooden floor smelt of old fashioned lavender polish. The high arched ceiling had simple mouldings and there were the faint remains of frescoes, just discernible, one on each side of the altar. The walls in between were of a freshly painted white.

"I never would have expected a chapel so far from habitation to be so well maintained, would you?" Adriana, standing in the warm sunlight, turned to look at Julian who seemed unusually mesmerized by their surroundings. He was silent for just a moment then he cleared his throat as if it had been constricted. He was nervous also, Adriana thought, whilst waiting and almost holding her breath, to hear what he had to say.

"Maybe Alec has something to do with the upkeep. Perhaps we should get married here, if it's allowed. I think it's about time don't you? After all, it must be nearly two years since I first asked you!" There was a loaded hush while he ran his fingers through his hair.

"But you told me, only the other day, that you wouldn't; not unless we could have children."

"I know what I said, but I think that perhaps I was being paranoid as, you're right, we could always adopt as a last resort and if nothing else works. That is, if you really wouldn't mind?" Adriana was radiant with happiness."

"I told you that I wanted to marry you, no matter what. I love you and always have."

"And I love you too my darling; I have from the day I first set eyes on you and I always will. Now come here. Standing with the sun in your hair you're just too good to be true."

He took her face in his hands and kissed her long and hard until her legs felt in need of support and they had to sit down together on one of the pews, breathless with emotion. Now, she felt, perhaps wasn't the best time to offer her own most important piece of news.

❋

Lunch in the pub was a jubilant affair with Poppy, Beth and Fergus and of course the long suffering Jessica. Dougie had made up a large table in a room the furthest from the bar. They decided on fish and chips all round, now known as 'Ginger's posh fish and chips', as he'd added his own special recipe of a very Scottish version of tartar-sauce. On the way back, Julian and Guy dropped in one last time to the incident room to say their goodbyes to Mac and the few investigative team still around. Meanwhile Adriana popped in to the chemist. To Emma's disappointment she appeared to come out with only cotton wool and a new tube of toothpaste and, annoyingly, she couldn't quite see if there was anything else in the bag. When they returned to the lodge everybody, except for Emma and Marc who were staying on a few days more, had to pack. Those driving were leaving early in the morning for the Lake District and Rose and Oliver were taking the overnight sleeper again the following evening. Alec was coming to dinner, with John, who had just arrived back from his visits in the South. Everybody was going to drop in to say goodbye to Mrs H on their way past.

Marc found himself left in a room with Adriana on a couple of occasions. But she'd said nothing; she had just smiled with her eyes as well as her mouth. In his opinion the odds were good and, incongruously, Emma had been the one to mention to him that she thought their friend might also be pregnant. The girls all looked content and rested. They'd had extra holiday, without worry. They had been well looked after and there was a huge feeling of relief all around at the successful outcome after all the dramatic events.

That night Adriana was in the bath when she called Julian to come and sit with her.

"There's something you might like to see."

"What's that sweetheart and where and what is it?" he asked looking around slightly puzzled.

"It's there on the shelf by the basin. Have a look." She was trying to keep from smiling too much and giving the game away, before he saw what was there, clear as a bell. He got up from the stool and walked across to the sink. His back was to her. She heard an exclamation and an intake of breath. He turned around holding the test carefully in his hands as if it was the most delicate piece of china which might easily break. His face bewildered in disbelief he asked in a hushed voice,

"Is this what I think it might be?"

"It most certainly is!" He continued to stare not yet daring to believe.

"So you knew, this morning in the church?"

"Not for certain then, no. I hadn't done the test. But I wanted to make sure that you wouldn't just be marrying me for our child you see," Adriana teased.

"Oh Arri, this is wonderful. Is it too early to tell the others?"

"I don't see why not. I'm perfectly healthy and there's no doubt about it, as you can see!"

"We'll tell them at dinner. But are you alright my darling? Is there anything that I should do? Should you see a doctor, perhaps Marc...?"

"No! No, there's nothing to do. I'll see our own doctor when we get home." Laughing she answered quickly. "You have done all that was needed. I'm as right as rain; blooming in fact as you might say and I'm starvingly hungry, so I'll get out and you can get in." Julian held the towel and watched her carefully get out of the bath. He had never been so deliriously happy and Adriana sensible and practical as ever, thought to herself, 'the baby could indeed be his and, thank God, either way they would never need to know'.

❄

That last night they all felt sad to be leaving. But it was time to go home. A lot had happened and much had been accomplished. New relationships had been forged and some had changed. A secret tryst had been entered into, but with another's best interests at heart and that which could have torn them all apart had, albeit subtly, achieved the opposite - a small miracle.

At the beginning of dinner when the wine had been poured, Guy stood up to thank both Emma and Marc for what, he said, could only be classed as a most remarkable holiday.

"Events on this particular holiday have been, once again, totally unexpected and things that have occurred made me realize just how important our friends and family are... so..." he held up his wine, "to wives and girlfriends, my god-daughter, friends and family." They all raised their glasses and drank deeply; then Guy sat down abruptly and a buzz of conversation began once more until Alec struck his glass with his fork.

"I also would like to say something." He looked around the table at each and every one sitting there.

"It has been nothing short of a pleasure having you all here. I have much admiration for the way this last month's difficult events have been so professionally handled and I have loved seeing so much of my great niece. As for Rose," they all looked at her, "I have seldom seen Hamish so pleased with his day out on the grouse moor. Well done. Please, all of you come again soon. You will be more than welcome." He paused for a moment before continuing, "Seriously though, I hadn't realised what an old recluse I had become since Caroline's untimely death. Even having a child in the house again has created an exceptionally happy atmosphere at Glencurrie and Mrs H has been in her element. I want to thank you, for this as well, because my life has taken on a new meaning and I now realize that... there's life in the old dog yet!" They all laughed and John looked thrilled to see his brother so cheerful once again.

Beth, as usual, had cooked another delicious meal - a paté of smoked salmon with crème fraiche, roast grouse and, everybody's favourite, her mouth watering chocolate mousse which they all had requested. After pudding had been cleared away and the coffee brought in, Emma suggested that they get Beth and Jessica also to join them for a toast.

The girls came in and Marc thanked them both for everything that they had done to help during the last very eventful month. Jessica had been brilliant looking after Poppy and Beth had excelled herself with the food. Beth had told of her plans as regards a job at the pub and a possible future with Fergus. They all liked Fergus and wished her well. The sisters then disappeared back to the kitchen to finish washing up, then to the television in their room.

Finally Julian pushed back his chair and stood up. They all stopped talking to watch with interest as the usually shy man, once more, ran his fingers through his fair mop of hair and prepared to speak.

"I also have something important to say, before we finish this excellent wine," he said looking at Alec, knowing that he had brought it over from Glencurrie. It was unlike Julian to make a public pronouncement thought Guy, but the girls were all grinning expectantly as if they knew something that he didn't. Julian glanced across at Adriana with such an undisguised look of love in his eyes, that the others were all momentarily stunned into silence.

"To Emma, Marc and Alec, our most generous hosts, thank you and..." clearing his throat, as he always did when something really mattered, "to my darling Arri, my future bride, who, I have just learnt, is carrying our first child." He stopped while they all took in what he'd just said. Julian, now even more embarrassed, finished quickly, "and we'll have a hard job choosing our godparents!" Adriana broke the silence by giggling, followed by Alicia who couldn't contain herself any longer.

"I knew it, I knew it," she gloated and jumped up to embrace her dearest friend. "Well done you two, that's wonderful news."

"And I too had already guessed. It was the kippers! You love kippers Arri! That's what did it for me," agreed Emma, also getting up and walking around the table to give them both a heartfelt hug, followed by Rose who whispered, "and I guessed too, not that I know much about these matters!" Guy, after thumping Julian on the back and kissing Adriana soundly, left the room to see if there was any champagne left in the fridge and Olly amused everybody by saying that he was beginning to feel quite broody himself, which instigated a playful whack on the arm from his wife.

"Συγχαρητήριο" called John across the table congratulating the couple in Greek. "That's wonderful, just what the doctor ordered." little knowing what he had just said.

"Meal a naidheachd, that's Gaellic," said Alec "And... Beannachd Dia dhuit, which means... Blessings of God be with you all!"

"Well, thank you, everybody. We probably shouldn't be telling you as its early days yet but, seeing as we're all together and I seem to be as fit as a fiddle..." Arri's voice trailed off.

The doctor then leapt to his feet, like an enthusiastic small boy. He raised his glass high above his head and grinned across at Julian.

"Congratulations. My most sincere congratulations to you both." Then he turned towards Adriana with a twinkle.

"And finally I... *shall dance at your wedding.*"

"We shall all dance at your wedding," Alec agreed and added firmly, "but you'd better get on with it, no more hanging around!" Everyone laughed again.

Thank God, thought Alicia – for this small miracle. She glanced towards her husband and caught his eye as he began to open the final bottle – the look he gave her, across the table meant the world. It said everything. As he watched she responded by gently placing her right hand across her heart. This was a secret signal between the two of them. 'All is right again within our little world and long may it stay that way'.

'THE SMILE'

ISBN: 978-1-4251-7153-7

Two women are thrown together through force of circumstance far beyond their control. With courage and determination they set forth to find out the truth and the whereabouts of the two men in their lives, suddenly disappeared, without trace, into thin air.

An unlikely boating accident in the South of France. A macabre funeral in Scotland. Unexpected and erotic happenings in Venice on the night of 'La Senza', the celebration of that city's marriage to the sea and a final, dramatic, scene on the island of Torcello, played out under the hot Italian sun.

'UNDER THE OLIVES'

ISBN: 978-0-9563366-0-6

Emma Brook, vulnerable and fragile, leaves a bad situation behind in England to explore the possibilities of a painting holiday in Greece for her 'Island Hops' travel Agency.

Underneath the olives Emma does indeed discover a whole secret world, just as the stranger on the plane implied. Who was the shy goatherd who never came out into the light? Why was he hiding? Who was the beautiful reclusive woman? And who were the mysterious little gypsies playing amongst the trees?

At the Hotel Stavros Emma meets an intriguing mix of diverse, irrevocably linked characters. In the hypnotic atmosphere of the olive grove she encounters tenderness, tragedy and unexpected drama. She finds the answer to a gripping riddle from the past and a certain magic for herself never before experienced.

Published by
Feel Good Books

'THE COLDEST NIGHT OF THE YEAR'

ISBN: 978-0-9563366-1-3

An idyllic winter holiday in a lovely hotel in the Swiss Alps becomes a nightmare. Early one morning a young woman finds suspicious and gruesome evidence in an otherwise beautiful winter wonderland. Unwelcome strangers, 'grey men' of questionable intent, infiltrate the area and an atmosphere of veiled threat engulfs the village in the valley. As the heavy snow clothes the mountains in thick layers of silent white, it both hides and protects those who wish to take advantage of its camouflage. A group of friends unwittingly becomes involved in unexpected events, when one of their party fails to finish a train journey and has to pit her wits against much more than the prevailing harsh weather. Friendship and love blossom as six people take part in an adventure which demands enigmatic skills, courage, determination and for some physical endurance beyond all imagining.

In the cold glorious surroundings of a land where few are brave enough to dare venture 'off piste' skiing becomes secondary to that most basic of instincts – survival.

Published by
Feel Good Books

For more information visit
Ginny Vere Nicoll's website

www.feelgoodbooksonline.com

www.thegreekvilla.co.uk

www.theswisschalet.co.uk

SONGS

Loch Island

The Smile

Under the Olives

The Coldest Night Of The Year

TOBIAH UK

www.tobiahuk.com

ABOUT THE AUTHOR

Ginny Vere Nicoll was educated in England. After leaving school she attended art-college. More recently she studied fine art at both West Dean College and privately in Italy. She exhibited successfully, in the West End of London, before turning her hand to writing.

Ginny has a large family and lives in an old farmhouse in West Sussex.

'I love to travel, anywhere, either by car, train, or even by foot, this is when I absorb the scenery and the colours and collect my material for my paintings and my books. 'Loch Island' is my fourth work of fiction. It is centred on an imaginary island off the North Western coast of Scotland, in the Highlands and also on the mystical Isle of Skye.

All of my previous novels are written around special locations. 'The Smile' is set mostly in Italy and across Europe and 'Under The Olives', in the beautiful Ionian islands of Greece. 'The Coldest Night Of The Year' takes you away to the spectacular Swiss mountains, in an exceptionally cold winter.

All four stories stand alone but are linked because, quite simply, I can't say goodbye to my main characters. I've come to know them all so well! I wouldn't be surprised if one of them walked through my door at any time! With each new novel the group of friends set forth on another unexpected adventure together.

Writing is another life into which I escape from the real world. I hope that I can take you on an exciting journey and transport you to these imagined places in the hope that, by the end of the story, you will have shared the 'feel good' experience' with me.'